SATAN'S MARK
THE COMPLETE CASES OF
SATAN HALL, VOLUME 2

SATAN'S MARK
THE COMPLETE CASES OF SATAN HALL, VOLUME 2

CARROLL JOHN DALY

ILLUSTRATED BY
JOSEPH A. FARREN

COVER BY
LEJAREN HILLER

POPULAR PUBLICATIONS · 2024

TABLE OF CONTENTS

DEATH BY APPOINTMENT

Satan Hall Knew, When He Struck
Chet Barloff in the Face, That He or
Barloff Would Die Before Morning

1

SATAN TACKLES A KILLER

CAPTAIN JAMES T. Harrington paced the back room of his precinct and told Detective Satan Hall exactly what was on his mind. Occasionally he looked at those sharp, slanting, green eyes; the tapering ears and the peculiar V-shape cut of the jet black hair.

"There isn't a man on the Force worthy of his stripes who wouldn't resent your being sent into his precinct Satan. That's natural. Even the man on the beat knows and understands. It's a reflection on my work. It wouldn't be human to look on it any other way."

"Then you don't intend to help me?" Satan asked.

"I didn't say that." Harrington squared his broad shoulders and threw back his gray head. "I've done twenty-five years in harness. The Commissioner sent you here to work out of my precinct. He didn't say I was to mother you. I presume you know what you're after."

"And I presume you do." Satan's thin lips parted slightly.

"Yes." The captain nodded vigorously. "You want the Barloff brothers. And so do I." Shaking his finger at Satan. "And I do resent your coming. If the commissioner has evidence that I haven't, I'm entitled to it. I'm entitled to the break. I don't see any reason for your horning in."

"You'll get the credit on the books. It's your precinct. There's no question of your honesty."

"No." The captain swung suddenly. "Then what is it? My intelligence? The Barloff brothers handle my district, certainly. But Zitto handles the city; the whole city. If I pinch one of the Barloff mob, Chet Barloff springs him. If I pinch Chet Barloff, Johnny Zitto springs him. Now—what? I never got orders to shoot Chet Barloff to death. You're a killer, Satan. No offense; that's common knowledge. If you are down here to shoot Chet Barloff dead, say so, Satan."

"The commissioner doesn't send men out with orders to kill." Satan stiffened slightly.

"Maybe not with such orders, but it's in his mind when he sends you. Leastwise, it works out that way. I've always been taught to enforce the law; not to suggest or encourage official murder."

"Official murder?" Satan straightened in his chair.

"Exactly! But this time a killing might not be so easy for you." Captain Harrington paused and ran a hand through his hair. "Chet Barloff's quick, Satan, and he's nasty. All your speed won't take his bullet out of your back."

"No." Satan grinned evilly. "I'll give him a chance at that

"Scram!" said Satan harshly. "I've got business with Barloff"

back of mine the first time I see him. It's part of a cop's duty."

"Duty!" Captain Harrington looked at Satan a long minute. "Well, you might as well hear it from me; it's common gossip along the Avenue. They say it's Mattie Hern that brought you down here."

Satan came slowly to his feet. His green eyes were narrow now; his thin lips a single red gash, but his voice was very steady.

"What else do they say?"

"They say that Mattie Hern was your woman."

Satan stepped slowly from behind the long flat table and stood directly before Captain Harrington. His right hand hung at his side; the fingers opened and closed spasmodically. The hand raised slightly.

Captain Harrington stiffened, but his gray eyes never

left the green ones of Satan. He knew Satan's reputation; knew those often repeated stories about Satan's method of "slapping down" a man. But he simply said:

"You asked for it and you got it." Then suddenly, "And take this, too, Satan. They say that Chet Barloff has his eye on her; that she's to be his woman."

"That's a lie; they're both lies," Satan said slowly. And then, much to the captain's surprise, who more than half expected some show of violence; mental, if not physical, "What else can you tell me?"

Captain Harrington laid a hand on one of Satan's broad shoulders. He smiled now and his gray eyes were kindly. **"YOU WORKED OUT** of my precinct, Satan, when you were a rookie," he said. "You were straight and honest and had a hatred for criminals; that was and is now, an obsession. You've done your duty as you saw it. You've rid the city of some of its most dangerous characters, but it's always been death and violence and spitting lead. It's kept you from the stripes of a sergeant. You're a one man law, with only the commissioner himself behind you. Don't you see, Satan? This time the girl will be used to—well, perhaps to kill you."

"She's a fine girl," was all Satan said.

"She's a crook. You can't deny that. She's fenced stuff with her father. Now that he's beat it she's deep in the racket. Hard as nails; clever and intelligent. Never done a rap, but crooked as a ram's horn."

"She wants to go straight; they won't let her. Chet Barloff won't let her. So—" Satan paused; rubbed a hand down a pointed chin.

"So if there wasn't any Barloff there wouldn't be any—"

Harrington spread his hands far apart. "Look out, Satan. Chet Barloff is bad. His younger brother, Ed, simply a common gangster pushed into authority by Chet. But they're both killers. They're not like Johnny Zitto. They don't weigh the possibilities before they act. They kill, trust to luck and influence to carry them through. So far, it has."

"*So* far," said Satan, "it has."

Captain Harrington shrugged his shoulders.

"The Barloffs know you're here, of course. They can guess why. As yet, they have no reason to act. When they have— I'd hate to see your career end in my district."

"And if it did?"

"It would be your own fault." Harrington shrugged his shoulders again. "But—"

"But—" said Satan.

"I'd get the guy who did it, of course. After all, Satan, you're one of the system. You're a copper."

Satan grinned broadly now.

"You never asked me of my interest in Mattie Hern; you don't believe the gossip, of course?"

"No," said Harrington, "I don't. There was a rumor that she pulled you out of a tough spot once. You don't like to be under obligation to anyone, Satan. I suppose you want to pay a debt."

"That's it. That's just it."

"Good luck! I know you. There's no use of asking you to play ball with me. You've got your own ideas, Satan. They're not mine. If you take first shot at Chet Barloff, let me know where to pick up the body. But he really likes the girl a lot. She can't play half the racket." And after a minute's pause, "Chet Barloff gave Cora Ryan the air. That can mean only one thing. He's getting himself a new woman. Now, if you're bent on it; if it's murder you want, go shoot him to death tonight."

Satan's thin lips set tightly. Green eyes narrowed to long, oblique slits.

"I don't go in for murder, Harrington," he said. "My record doesn't show that; Every 'gun' has had his chance; the first draw. They've died with guns in their hands. I kill because I have to kill, to live. I don't murder, but I don't contemplate suicide either."

"No?" Harrington dawdled out the word. "Well, you might get young Ed Barloff to draw on you. He lacks sense. But not Chet, He'll put a bullet in your back. Of course I wasn't suggesting that you kill Chet offhand, though it might help matters no end. I was simply stating a fact. To help the girl you'll have to act quick."

"Chet Barloff will have something else to think about besides women after tonight," Satan said emphatically. Then thoughtfully, "Hell hath no fury like a woman scorned. You think, now that he threw Cora over, she'll talk?"

Harrington shook his head.

"I've been wondering," he said. "I thought of that myself. She may, if she can. You see, in the underworld they say that Cora took it so hard she just dropped out of things. Anyway, I can't find her."

"You think—"

"I think just what you think; what everyone along the Avenue really thinks. That Cora Ryan won't ever talk."

Satan grabbed his hat and adjusted the gun under his left armpit.

"I'm going to find Cora Ryan," he said as he started for the door.

"That's a tough assignment," said Captain Harrington.

"Not so tough," Satan told him with a nod. "I know where she is. That's why I'm down here."

"You think she'll talk?"

"I think so," said Satan. "You see, she sent for me."

2

APARTMENT 3-D

DETECTIVE SATAN HALL walked three blocks north, turned east, and flat-footed it along the dismal side street for a block and a half. Few figures were on the darkened street, but to those few figures Satan gave his attention. Twice he slowed down, and let men pass him. It didn't seem as if he were followed.

Three houses from the corner Satan turned quickly and passed into an alley between two tenements. A couple of times he peered out cautiously, looking up and down the street. Then he leaned against the sagging wooden fence, and, shoving his brown felt hat far back on his head, gazed up at the blinking stars.

Satan had no illusions about hunting men. You got the breaks or you didn't get them. If you didn't get them, you hunted up a stool-pigeon. Persistence and patience brought success.

Feet scraped far back in the alley. A bent, emaciated shadow slipped along close to the fence. Satan didn't move until the figure touched his arm. Then he said:

"Well, where is she?" And when the man did not answer, Satan gripped him roughly by the shoulder. "Don't try and two-time me, Pinkey."

"I don't know. Afore God, I don't know yet. She give me a jingle at a Speak; like she did before, Satan. She says she won't tell no one but you where to come. She wants you to be at Joe's cigar store at eleven o'clock sharp. She'll buzz you there."

"She didn't say where she was?"

"No. She said—" The small stooped figure paused and rubbed a hand across his lips.

"She said what—what?" Satan's fingers bit into the man's shoulder.

"She said she couldn't trust no one; not even me. Me, what—"

"I see." Satan dropped his hand from Pinkey's shoulder. "She would not trust you. And Cora's right. I'll be there." He started toward the street. Pinkey plucked at his sleeve.

"Barloff would kill me," Pinkey whined. "Deader than hell."

"I'll send you a wreath."

"Listen, Satan. Cora's going to talk plenty words. She's mad. It'll be a big thing if you get Chet Barloff. He's looking for her now. I hear as how he'd give five grand to the lad that knocked her over. I'm broke. I ain't eaten in two days. Can't you spot me a saw-buck?"

"Ten dollars!" Satan swung on him almost viciously. "Do you think I'm Rockefeller? If I open my mouth you'll do life."

"Life for lifting a couple of cheap tickers? That ain't right, Satan."

"You're a four-time loser, Pinkey. Right or wrong, that's the law. And you ask me for money!"

"A fiver then." Pinkey was persistent.

"Here!" Satan thrust three tightly wrapped one-dollar bills into the eager, twisting fingers. "Don't get hopped up on it and talk big." And as he jerked his arm free, "If things break right I'll slip you another buck. Some of you guys think a copper owns the mint."

And Satan was gone. Joe's was only six blocks back across town, and he had over half an hour to make it.

Joe's was a cigar store in front, a billiard parlor in the middle and a Speak in the back. A few old magazines lay on a stand, by the door and two or three slot machines dropped colored balls into your hand that some time back were made to eat.

Three times Joe came out to the front of the shop. The third time he spoke.

"Cripes! Satan," he complained, "are you going to stand there all night and kill business?"

Satan looked at the clock.

"I've been here twelve minutes," he said. "What's eating you, Joe? There's no law in this State against peddling varnish. I'm not a Federal dick."

"Yeah. I know. But just your being here gives the dump a bad name." And putting his shrewd little eyes on Satan, "I'd be glad to lend you a ten-spot if you're broke and want to go places."

Satan laughed.

"I've got money in the bank, Joe. Honest dough. You—" He paused. The 'phone behind the dirty glass window of the booth rang. "I'll take it." Satan's long arm swept Joe back against the counter. "That's what I've been stalling for."

"Yeah?" Joe seemed relieved, yet he leaned against the

counter and watched Satan; tried to study his face through the smeared window. He half decided to run a damp rag over the glass in the morning.

"DON'T YOU WORRY, Cora," Satan was whispering over the 'phone. "I'll hop the subway, right up. You're going to make my trip worth the nickel?"

"Worth the nickel!" And her laugh rasped over the wire. "I'll give you enough to roast Chet Barloff over and over." And then, "But I'm scared, Satan. I told Chet where he was heading in when he threw me out. He couldn't do anything then, but I can see his eyes now. He'll kill me, Satan. I know it. You've got to put the finger on him. I'm scared."

"That's the girl!" Satan soothed. "You talk and I'll act."

"Hurry then—hurry. I keep imagining people; seeing Chet's boys. I'm going to die. I know I'm going to die."

"Easy does it, kid." Satan felt, more than heard, the terror behind her words. "I got the number straight?"

"Yes, yes." Cora Ryan hardly breathed the words. "Third flight. In the back, on the right. Apartment 3-D. Got it?"

"Sure, Sure! Just sit tight. I'll see that you're taken care of."

Satan stepped out of the booth, whistling softly. He grinned at Joe and poked a finger against his stomach. Then he leaned over the counter, put his fingers into a box of cigars and gingerly felt a few of them, dropping them back in the box.

"It'd pay you to put in good stogies, Joe," he said, as he pulled open the street door. "Flannigan, on the beat, is getting fussy about his smokes."

Joe showed yellow teeth and nodded, his big head.

"Flannigan makes enough to buy the best cigars," he

said. "Don't worry about him. He's a copper that knows how to take care of himself."

Satan was feeling pretty good when he left the subway station up in the Bronx. Mattie Hern! Well, he didn't exactly know that he owed her anything. After all, he had done as much for her as she had done for him. He liked the girl. At least he thought that he liked her. She was a crook, all right. There were no two guesses about that. Satan grinned; the thing was new to him. It had never been his job to save a crook for society. His duty was simply to apprehend the criminal, for the State to punish. Yes, he guessed he liked Mattie. Maybe she wanted to go straight and maybe she didn't. But with Chet Barloff out of the way the choice, at least, would be Mattie's.

Satan turned up his coat collar and pulled his hat far down over his forehead as he passed the walk-up apartment, the number of which Cora had given him. There were several cars on the block, but that meant nothing. The police department were permitting all night parking in these times. It was bad business for the garages, perhaps, and sometimes expensive for the owners of those cars. Tires were all too often found slashed to ribbons in the morning.

No, Satan couldn't see anything suspicious about those parked cars; there were too many of them. But he was suspicious. The thing, after all, might be just an elaborately planned trap to gun him out. Chet Barloff might have cooked the whole thing up with Cora Ryan. But Satan-didn't think so. He had never given the boys all that trouble for a shot at him. He wasn't hard to find and wasn't hard to shoot at. Satan grinned to himself. Just the same, he wasn't going to make his death easy for them. He thought every man should work for what he wanted. Even a murderer.

So he passed the house again on the other side of the street. Then jumping a gun from a shoulder holster to a jacket pocket he crossed the street and entered the apartment.

He spotted the 3-D bell almost at once and pressed it. His finger hardly left it when the lock clicked, and turning the knob Satan entered. He walked down the narrow hall, looked behind the stairs and even gazed through the glass top of the little back door leading to a court a dozen steps below, before he started for the third floor.

THINGS SEEMED ON the up and up, but Satan clutched his gun tightly in his pocket as he mounted those stairs. At the second flight he paused and listened. Not a sound. He went on up, whistling silently to himself. What a break! The commissioner had wanted Chet Barloff for some time. Here was Satan's chance to do a little "fancy" police work. No shooting; no violence. Just drag Barloff in, build up a case or several cases from what Cora Ryan would tell him, and let the State pay the electric bill. It looked easy. Almost too easy. Satan frowned.

He didn't go directly to apartment 3-D when he reached the third floor. He went first to the front of the house. At the foot of the stairs leading to the fourth floor he paused and looked up. He even listened. Then, with a shrug of his shoulders, he turned and proceeded directly to the rear and apartment 3-D.

He was close to the end of the hall there, and by turning sideways could cover its entire length and also see the

door of the apartment almost directly opposite the one he
sought.

He raised his hand and ran his fingers lightly along
the door; just the slightest scraping noise. It would not be
heard inside the apartment unless someone was listening
close to that door. Cora Ryan would be listening. Satan
was surprised that she had not been waiting there. The
door open a crack. But she mightn't do that. She'd want
the door locked and bolted.

And Cora Ryan wasn't waiting by that door. Satan raised
his hand to knock, hesitated, and decided that the bell
would be less apt to call to the attention of others on the
floor that there was a visitor for apartment 3-D.

He pressed the bell in one quick stab. It buzzed sharply
for a moment back in the apartment. Satan waited and
listened. There were no hurrying feet; no frightened voice
inquired who was there. He glanced again at the number.
It was 3-D, of course. His eyes narrowed to oblique lines,
his lips set grimly, and his left hand closed about the knob
of that door. The knob turned, and the door gave slightly.

Things were not right. Far from right. Cora Ryan had
clicked the lock almost the moment he rang the bell. Now,
why didn't she open that door? Satan knew that something
was wrong; terribly wrong. He thrust open the door and
stepped into that apartment. Right or wrong; trap or no
trap, he was going in.

Blackness and silence greeted his entrance. He didn't
call out. He just stepped quickly from that lighted hallway and let the door close behind him. Then he waited
and listened. Still silence; still blackness. Yet, someone had

been in that apartment less than—well, not more than five minutes before.

Satan shrugged his broad shoulders, jerked his pocket flashlight into his left hand, and with his gun in his right slowly followed the beam of light down that hall a few steps to the living room.

The flash picked out the heavy velvet curtains, slightly parted in the center and swaying as if in a sudden breeze; yet there was no breeze.

Carefully, very carefully, Satan searched out the edge of one of those curtains, clicked out his flash and shoved his hand beyond that curtain into the living room. Along the smooth white trim he ran his fingers, felt of the wall paper beyond it, and finally located the cold, oblong bit of celluloid that held the light switch.

He waited a second or two, thrust his gun between the wall and the curtain, set his eye to the tiny slit and pressed the light switch. The living room was suddenly bathed in an almost brilliant glow. And something was wrong; decidedly wrong.

With eyes accustomed to covering an entire room with a single glance, Satan took in the two windows with their shades tightly drawn, the wider door to the left and the smaller one to the right. He saw, too, the low couch, the table, the two easy chairs, the high backed stiff looking pair of chairs to either side of the window—and then the thing that lay on the floor.

3

THE FACE IN THE LIGHT

AND THAT THING was a woman. The light shone full upon her face; the wide, frightened eyes that stared unblinkingly straight up at the light. Someone had dragged a knife across her throat. It was Cora Ryan, and she was dead. Satan shook his head. She had waited too long before sending for him.

He stepped quickly into that room, watched the door to the right as he slid along the wall and passed through, the wider one to the left. His flash covered that room until he found the light button and pressed it. It was a dining room; no man hid there. Beyond it was the kitchen. A quick look showed the kitchen to be unoccupied.

With quick, cat-like steps Satan passed back through the living room and into the bedroom at the right. A glance under the bed and another into the closet finished his inspection of that room. He was not looking for clews then. He was looking for someone who might be hidden in that apartment. The murderer of Cora Ryan.

And all the time Satan walked softly and listened. When he came into that living room again his eyes were riveted on the drawn shades before the two windows.

Ears alert, gun in his hand, he looked down at the dead

body of Cora Ryan. She wasn't beautiful in death. Her face was hard and lined, and her mouth was slightly twisted in a sneer.

Chet Barloff, Satan thought; then shook his head. Ed Barloff it might be. Satan knew his underworld and knew that criminals generally ran true to form. Chet always used a gun; it was Ed who was handy with a knife. Ed, yes; the silent, creeping, slimy killer that he was. And while Satan stood above that body his ears were straining to catch the slightest sound; a sound that did not come. Although his eyes seemed fastened upon the dead woman at his feet, they were actually watching the drawn shades before those two windows.

Satan straightened, laid his flash on the table and appeared for the first time to notice the phone upon the small stand in the hall. He stroked his chin as his eyes went to the phone.

Then, with a shrug of his shoulders he abruptly turned his back on the two windows and started toward the phone. For a fraction of a second Satan's back was toward those two windows. Then he swung and faced them, his gun raised; his green eyes narrow slits of brilliance.

For a split second, green eyes glared at the whiteness of a face beneath a lifted window shade; glared too straight down the flat nose of a heavy automatic. Two guns roared, two streaks of orange blue flame seemed to meet in that lighted room. The head at the window moved suddenly of its own accord; then jarred back, taking the body with it. A body that made a queer thump as it tumbled upon the fire escape landing and thudded against the iron supports.

Satan turned once and looked at the hole in the wall

above his head. Not much of a contest when a man with a gun faces a rat with a gun, he thought, as he crossed the room. Jerking up the shade he flashed his light, which he had taken from the table, upon the silent form that lay there.

"Not Chet," he muttered as he looked down at the dead face of Ed Barloff. "Well, it wouldn't be, Chet just sent him to do the job."

Satan suddenly jumped through that window, and, straddling the body of the dead gunman, looked over the rusted iron railing and down into the court. Plainly he had heard the sudden jolt of feet as they hit the paved alley below.

And the figure! Yes, he saw the moving figure, running toward the sidewalk; almost on the sidewalk. The figure was stumbling; frantically fleeing from the apartment. In the street it straightened and slowed to a walk. Plainly, in the light from a street lamp, Satan saw the long blue trousers, the snug blue jacket, and even the gray fedora hat. The gray fedora that the figure pushed slightly back as it rubbed a hand mechanically across a forehead.

Ed Barloff had an accomplice then. He had not been alone on his mission of death. As Satan nodded at that thought he leaned far over the iron support, and, raising his gun, drew a bead almost in the center of that back. Was he going to get Chet Barloff after all?

In another moment that figure would pass from view down the block or slip into one of the many parked cars and drive away. In another moment, yes. But Satan knew that there wouldn't be any other moment. His finger tightened upon the trigger. The figure turned almost under the light; turned and looked back at that fire escape. But Satan could not be seen in the darkness. Yet he could see the figure; the white face was directly in the light.

Satan's finger loosened; the hand that held the gun dropped to his side. His breath whistled in his throat. The figure that had dropped from the fire escape was not a man, but a woman. It was a woman's face that had involuntarily cast a fleeting glance, back at that window. It was the face of Mattie Hern.

Windows were going up; people were calling. There were voices in the hall; running feet upon the stairs. Somewhere a police whistle shrieked; then another. A baby cried, and a man cursed.

Satan dropped back into that room. He had very nearly shot Mattie Hern through the back. He had very nearly— And now he rubbed the cold sweat from his forehead, much as the girl must have done beneath the light. Mattie was a crook. He knew that. But she wasn't a murderer; she wasn't— And yet it was Satan's own statement; his own belief that all crooks are potential murderers. It is only prison that saves them from being caught in that maelstrom of crime that in the end must lead to murder. But Mattie Hern! Surely she wouldn't; couldn't—

SATAN OPENED THE door to Patrolman Whalen.

"It'll be another of them unsolved butterfly murders," Patrolman Whalen said, after he had driven back the crowd who, once the law had arrived, found courage to gather before the door of apartment 3-D.

"I guess you didn't get a good look at the lady," said Satan. "It's Cora Ryan; and on the fire escape," he jerked the window curtain farther back, "is Ed Barloff."

"He's dead?" said Whalen in an awed voice. "Chet Barl-off's brother?"

"Of course he's dead." Satan nodded. "You wouldn't expect him to be walking around with a hunk of lead in his brain."

"Was he alone?" Whalen was looking down at the body as he spoke. There was nothing in his question, to make Satan straighten suddenly and hesitate over his answer. But he did hesitate just the same. Then he said:

"If he wasn't alone, you can rest assured that the one with him will pay for the crime." And as Whalen looked up at the sudden change in Satan's voice, "I'm the law!" Satan said.

Then he turned, told Whalen that he would make his report later and strode from the room. He pushed through the crowd and went determinedly down the stairs.

"The name of the lad who killed the girl is Ed Barloff," Satan explained to a sergeant who had just alighted from a radio car. "Try to keep from identifying him for an hour or so."

And when the sergeant inquired why:

"I thought I'd like to surprise his brother, Chet, that's all," Satan told him.

Satan had seen very little of Mattie Hern during the past three months. That the girl liked him he knew. That she was in love with him seemed absurd. That environment played a big part in her criminal career was entirely a matter for the sociologist, and not for a copper; a hunter of criminals. Satan liked the girl. He didn't know why; he didn't try to figure out why.

Now, Satan clenched his hands at his sides as he rode

down town. It was a tough break, that was all. He didn't look on it in any other way. It never entered his head that justice had been served; that the murderer was dead. He was going to arrest Mattie Hern for murder; at least, as an accessory after the murder.

Satan knew exactly where to find Mattie. She would get to Chet with the news of his brother's death as soon as she could. No. She couldn't tell him that; she couldn't know that Ed was dead. She must have been ready to drop to the court when the shots were fired. But she would know that something had happened.

It was Satan's hope to see Chet Barloff first. He wanted to see how Chet would take it.

Satan went straight to the Club Venice, one of the numerous places owned by Johnny Zitto. The manager stopped him as he passed the girl at the check room.

"You're not making any trouble, are you, Satan?" The man was rather nervous.

"Would you stop me if I was?" Satan grinned evilly at the man. "I want to see Chet Barloff. He's here, isn't he?"

"Sure. Sure!" Satan was surprised at the readiness with which the manager admitted the presence of Barloff; generally they were all very reticent on that subject. But the man's next words gave Satan the reason. "He's having a little dinner. Just a few friends; a politician or two." The manager poked Satan in the ribs. "You understand."

"Sure!" said Satan. "I understand. An alibi!"

"An alibi?" The manager was grieved and it showed plainly on his face and in his words. "What would he need an alibi for?"

"That's his business," said Satan. "Tell him I've got news for him."

"He may be engaged for some little while." The manager was politely solicitous. "Another time, maybe?"

"I'll wait," said Satan. "Wait until I get tired, then I'll go find him. I'll take a seat inside. I could go a bite to eat."

The manager's hand fell on Satan's shoulder.

Satan whirled suddenly, knocking the hand from his shoulder. His green eyes flashed so dangerously that the man involuntarily stepped back.

"Never do that. Never do that!" Satan seemed to be thinking aloud, but the second time he repeated the words his voice was not unfriendly.

"No?" said the manager. "Well, don't get up-stage about Barloff. Johnny Zitto is upstairs tonight. He's a little big for even you to handle."

"Yeah? I wonder." Satan tapped his right hand against his left armpit. "I know a way to make all men equal." He turned and walked into the main room.

4

"ENOUGH TO KILL A MAN"

THE FIRST PERSON Satan saw when he entered the room was Mattie Hern. She was seated alone at a booth table in a far corner, well back from the dance floor. She held a vanity case in her hand and was dabbing at her face. Occasionally she cast furtive glances toward a small door across the room.

She didn't see Satan until he had almost reached her table. Her face was deadly white but for the blotches of artificial red that stood out vividly on her cheeks. Her deep black eyes were fastened on Satan's green ones. He saw the haunting fear of a trapped animal far back in their depths, before she lowered her head.

Satan pulled out a chair and sat down.

"Hello, Mattie," he said. "I'm going to make it easy for you."

"Satan!" The girl looked up. "Frank Hall." She was one of the few people who ever used his Christian name. Then suddenly, "What do you mean, 'make it easy for me'?" She tried to smile.

"You're afraid of Chet Barloff, aren't you? You've got a crooked quirk in your brain, Mattie; but your body's clean. I'm going to take you away from him. He won't be able to bother you, Mattie. It's tough; but it's easier, coming from me. I'll see that you're not—not put over the hurdles." And when her mouth only opened, "Yep, Mattie, that's it. It had to come. It's a pinch."

"A pinch, Satan." Her hand moved across the table and settled on his wrist. "You wouldn't; you couldn't. What for?"

"I won't ride you, Mattie." Satan was very serious. "I won't trip you. Cora Ryan was murdered tonight; her throat was cut. You were there."

"Satan, you don't think—you don't believe I did that? You—you couldn't."

He nodded emphatically, but his voice was very grim. "You couldn't have done it. Maybe you even thought he was only going to scare her. But Ed Barloff went there to kill. What part you played I don't know. But—"

The girl raised her head now.

"I wasn't there, Satan!" she said defiantly.

"I saw you. I stood on the fire escape and watched you leave. You looked back while you were under the light. You were dressed like a man. Blue suit, gray hat, tan oxfords. I'm sorry, Mattie."

Mattie Hern's lips twisted slightly; even, white teeth drew in her lower lip.

"You told me once, if I ever needed you you'd come. And I do need you. I told you that I was afraid of Chet Barloff; that I wanted to get out of the racket. Yes, I'm a crook. I've always been a crook. But I don't go in for murder, and I don't—" Slender, almost childish shoulders shrugged. "Cora Ryan was all that stood between me and—well, between me and Chet Barloff. She was my protection. Now—she's dead, isn't she?"

"Yes," said Satan, "she's dead."

"I went to Cora's apartment tonight to prevent a murder. I knew where she was. Chet told me. He hinted that she—yes, more than hinted that she wouldn't stand between us any longer. I had to see her, I wanted to warn her, I—I was too late, that was all." And suddenly, "Well, look at me, Satan; look at me. Tell me the truth. You believe me?"

Satan raised his eyes and looked at her; long and steadily he looked at her. Never once did it enter his head to spare the girl because of his liking for her. That was a personal matter. This was the law; the law he served. He was simply looking at her. If he felt she was guilty, nothing would keep him from dragging her in. If she told him the truth, and reason told him that she lied, why—

A shadow crossed the table; a man spoke.

"Good evening, Satan. Hello, Mattie. Better run along, like a good girl. Satan wants to talk to me."

Satan Hall looked up at the wide, hard face of Chet Barloff. Chet was still a young man, but dissipation was already beginning to take its toll. Flesh was beginning to form beneath his hard, set jaw; little pouches were already visible beneath his eyes, and an unlighted cigar which constantly ran back and forth across his mouth only partially hid the sneering curve of his lips.

Mattie Hern came slowly to her feet.

"Well?" she said, as Satan looked back at her.

"Well?" Chet Barloff mimicked her word. "You're not in a cop house now, Mattie. You don't have to take orders from this flatfoot,"

"No, Mattie. That's right." Satan nodded very seriously.

"I guess I just dropped in as a friend, not as the law. See you some more."

"You take quite an interest in that girl," Chet Barloff dropped into the seat across from Satan when Mattie left.

"Sure!" said Satan. "An interest that would surprise you."

"Yeah." Barloff's cigar raced across his mouth. "We're alone here, copper. You can speak plainer, if you're not afraid."

"Well," said Satan very slowly, "I take enough interest in that girl to—to kill a man."

"You mean 'murder'?" Chet Barloff's eyebrows went up.

"That wouldn't be necessary with you, would it?" Satan leaned across the table now.

"LISTEN, COPPER." BARLOFF took the cigar from his mouth and pointed it straight at Satan. "You can't pull your tricks on me. You can't get me to jerk a gun on you, and take a dose of lead in the stomach. I know your racket. I know it well. Guys that cross me, even coppers, live to regret it. And sometimes they don't—don't live to regret it."

"Like Cora Ryan, eh?" Satan's green eyes watched him.

"Cora Ryan?" Thick eyebrows went up. There was just the right inflection in Chet Barloff's voice. Satan knew that he was prepared for that question.

"Yes." Satan nodded. "She was found dead tonight; her throat cut—murdered."

"Murdered! Cora?" Chet shook his head. "That's tough! She left me in a huff, too, but I understood she was coming back. Got a little jealous, Satan. Oh, well." He stifled a yawn with his hand. "Mattie's a nice bit of goods at that."

Smack! Chet Barloff's head crashed against the side of the booth as Satan's open palm struck his face, and Chet had never seen that hand move from the table. The white marks of fingers stood out on the sudden red of Barloff's cheek. His right hand half raised and jerked quickly toward his left armpit. Then it stopped.

"Go on!" Satan encouraged. "Pull it out. You've got a license to carry it. Let's see you use it."

And the temptation was strong for Barloff to draw that gun. Satan's hands were upon that white table cloth. People at the adjoining table had seen the blow; some of those at other tables' must have seen it. There was provocation there. Johnny Zitto would spring him; high priced lawyers would keep putting the trial off for weeks and months. Just a jerk of his hand and the slightest pressure of his finger, and Satan would bother him no more. Yes, Chet Barloff was fast. He felt that he could get that gun out and squeeze lead between those sinister green eyes even before Satan could lift his empty hands from the table.

Empty hands. Hands— And in the second, perhaps, that such thoughts rushed through Chet Barloff's brain, another thought followed them. Friends of Chet's; boys with guns and the wills to use them; boys fast on the draw had looked at Satan's empty hands and—and died. Died with their guns half drawn from their holsters.

The red left Chet Barloff's face and the frenzied lust to kill left his eyes. Just hatred remained. But most of all, his hand; his right hand left his arm-pit and dropped quickly onto the table.

"So you're a rat," said Satan. "You haven't got the nerve for it. You're like your brother Ed; you want a shot at a man's back. Just like Ed wanted a shot at a man's back after he killed Cora Ryan."

"What do you mean?" Chet Barloff's eyes blazed. Then he smiled. "No, Satan, it won't work this time. Some day I'm going to get you. But you can't hang that Cora Ryan killing on me or on my brother. I've got friends to swear that I was here all night; names that will mean something in court."

"And Ed? Will they swear that he was here?"

"Maybe." Chet Barloff stroked his flabby neck. "Maybe he was in the room in the back, doing some figuring for me. He was in and out of the private dining room a lot. Laugh that one off."

"I won't be questioning Ed," Satan cut in, and turned to watch the three men who had sauntered into the room and dropped down at a nearby table. "I've got a little surprise for you, Chet. Ed's alibi is shot for tonight, and so is Ed. He meant to take a shot at my back tonight, but I turned around." Satan's long arms came far apart; his palms opened. "He was yellow when show-down came. He's lying dead on Cora Ryan's fire escape. Laugh that one off, Mr. Chet Barloff."

Satan came to his feet, swung on his heels, parted his lips slightly at the three muscle-men who eyed him belligerently, but also a little apprehensively, and walked toward the door. He turned once and only once. But Barloff still sat at the table; his eyes were fastened on the white cloth and his hands were plainly visible.

Satan grinned, yet he knew that Chet Barloff was a dangerous man; a killer, and maybe doubly dangerous because he'd wait his time; carefully choose his time before he killed. But Satan's thought as he reached the check room was, Barloff's time is my time.

At the check room Mattie Hern met him and pulled him into a dimly lit hall.

"I'm not going to thank you, Satan, because what you did you couldn't help doing. I know that. You believed me; believe in me? I'm afraid of Barloff. If I quit the racket Barloff will get me, or—well, there's my father too, Satan—Oh, I know you think he's just a common fence, but Barloff knows where he is and will slip the word along to the police."

"You've got to stand on your own feet, Mattie," Satan told her. "Let me know you're going straight, and—and I'll stand squarely behind you. Why not give me your hand on it tonight? I'll believe you, Mattie."

"I can't. I can't. But I can be protected from Barloff. Don't you see? If it wasn't for Chet I'd be clear of the racket. It's been my life ever since I was a child, Satan. It's hard for me to distinguish between the right and the wrong of it. It's been my living. Barloff keeps me in it. But I can be free of Barloff, Satan; free of him for good. Will you help?"

"How? Barloff hates me."

"That won't matter. I'm panicky tonight. I took a chance and went to see Zitto. He— But it's you that can free me from Barloff before—" And as Barloff came from the dining room and turned toward the bar, "Go up and see Zitto. He's upstairs, now, expecting you. I told him you'd come."

And she was gone. Lost somewhere in the labyrinth of passages which the Club Venice provided, for steady patrons who were useful to Johnny Zitto.

5

JOHNNY ZITTO

SATAN HAD NO trouble in reaching Johnny Zitto's private room on the floor above. A broad shouldered, flat faced man lounging through the narrow, brightly lit hallway told him to go right to the end of the corridor and step in on Zitto. But Satan knew that, if the occasion warranted it, that same hall would be dimly lighted; well oiled steel doors would block the passage, and the indifferent flat-faced man would become an alert, dangerous gunman.

The door at the end of the corridor was ajar. Satan pushed it open and stepped into the big, comfortable, but not gaudily furnished room. Johnny Zitto looked up from the other side of the polished desk; smiled, nodded, and continued slowly with the game of Canfield he was playing.

"Take a load off your feet, Satan." He extended a hand and shook Satan's heartily. "It's a sucker's game, this. Ever play it?"

"Not for money." Satan dropped into a chair upholstered in black leather and looked at the city's ace of public enemies.

Johnny Zitto had a good face. The forehead was high,

the features well defined though slightly sharp, with soft blue eyes that were set a little too far apart.

"A cigar?" And when Satan took one and put it in his pocket, "Don't smoke them myself any more. Doc Runyan says that's what gives me the bad taste in the morning. Nothing to drink, eh?" Zitto laid a red jack on a black queen. "I'm off the stuff too; a glass of wine or two occasionally, but nothing more. Played hell with my game. I did a 91 this afternoon." He looked up at Satan. "On the Ritz Meadows' course. Yes, I'm a member there now. Swankiest club in the East. It's not my social standing, Satan; it's my money and the depression. The lawyers made it very clear to the board of governors just who was lending the club money. I would have been in the eighties today for the first time, but I got in the rough on the fifteenth."

"So you've gone in for golf."

"Gone in for it!" Zitto's thin eyebrows raised slightly, "Played it every chance I got when I was a kid. Caddied at most of the public courses. Just getting back in form, that's all. When I was a kid, Satan, they tossed me out of the Ritz Meadows for stealing balls. Now—" He shrugged his shoulders and smiled. "Now look at Johnny Zitto. But what's on your chest?"

"Mattie said you wanted to see me."

"She did! No, you can't pass the buck on to me." And shoving the cards suddenly together with his left hand, "You rubbed out Ed Barloff tonight. Why?"

"Had to." Satan shrugged his shoulders. "Ed would have it that way. Sore?"

"No, no." Johnny Zitto pulled at his lower lip. "In a way

he was a nuisance. Fancied himself a bit too hard. Often told me he'd blow you over some night."

"And what did you say?"

"Oh," Johnny Zitto leaned back in his chair and chuckled, "I told him I'd send him the best wreath money could buy, and I will too. How did Chet take it?"

"Not so good. Going to fix me, and all that." Satan grinned.

"He's not Ed." Zitto shook his head. "He shoots faster, and has more nerve, I'd sort of hate to see you go out, Satan. I rather like you. Besides, it would cost a fortune to fix up a cop killing. Chet really liked that brother of his."

"I gave Ed his chance. Chet's entitled to his when he wants it."

Zitto's shoulders moved.

"Guys are just as dead with a bullet in their backs as in their stomachs."

"I rather like you too, Johnny," Satan said. "I guess I'll be sorry the day I put the finger on you. But you've all got to come to it."

"Nonsense." Johnny Zitto frowned. "Every cop on the Force knows I'm too hot to handle. I'm not shooting my way through life any more, Satan; I'm greasing it. Now," he fairly drawled the words, "I'm giving you a tip. Chet Barloff's a killer; even a cop killer. Lay off him."

"That's a threat?" Satan stiffened.

"No. That's friendly advice. If you want a dose of lead you're welcome to it. But you wanted to talk about Mattie." And when Satan would have cut in he raised his hand.

"You're not new at the game. You know the racket. The kid's in it. She must know what to expect."

"YOU'RE A WHITE man, Zitto; or at least they say so around. A word from you," Satan snapped his fingers, "and like *that* Chet Barloff would lay off her."

"I never interfere with the boys and their women. Mattie's clever; she's bright. She's got more brains than any dame on the Avenue. She comes from good stock, too. There never was a receiver in the business that played straighter than her father, Jake Hern. He got panicky and did a run-out. I'll have him back in another month. You had as much to do with his run-out as anyone else."

"But Mattie said you'd fix it for her if I—if I would help."

"That's right." Zitto nodded. "I've known Mattie for years; watched her. She's a cute bag of tricks. If she wants to work with me, she can." And as Satan half came to his feet, "That idea comes straight from Mattie, Satan."

"I thought," said Satan slowly, "you didn't go in for women."

Johnny Zitto's lips curved at the corners.

"I go in for brains. Mattie's got them plenty. Man or woman, I can always use brains."

"And you'd tell Chet Barloff to layoff?"

Johnny Zitto smiled.

"If she was working for me I wouldn't have to tell Chet Barloff to lay off. You know that."

Satan nodded his understanding.

"And where do I fit in the picture?"

"It's like this. And I'm not trying to be offensive. You've got an interest in Mattie. Since Chet went soft on her you've been riding him. I know that. You're down here now to get him. You had Cora Ryan lined up for a squeal. I won't take Mattie over if you're going to sit down on my tail. They took me in at Ritz Meadows, but they'd draw the line at having a copper romping around a high class locker room in his underwear."

"I'll always bother you, Johnny, until—" Satan spread his hands apart.

"Sure. Sure!" Johnny Zitto nodded. "I've got no kick on that. I know, I know. You're the law and all that. Fine! But stick to the law."

"Mattie—Mattie should have a chance to go straight."

"Damn it! Satan, you'll be writing tracts after a while. She was born in the racket. I'll bet Jake Hern had her appraising rings before she was five. And there's another thing. A thing Mattie understands; a thing you've got to understand." Johnny Zitto leaned far over the desk now, and those soft blue eyes grew cold and hard. "Johnny Zitto has only friends and enemies. There's no 'in between' course. Mattie can work for me or not. But she can't jump in temporarily for her own convenience. If she comes in with Johnny Zitto, she sticks. I made that clear to her; I'm making it clear to you now. What do you say?"

"Mattie's got her own life to lead," Satan said slowly as he came to his feet. "I won't interfere."

"Then that's that." Zitto shuffled the cards and started laying them out in seven rows again. "You've got nothing personal in the matter?"

"No!" said Satan. "Nothing personal. Just the law."

"Okay, Satan. But remember; Chet Barloff's really bad. That's just a friendly warning."

"Give your warning to Chet. If he's half the man you think he is, or one tenth the man he thinks he is, you'll have another handsome piece of change to pay out for a wreath. Goodnight."

"Good night, Satan. Help yourself to a handful of those cigars. They cost me a dollar apiece. Got my name on the band now. 'Made especially for Johnny Zitto.'"

And Satan admitted as he went down the stairs that he didn't and probably never would understand Johnny Zitto; but that the day would come when he'd get him, or the law would get him, he never doubted. Only criminals scouted the old adage, "Crime does not pay." Satan had been long enough in the game to know that they all took the rap in the long run. But he knew also that younger men with warped, twisted brains were ready and eager to take the places of those who got the jolt—or burned. Ready, too, to scoff at the old adage until the iron doors closed behind them or a prison guard slit their trouser leg up the side. The racket, in the long run, was a good racket only for the undertaker.

But Satan dismissed Johnny Zitto from his mind. It was Chet Barloff he had to think of. And Mattie— Yes, Mattie had brains. She had discovered the one way of saving herself from the unwelcome attentions of Chet Barloff. She couldn't do it by stepping out of the racket. But she could do it by stepping deeper into it. By mounting the ladder of crime and working direct for Johnny Zitto. Chet mightn't like it. But then, there were a lot of people who didn't like the things Johnny Zitto did. Yet they had to grin and stomach them just the same.

AT THE FOOT of the stairs Mattie met him. Her face was very white; her black eyes shining brightly. She pulled him down a side hall and into a room.

"Well," she said, "what are you going to do?" She clutched at his shoulder.

"It's what are you going to do, Mattie? I saw Zitto. He knows you're valuable to him; knows I like you, and thinks anything you swing will be safe from me. By getting you he thinks he ties me up."

"No, no. That's not true," the girl cried out. "He told me, Satan, that he didn't expect you'd live long. Chet's going to kill you, Satan. He's got to now. You killed his brother and came here and threw it in his face. Why did you do that? I'm afraid of him, Satan. It's the first time I've ever been afraid of any one in my life. I—I—"

"Mattie," Satan lifted up her head, "why don't you chuck it? Only Barloff stands in the way of your freedom. I know, I know. You've worked for him; you've been pretty close to him. You know the deals he had with your father. Now, just a word; just a hint, and I'd be able to take him out of your life." And very slowly, "Out of everyone's life. It wouldn't need to come through me. I—"

Mattie had stepped away from him. Her great black eyes were wondering; puzzled.

"Satan. Satan!" she cried out. "You—you wouldn't make a rat out of me. You don't want me to two-time Chet Barloff; two-time the boys. Break the only code our kind, my kind, ever knew!"

"He's making more than a rat out of you. You've got a twisted brain, Mattie. Barloff wants you. He's going to get you."

"No," she said. "He's not. I'm going to Johnny Zitto. He likes me; likes my work; likes my father. I'm going straight to Johnny Zitto."

"Wait!" Satan laid a hand upon her shoulder. "I killed Chet's brother. He knows that; his mob knows that. I came here tonight and threw it in his face. He's been shooting his mouth off about getting me for a long time. Now he'll have to make good. Don't go to Zitto yet. Wait. You understand, don't you, Mattie?"

"Understand what?"

"The city isn't big enough to hold both Chet Barloff and me any longer. One of us must die."

She shook her head.

"I can't wait." She gave a little stifled cry. "It's— He told me to go to the apartment; Cora Ryan's apartment. Look!" She thrust out her hand. Satan saw the warm glow of pearls. "He tore them from Cora Ryan's neck the night he threw her out."

Her eyes grew wide with fear.

"They say her throat was cut, Satan; her white throat slashed with a knife." And suddenly she was close to him. "Take me away. Take me away!"

Soft hair brushed his cheeks; arms clung tightly about his neck. The girl was crying; sobbing. He pushed her from him and held her straight before him.

"Don't, Mattie!" he said stiffly; awkwardly.

"You couldn't care for me like that. That's it, isn't it?" She laughed a little hysterically, dabbed at her eyes, jerked herself from the hands that gripped her shoulders.

"All right. I was a fool. Forget it!" She turned toward the door.

"Where are you going?" Satan demanded gruffly.

"I've lived clean," she said, and with a curve to her lips, "At least, as I see clean living. Maybe I just thought I wanted to go straight. Now, I'm going to climb the ladder; I'm going to the top. I'm going to forget Barloff; drop him out of my life. I'm going straight to Johnny Zitto."

"Wait!" Satan's eyes were thin green slits.

"How long?" Mattie turned at the door.

"Just—just tonight."

"Just tonight!" Mattie said very slowly. "Why?"

"Tomorrow— Well, I don't think Chet Barloff will bother you again."

"Satan," she said, "you're going to kill him."

"No, ho!" Satan said very thoughtfully. "I don't think so. You see, Mattie, the law can't go in for murder."

"He's bad, Satan. Worse than you give him credit for. And he's got twice the nerve Ed had, and—and he was very fond of Ed."

She turned suddenly and left, Satan followed slowly. He saw Mattie again, standing at the foot of the stairs which led to Johnny Zitto's private room. He didn't know if she saw him or not. But when he reached the stairs she had disappeared.

6

AT THE VENICE BAR

SATAN BRUSHED A hand across his cheek. The skin seemed to tingle where Mattie's soft hair had brushed it. He shook his head and whistled softly. Mattie—that was funny! But he didn't laugh. He went straight down the hall toward the bar. The door swung back and forth as a customer came out. A man lounging close to it looked at Satan and said:

"God! Satan, you're not going in there tonight. Chet and some of the boys are at the bar."

"Yeah?" said Satan. "What of it?"

"After knocking over his brother! Ain't you got no sense of decency? Besides, there might be trouble." And, in a lower voice, "Johnny Zitto's upstairs. He won't like it none."

"If he makes a complaint to the manager, let me know." Satan shoved the man aside, turned before he went into the bar and looked at the hand that hesitated, half-lifted toward the left armpit. "You'd be making a mistake, Tony; a mistake you never could rectify."

"I guess that's so." Tony showed white, even teeth; but his swarthy face had gone suddenly pale.

There were only a few people at the bar when Satan entered. Things were very quiet. The bartender looked up, muttered something under his breath and started wiping down the bar.

Two or three heads turned and a man cursed softly. But Satan strode easily down the room, straight to the high-backed booth. His green eyes held the blinking, mud-colored ones of Chet Barloff. Despite the sneer on Barloff's lips, Satan saw that they trembled slightly.

Barloff had been talking, but he stopped. The man across from him jerked his head back over his shoulder and his mouth snapped open. Two other men were in that booth, as Satan saw when he paused directly beside it. He knew them all. Johnson Kohn, the lawyer; a shrewd, methodical man who had lived a long time in the racket—too long. Butch Delaney, who had started out as a muscle-man in Brooklyn; and Willie Hersog, who was young and coming, and affected a perpetual sneer on the right side of his mouth.

"Hello, Chet." Satan stood directly before Barloff, both his hands hanging at his sides. "Been hearing that you're shooting your trap off about me; about fixing me up with a dose of lead. Well, when do the fireworks begin?"

The color came slowly back into Chet Barloff's cheeks. When he spoke it was very slowly and distinctly, and he was careful to have both his hands plainly visible upon the bare surface of the table.

"There's time enough for all that, Satan," he said. "I've got other things besides a flatfoot to think of tonight."

"That's right," said Satan. "That's what I wanted to talk to you about—alone." He jerked a thumb back over his shoulder. "Move along, boys." Satan eyed each one of them in turn.

Johnson Kohn came to his feet; Butch Delaney half got up. But Willie Hersog sat tight and spoke through the side of his mouth.

"You're not giving orders around this dump; not to me."

"You're young and you're new." Satan leaned suddenly along that table; his left hand shot out and fastened upon the youth's throat. There was a curse, a choking cry, and Willie Hersog was dragged out of his seat across that table and sprawled upon the marble floor.

"Scram!" Satan eyed the other two men. "I've got business with Barloff."

Chet Barloff bit his lip before he spoke.

"Get over to the bar, Willie," he finally said, and then, to the others, "You, too. I'll listen to this copper's chatter. Stick around!"

Although his voice was steady and his body outwardly calm, Chet Barloff trembled inside; trembled with rage, and perhaps just a touch of fear. He knew Satan; knew his reputation. Knew, too, that he was there for one purpose; to get mussy. For the first time he began to have fears; real fears. But he mustn't show them. An hour more; a few hours at the most, and then— He tried to shrug his shoulders indifferently as Satan slid along the seat opposite him; far into the corner, where he could not be seen except by those very close or directly opposite the booth.

"Barloff," Satan said slowly, as he glared straight into the muddy eyes, "Mattie Hern's a crook. Maybe she'll always be a crook. But some day, I think, maybe she won't, and then—" he spread his hands far apart. "You've got an apartment uptown that used to be rented for Cora Ryan."

"Yeah!" said Barloff. "Cora won't be using it any more. I've got a new tenant in mind. It ain't for rent."

"But it's going to be, from right now on. Understand!"

"Maybe not, exactly. You see, I'm thicker than hell, Satan. Never went in much for education."

"Then I'll make it clear. I can't just shoot you to death, Barloff, though the temptation is strong. But I'm going to drive you out of the racket; out of it for good. You've heard about my slapping guys down; yellow guys like you, Chet. I'm going to slap you down every time I see you. You've fooled the boys, and I'm going to let them see inside of you; let them see what a punk you are. And I'm beginning right now."

Chet Barloff's face turned from sudden red to white; then to a pasty yellow.

"I'll kill you if you do. I swear to— Take your hands off me."

But Satan's hand was already across that table; long strong fingers were fastened on that flabby neck. With a single motion he jerked Chet Barloff to his feet. Then he swung him around so that Chet's side would be to the bar.

And a voice spoke; an easy, slow, unexcited voice.

"Come, come, boys. No rough stuff here. I mean it, Satan!"

Satan's hand dropped from Barloff's throat. He knew that voice, and he knew also that it came from behind him and that the man must have entered from the private door close to the end of the bar. It was the voice of the one man who would draw a gun and shoot it out with him. Not that Satan wasn't willing to shoot it out with any criminal who packed a gun. But did the man behind him have him covered? And Satan didn't want to die. At least yet; while Chet Barloff lived.

SATAN DIDN'T KNOW if the man who had entered carried a gun in his hand or not. There was no threat in that voice; no order to throw up his hands. Satan dropped his hands to his sides; turned and faced Johnny Zitto. He saw, too, the dull outline of the gun that Zitto dropped back in his jacket pocket.

Johnny Zitto looked the bar over. All the customers were "regular" tonight. The man at the door had seen to that. There was much to discuss that was not for the public to hear.

"I've got a little news for the boys," Zitto said. "For you too, Satan, because it might as well be known in certain quarters if she should get a ticket for speeding. Mattie Hern is working for me from now on. Straight from me, understand. And she gets orders only from me."

"Mattie Hern. Mattie Hern!" Chet Barloff gasped. "Why, she—" And seeing the blue eyes of Johnny Zitto freeze to ice, "She's friendly with this dick here. Satan Hall."

"Sure she is. Sure she is!" Johnny Zitto nodded vigorously. "Aren't we all? Set the house up, Oscar. Come on, Satan!" Johnny turned and walked to the bar, leaning against it.

"Turn my back on these gorillas!" Satan slipped along the bar.

"Sure. Sure! They won't bother you now."

"Cripes! boss." Chet Barloff's voice was plaintive but his muddy eyes smouldered. "This dick, Satan, killed my brother tonight."

"Don't we all have to die?" Johnny Zitto swung from the bar and winked deliberately at Chet Barloff.

But Barloff didn't wink back. He stood for a long time, staring at the back of Johnny Zitto's neck and the side of Satan's face. Then he swung, and without a word left the room.

"And that's that," said Johnny Zitto, as he and Satan moved to one end of the bar. "Barloff will kill you, of course. He'd have to now."

"When did Mattie make this decision?" asked Satan.

"Right out in the hall, less than five minutes ago." Johnny Zitto smiled. "She likes you a lot, Satan, or she likes Barloff, or maybe she just wanted an excuse to work in with Johnny Zitto, though I put the proposition up to her several months ago. The idea wasn't a new one with me."

"Just why did she do it?"

"She said she didn't want you committing murder tonight."

"Me!" said Satan. "Me? She did this because of me?"

Johnny Zitto laughed.

"There's no understanding the reasons of women," he said. "Who'll think a copper would go to all the trouble you have because of a bit of dress goods?"

"You should have given her more time."

"Listen!" Johnny Zitto swung and faced him. "It's my racket. I like the girl. I'm giving her the biggest chance of her whole career. I've got big people working for me. Only the best. She knows the ropes; she wanted to come in. You let the cops know, so they'll lay off her and keep their jobs."

"I wish," said Satan, "she had waited until tomorrow."

"Why? You thinking of dumping over Chet Barloff tonight?"

"Not exactly," said Satan. "But he was thinking of getting me, and that would amount to about the same thing."

"Well, he'll still think of it. Don't shake your head. You killed his brother. You know what that means. Now, he'll figure it out that you had something to do with taking his woman from him. He'll treat you right." Zitto grinned. "He'll lay some lead up and down your spine the first opportunity you give him."

"Yeah?" Satan took a long drink of celery tonic. "A lot of good that will do Mattie now."

"Hell! the girl's—" And suddenly, "Look here, Satan, I'll make you a sporting proposition. You think the girl wants to quit the racket. To me it sounds stupid. But it's like this. If Barloff goes after you tonight; if— Well, if Chet turns up dead in the morning, I'll let Mattie withdraw her proposition. How's that?"

"You'd like to get rid of Chet?" Green eyes narrowed.

"You cops are always suspicious. Still, I didn't like the way he looked at me. I never thought the woman meant so much to him, or—" He paused and drew his upper lip between his fingers. Then, "Again, Chet might dump you over and feel pretty good all around."

And suddenly, turning to the bartender, "What was Chet drinking, Oscar?"

"Water, Mr. Zitto. Water. He turned down the champagne cold after he learned that his brother was croaked by that lousy—" Oscar paused, stuttered, looked at Satan apprehensively, and finished, "after he learned his brother was killed."

"There you are." Johnny Zitto made a grimace. "You're getting all the breaks, Satan. When he's on a 'kill' he lays off the stuff. He'll do it alone too. It looks better."

"You think he'd have the nerve to get me?"

Johnny Zitto laughed.

"That's the trouble with you, Satan. You've had too much luck; too big a reputation. Chet's got to take a crack at you to save his face now. You knock over his brother, then come down and gloat over it. I know, I know. Killing a woman seems a mess, but words are words, and they roast you just the same if they come from a man or a woman. Cora had to go out. I'm a fair minded man and I can't see it any other way."

"It was kind of a shock to me," Satan said slowly, as if he were thinking. "I won't be able to sleep so well tonight. I'll go up to Rafferty's Speak and stick around until I get sleepy."

"You will. You mean that?"

"Never meant anything more in my life."

"All right." They both turned and walked from the bar out into the hall. At the entrance Johnny Zitto said, "No chance that I misunderstand you?"

"None at all," said Satan. "I wouldn't want too many knowing it, that's all."

"Okay. Goodnight, Satan." He stuck out a hand and gripped the detective's. "Goodby, then, if I don't see you any more." And just before the door closed, "I'll drop Chet a word about Rafferty's. He drops in there occasionally. It's a quiet place."

7

THE MURDER TRAP

JOHNNY ZITTO TURNED back to the bar, strode leisurely in and spoke to the boys.

"The place is getting crummy lately." He rubbed his hands together and smiled pleasantly. "All kinds of riff-raff dropping in. We'll have to put a stop to it." And just before he left, "I want you boys to be able to tell where you were tonight, from now on. You know! In case the police should want to know."

Johnny Zitto didn't say any more. He left the bar and turned toward the stairs to his private office. The flat faced man met him and whispered hoarsely as he jerked his head toward the stairs. Then, slightly louder.

"Want me to go up with you, boss? First his brother, then his woman. Chet's bad."

"I'll go up alone." Johnny Zitto nodded, and with one foot on the stairs, "Chet's all right. You don't understand him, that's all." And with steady, even steps Johnny Zitto mounted those stairs.

He went straight down the hall to his office, slammed the door shut behind him, and with one quick glance took in the entire room. His eyes settled on the partly open door of the small wash room. Then he dropped into the chair behind his desk, set his lips rather grimly as he looked at the crack in that door, and spoke.

"Drop that gun into your pocket, Chet," he said evenly. "Then come out and give me a good look at you."

Feet scraped for a moment; the door opened, and Chet Barloff came into the room. His face was slightly red and his muddy eyes still smouldered.

"I didn't have any gun—out. I just wanted to talk to you," he said.

"All right. Talk. I'm listening."

"Mattie's pretty close to Satan. I'm afraid she might spill over some night."

"No, you're not." Johnny shook his head. "Mattie was born in the racket. You know she won't 'rat' on me, or even on you. What next?"

Chet Barloff scowled.

"That's all," he said sullenly.

"No!" said Johnny Zitto. "That is not all. Mattie's working for me. You don't like that, do you?"

More red shot into Chet Barloff's face, but he didn't speak.

"Well?" Johnny Zitto's blue eyes held his.

Chet Barloff's tongue came out and wet his dry lips.

"No," he said, "I don't like it. I went to a lot of trouble for Mattie; the boys all know it. Now, you drag her away from me. Why?"

"Why?" Johnny Zitto came to his feet. His eyes were on Chet's hands. "You're asking me to tell you why! So you're a guy who wants to know things, now. Wants to know why Johnny Zitto does things."

Chet Barloff's lips curled. He was watching Johnny Zitto's hands too.

"Yes!" he finally said. "I want to know why."

For a long moment eyes locked. Johnny Zitto's were the first to drop. He laughed, and stretching out a hand placed it affectionately on Chet's shoulder.

"You've got nerve, Chet. Plenty nerve. I like a guy with nerve. And I'll tell you why. You've been a valuable man to me. I want to keep you so. I want to make a pile of jack for you. Lately you haven't been so valuable. Satan's out to get you. He's going back over your life with a fine tooth comb. I can't make use of a guy who always has Satan Hall sitting on his tail."

"He ain't going to be sitting there much longer."

"Why?" Johnny Zitto fairly snapped.

"I'm going to get him. Rub him out!" Chet's flabby chin shot forward; his eyes blazed with hate.

"Yeah? You've been feeding the Avenue that line for three months. It's so old it's beginning to smell."

"It's different now," Chet Barloff shot in. "He killed my brother. I'm going to get him—the first chance." And when Zitto just looked at him, "I'd a done it tonight if you hadn't horned in."

"Down stairs to my bar! That's a bright thought. You and Satan have got feelings about each other: He's willing to meet you half way, Chet. He'll be at Rafferty's tonight—"

"He will!" Chet Barloff brightened. "Good! I'll take a car load and blast him out as soon as he sticks his face onto—"

"No!" Johnny Zitto cut in. "You won't do that, Chet; Satan's not a rookie. That's been tried many times; he's always ready for it. Tonight he'll be expecting trouble; waiting for it. You'll have to do it alone."

"Cripes! Go up to Rafferty's and shoot it out with Satan? Why, he'd pop me out before I got my gun half drawn. That's his way; that's his meat." And eying Zitto, "You ain't particular about me, eh?"

"You're not any good to me with Satan around," Johnny Zitto said, indifferently. "He's horning in more than I like. I can't fix him and I can't break him. He works straight from the commissioner. I expect you to go to Rafferty's and shoot Satan through the back."

Chet's laugh was not a hearty one.

"And him expecting me?"

"It's like this. Satan's going to Rafferty's gives us a break. You remember the private hall behind the back room."

"A break! Rafferty stools for Satan. You know that."

"YEAH! THEY SAY that." Zitto nodded. "But he couldn't stool for a dead man; and Rafferty don't like to stool. But he'd rather stool than do twenty years. That's only natural. Now, listen!"

For five minutes Zitto talked and Chet Barloff listened.

"It's as sure as a guy can make it with Satan," Zitto said. "Nothing can go wrong. They've been riding Satan in the papers a bit. But he never shot a guy who didn't have a gun in his hand."

"Hell!" said Barloff. "I'll have one in mine."

"Smack on Satan's back. You can't lose out. Just remember your weakness, Chet. Don't try and talk him to death."

"Gawd!" said Barloff. "I'd like to see him on his knees; squealing, on his knees. I'd like to empty that damn gun in his belly."

"You empty it in his back. Remember that. If he sees you, he kills you. Don't sneer. Better 'guns' than you have thought different. Now," Zitto lifted the receiver, "a word with Rafferty before Satan gets there."

For some little time Zitto talked over the phone. Finally his voice changed; grew hard.

"I'm not asking favors. I'm telling you what to do. Just leave the key so the lad who comes can get into your private hall. He'll know what to do. Listen. Do what you're told if you want to take that kid of yours to the country for her health."

And a moment later Zitto said, in a more friendly tone:

"You won't even know who it is and you won't be blamed if things go wrong; naturally wrong. It'll clear things up for you, Rafferty. With Satan out, you can come back in the big money. I'll do the handsome thing by you." And slamming the receiver onto the hook, "That's fixed!"

And Chet Barloff began to argue. They'd know who did it! Every cop would suspect him! Zitto knew what they did to cop killers!

"Satan isn't liked any better on the Force than he is on the Avenue. But I'm taking care of you, Chet. There'll be an alibi. After the fracas, breeze right up to—" he whispered a name and Chet gasped. "Yes, that's the way Zitto does things. He'll swear you were there at the time of the killing. That's me! I don't leave things to chance."

"And— But they'll—the cops will want a fall guy." Chet Barloff had planned this killing for a long time, but his planning had only been a mental picture of Satan's death scene.

"They'll have one." Zitto nodded. "That kid, Willie

Hersog. He's getting up-stage, Chet; thinks himself pretty tough. It's the hard ones, like him, who crack when they sweat them. I'm having a message delivered to him that the doll he likes, Freda, wants to see him uptown. It's right behind Rafferty's. Besides, Satan handled him rough tonight. It'll look like a natural, with your alibi. You've got two hours yet. Want to go down to the morgue and take a look at Ed? I understand he doesn't look so bad."

"No, no!" The hatred came back in Chet's eyes again. "I swore I'd never look at his face again until I got the louse that killed him."

"Well, you've got business tonight then." Johnny Zitto shrugged indifferently. "You better run uptown and start working out that alibi. Twenty minutes out of the house should cover the knockover."

"Yeah. Yeah. It ain't every guy who can get a state senator to swear him clean of a killing,"

"No," said Zitto. "But then, it ain't very often that a state senator has to. On your way!"

Chet Barloff paused in the doorway.

"You must want this guy, Satan, bad to do all this for me, Johnny."

"Not so bad, Chet; not so bad. He's dangerous, yes. But it's you I'm thinking of. The boys would run out on you if you didn't make good now. I can't have a guy giving orders for me who looks yellow. And, Chet—"

"Yeah, boss?"

"You make good and we'll give you a party tomorrow night, A real party; for you and Mattie."

"Mattie!"

"Sure! She's a nice trick and a square shooter. Remember that when you press the trigger, and remember that live dicks aren't good company for a guy's girl. Good night."

"Cripes! Johnny." Chet Barloff gripped tightly at Zitto's hand. "You're one white guy; one white guy."

"I manage to take care of my boys," Johnny Zitto said carelessly as he watched Chet Barloff's broad back pass down the stairs.

Then he shrugged his shoulders and walked back into the room. He lifted the phone and called the bar.

"That dame, Freda, wants Willie Hersog to meet her up at her apartment at two o'clock. Tell him he's not to go: that I said so." Then Johnny banged down the receiver and picked up the deck of cards. He knew Willie and he knew that it would not be the first time that he disobeyed his orders. But he had a feeling that it would be the last time. Besides, he would see to it that Freda spent the night in Jersey.

Slowly he dealt the cards in seven neat piles. Satan wasn't a bad guy. No. As dicks go, Satan was all right. But he shrugged his shoulders as he placed a red five on a black six. Satan had asked for it. He was supposed to own a charmed life. Well, he'd need it tonight. Chet was a killer.

8

IN RAFFERTY'S BACK ROOM

RAFFERTY'S BACK ROOM was small. It had five or six tables with plain wooden chairs pulled up to them. The single window was tightly boarded on the outside and was heavily curtained inside. What air was there came from the open door which led down the hall to the bar. The private door, which led to the stairs and to Rafferty's sleeping quarters, was closed and locked.

Satan knew it was locked, for he had spun the knob the very minute he entered that room. Then he pulled out a chair and sat down so that he faced the door to the bar and the locked door was to his right. With just a shift of his eyes he took in that private door and also the boarded window. His back was some six or seven feet from the wall. He was the only occupant of that little room. It was always that way when he visited Rafferty's.

Satan took a certain pride in Rafferty. Rafferty, he felt, was his single weakness. Rafferty had killed a man and Satan knew it. He could have laid a hand on Rafferty's shoulder a few years back and sent him up for at least twenty years. But he didn't do it. Satan also felt that the man who Rafferty killed had needed just that; just one good killing. He grinned too as he looked up at Rafferty's fat, round face. Even in the Department they thought that Rafferty was stooling for Satan. But he wasn't. Satan had never threatened him; never even told him he could have given him the long jolt. Yet Rafferty did know. There was an understanding between the two men that was never put into words. They liked each other.

Occasionally Rafferty would wipe down that table and talk. He heard things around. More than once he had tipped Satan off to attempts on his life. It was always done in a round-about fashion; a light bantering sort of a conversation that Satan would have to digest and reason out.

Now, Satan leaned his elbows on the table and looked up at Rafferty. The round face, the snapping bright little eyes, and the folds of thickness beneath the heavy chin.

"No one looking for me tonight, Rafferty, eh?" Satan asked.

"No, there wasn't. And if you drink any more of that swill you'll bust. I don't see how your stomach stands it."

"You've had me for a customer for a long time. I guess I'm about the only flatfoot who pays cash."

"That pays at all," said Rafferty. "But if they all drank sarsaparilla, like you, I wouldn't mind."

"Johnny Zitto still supply you?" Satan toyed with his glass. "And I don't mean with sarsaparilla."

"Johnny Zitto! Who told you he ever did?" Rafferty's face registered movie picture innocence.

"Johnny sells everything. You get your stuff through Fitzgerald, don't you? Well, that's part of Zitto's racket."

Rafferty shrugged his shoulders and looked at the clock.

It was ten minutes to two. "Going to spend the night here, Satan?"

"Maybe. I like it. How's the wife and kids?"

"So, so. The girl's not so good." Rafferty frowned. He was thinking of Zitto's words. "That's why I'm anxious to get her away."

"You close up at the end of the month." Satan nodded. "It must be a good business to be able to retire at your age. You should have a celebration to go out with. Maybe I'll give you one."

"You're not—not looking for anyone here tonight? Not going to start anything here?"

"Hell!" said Satan. "I never start anything. I finish it."

"What's this talk about Zitto, tonight? Why bring his name up?"

"I was wondering what you knew about him."

"I don't know anything about him. He never comes here."

"But he used to own the place at one time. You know him, of course?"

"Just like anybody knows him. He's a big shot; a bad man to cross. I'll be glad to get up on that farm I bought. It's a rotten racket, Satan."

"Then you wouldn't cross Zitto?"

"Me?" Rafferty hesitated. He was thinking of his girl again. "Hell! I don't know him. How could I cross him?"

"I'll probably find that out tonight. It's a good thing you're moving. They may be pointing this place out as the joint a guy got bumped in."

"Who got—" Rafferty started, then stopped.

"MAYBE ME; MAYBE not." Satan shrugged his shoulders

and finished his sarsaparilla. "Give me another load of that; and I'll open the bottle myself. You've got nothing to worry about, Rafferty. If a guy came down that hall from the bar and started fireworks in here; why, you've got an alibi. Mostly family men at your bar tonight, eh? Family men afraid to go home."

"SATAN—" RAFFERTY STARTED again and stopped. Then suddenly, "I wish to God you'd go home. Who do you expect to come down that hall?" And, leaning closer, "And who in hell would have the nerve to try that on you? Use your head!"

Rafferty turned suddenly and left the room. He was some time coming back with the sarsaparilla. Then he said, in a strained voice:

"You shouldn't a picked my dump tonight for—for whatever's on your mind, even if I am closing up." And quickly, "I've changed things around here a bit. The next lad may not be so patriotic. George is gone."

Satan looked up from his seat and at the wall across from him. Yes, the picture of George Washington had gone. In its place was an oblong mirror with a dirty white border.

"Going to turn the back room into a boudoir?" Satan nodded.

"Don't like it, eh?" Rafferty picked up Satan's dime, and, spinning it in the air with his thumb, caught it in the palm of his hand. "It took me close to an hour to hang that right, just right. Call me if you want anything."

"Stay out front at the bar," said Satan. "You expect me to admire myself in that dirty bit of glass?"

"Dirty?" Rafferty paused by the door. "There ain't a speck on it. Yeah, I expect you to look in it." And he was gone.

Satan's green eyes narrowed, searched around that room and came back to rest on that mirror. He looked straight at his own sinister green eyes, at the dark paneled wall behind him, and the dust on either side of the glass where the larger frame of George Washington had rested.

Then Satan's eyes turned slightly and for five full minutes he stared at the door. The door through which Chet Barloff must come, if he came. That was it. Satan scowled. He wouldn't come of course. At least, not into Rafferty's back room. Chet Barloff might try to gun him out on the street; shoot from an alley as Satan was on his way home. That is, if he went home his usual way.

Both his elbows on that table, his chin resting on his hands, he thought that one over. Chet Barloff was bad. Chet Barloff was a killer. Three times, least, Satan was sure that he had Chet for murder, and then the Johnny Zitto money; the Johnny Zitto influence. Those alibis. Big men; well thought of men; even trusted officials had perjured themselves for a murdering rat. Why? And the answer to that was simple. It is human to err. Big men; trusted men have made mistakes. Some of those mistakes were known to Johnny Zitto.

And Mattie—Mattie Hern! Was she safe from Chet now that Johnny Zitto would take her over? And Satan wondered. But he'd go home his regular route. If Chet Barloff wanted a shot at him, he guessed he'd better give it to him. But he'd be mighty careful that he didn't turn that back of his on Chet Barloff. He half lifted his sarsaparilla in his right hand.

A glass dropped at the bar outside; a man laughed

drunkenly and a voice spoke. A voice directly behind Satan; a voice that he recognized.

"Don't so much as move a muscle," said the voice. "My gun's less than six feet from your head; just the right distance to blow the top of it off." And the voice was the voice of Chet Barloff.

Satan never moved a muscle. His eyes just raised and looked straight into the mud-colored ones of Chet Barloff; straight down the black mouth of a snub-nosed automatic. The face seemed a long ways off; but Satan knew that it was less than seven feet from him; from his back; from the back that he wasn't going to turn to Chet Barloff. Yes, clearly reflected in the mirror that had taken the place of George Washington's picture, Satan Hall saw those sneering lips; those gloating eyes. A panel in the wall behind him had slipped noiselessly back—a panel wide enough to admit the head and shoulders of the killer; a necessary device of pre-Volstead days for a Sunday can of beer.

SATAN DIDN'T MOVE and he didn't speak. He simply watched that gun in the mirror. Chet Barloff laughed deep back in his throat as Satan sat there, his half filled glass of sarsaparilla partly raised in his hand—his right hand. He cursed softly beneath his breath. If his right hand was only free! But it wasn't free. He couldn't set that glass upon the table without attracting Barloff's attention to the move-ment—and perhaps the reason for it.

As Barloff talked, Satan's left hand began to move, slowly, cautiously down from under his chin; but he was careful that his left elbow, firmly set upon the table, or even the part of the arm visible to Chet Barloff did not move with it.

"Wise guy! Wanted me to walk in that open door—then gun me out. Wanted to force me into a draw with you by throwing Ed's death in my face, marking me yellow before the boys. How do you like it now? One movement and I'll blow you out, you dirty dick."

And all the time that Chet forgot or disregarded Johnny Zitto's warning not to talk, Satan Hall's left hand was moving; creeping beneath his right arm-pit; stiffly, awkwardly clutching the butt of his gun as his elbow remained firmly set upon the table.

"You won't get away with this murder," Satan said, to gain time, as he saw the narrowing eyes, and saw, too, the finger beginning to tighten upon the trigger.

"Won't get away with it!" Barloff chuckled. "It's in the bag. Alibi; even the fall guy who'll take the rap for your knock-over. Nothing left to chance."

"SO ZITTO WANTED it that way?" Satan's gun was out of its holster; already it was turning in his hand, just his wrist moving; the nose of the gun tight against his chest, creeping slowly up to his right shoulder. A desperate chance; perhaps a hopeless chance to sight that gun in the mirror, toss the nose suddenly over his right shoulder and gun Barloff out. Yes—Satan knew that. But he knew also that it was his only chance—a chance that his lead might find Barloff before he died. If it was his right hand that held the gun and his left that held the glass of sarsaparilla if—

But Barloff was speaking.

"Sure," he said. "Zitto said you wanted me to pull a rod on you. Well, I have. We know you can dish it out, Satan. Now—we'll see how you can take it."

Satan knew that death was a matter of seconds; maybe

less. He had looked into the eyes of a killer before—now in those contracted pupils he recognized—the will—the lust to kill. He didn't have a chance unless— He spoke quickly.

"But you lose Mattie. She's safe." He felt that he got that out just in time to stay the pressure of Barloff's finger.

"Sure, she's safe." Chet Barloff nodded his head and grinned. "Safe, for me. The little girl you think I don't mean right by is my reward for your death. Zitto wants it that way too."

It was coming. Death, sudden and violent. And Mattie! What of Mattie? Mattie, who had cried out piteously for Satan to take her away; Mattie who—

Satan had it. He'd plead for his life. Whine, as Chet Barloff would like to hear him whine. That would give him time. Chet hated him; hated his nerve. He'd like to see Satan cringe and hear him beg for mercy.

And Satan would! It would give him time. It was for Mattie. Twice he licked his lips and tried to speak, and twice he failed. And then the whimpering words he would have spoken; wanted to speak, turned into something else.

"You lousy, yellow rat!" he cried. "You—"

Satan stopped. Chet Barloff's eyes had raised from the back of Satan's head and were looking straight into his eyes; straight into the mirror across the room. There was puzzled wonder in them. Then Barloff's gaze dropped and rested on Satan's left hand; on the gun that left hand held; on the gun that was ready to creep over Satan's shoulder.

And things happened. For a split second Barloff's eyes were fastened on Satan's left hand—on the gun that left hand held. The right hand was forgotten.

Satan let his right hand fly back as he pitched himself

forward onto the table. He heard the roar of Chet Barloff's gun, the curse too that preceded it. For a split moment in the mirror Satan saw his glass strike the wall above Barloff's head—saw the bits of glass scatter and the dull brown liquid run over Barloff's face.

There was the smell of burnt powder in Satan's nostrils, and a cold stab along the side of his face as if a piece of ice had been dragged across his cheek. Then as something warm trickled down his neck and under his soft collar Satan Hall hit the floor in a tangled mass of two chairs and a table.

But Satan was twisting his body even as he fell. If his legs were partly caught in the wreckage of his own making the table itself protected his body. And his left hand was free—the left hand that raised the nose of that gun slightly as he looked into the eyes of Chet Barloff.

Satan didn't see the lust to kill in those eyes now. He saw fear—even terror.

Satan's green eyes narrowed; his thin lips were a single straight line. His finger closed once upon that trigger.

They fired together. Barloff with a hand that shook—with a finger that closed frantically—desperately.

A chip of wood from the table tore across Satan's neck. He nodded grimly and his lips parted. Clearly he saw the round hole almost in the center of Chet Barloff's forehead; a small round hole that was growing larger and turning red. Mud colored eyes were dimmed to a dull sandy shade, with a film over them. Chet Barloff did not fall at once. He just seemed to stand there and stare unseeingly at Satan. But he was dead. Satan knew that. Just as Johnny Zitto had warned him, Chet Barloff had talked himself to death.

As Satan climbed to his feet and dabbed his cheek with his handkerchief, Barloff's almost erect body slipped from the opening in the paneled wall. The weight of the body dragged back the head and shoulders and Chet Barloff disappeared, crashing into the hall beyond.

"Just as I always said." Satan thought, half aloud. "No nerve. When he faced the gun in my hand he turned yellow."

Men were in the room now; white, frightened faces were staring at Satan. And, behind them, Satan saw Rafferty lift the mirror from the wall and put the portrait of George Washington back in its place.

He saw, too, the questioning, apprehensive, almost fearful look in Rafferty's small eyes.

Just before the cop barged in, Satan winked reassuringly at Rafferty. He understood. After all, Rafferty had given him a break; a sort of break, anyway. More of a break than a cop who worked against the racket was entitled to.

Besides, Rafferty had a wife and kids; one kid he wanted to get to the country. It wouldn't be hard to convince Johnny Zitto that Chet Barloff had talked himself to death.

SATAN'S MARK

*Satan Hall Swayed Weakly as He Stole
From His Hospital Bed into the Night.
He Must Rescue Mattie Hern—She Was
Held Prisoner in a Deserted House*

1

HIS LAST WORD

JUDGE RICHARD LANDON couldn't sleep. There were times when he was glad that he couldn't.

His dreams were not pleasant ones. Twice he had cried out in the night. The second time, his servant had run frantically into the room. He was sure that in these nightmares he had not said anything; that is, anything that shouldn't be heard, but his servant had looked at him queerly. There might be gossip. That was why he had sent the servant home at night; that was why he was now alone in his old-fashioned brown stone front.

For an hour he had paced the living room, making and changing decisions. There were times he flatly decided not to see the man, and times when he was just as decided that he would see him. It was exactly ten-thirty P.M., and he had reached another "final" decision not to see his expected visitor, when the doorbell rang. Almost before that single sharp peal had died away, Judge Richard Landon had again reversed his decision and walked toward the door.

The man at the door was tall. He was heavy set. His mouth was large, his lips thick, his nose flat on the end, and his wide staring eyes were steady, unexpressive, mud-colored balls. His foot was set against the door; a huge shoulder thrusting it open as Judge Landon tried to force it closed again.

"I thought—thought that Zitto was coming." The judge

"I'm sorry, Satan,"
Johnny Zitto said, "that
it had to come like this"

half stammered the words.

"Zitto. Johnny Zitto!" The man laughed as he closed the door and carefully placed the chain across it. "Not him. It ain't necessary, when he has me to—to suggest things, and you to listen to them suggestions."

"It's about the Carver case—still?"

"Sure—sure. About the Carver case."

"I thought I had said the last word on that." Judge Landon straightened somewhat, but his attempt at judicial dignity was not very convincing.

"You haven't—yet. We'll chin in there, eh?" The big man jerked a thumb toward the living room.

"It's useless," said Landon. "I have made up my mind. I shall not betray my trust." And in the brighter light of the

"Coppers ain't the only ones who use bracelets— and guns," Krause added

living room, as he looked at the man, "You're Al Krause, of course. Gunner Krause?"

"Gunner Krause. Of course!" There was emphasis in Krause's voice. "And that's a pretty thought about 'your trust.'" He threw himself into a big chair, lifted the cover of the humidor on the table and stuck a cigar between his teeth. "You're the sort of a man the people want on the bench; that is, the right people. Johnny Zitto could send you a long way." And after a moment's pause, "A long way in either direction; up or down."

"Get to it!" Judge Landon remained standing.

"It's like this. Johnny Zitto thought as how you might sign a habeas corpus writ on Howard Miller, the jeweler's clerk who—"

"Who saw Ike Carver shoot the old jeweler to death right in his own store! Howard Miller, who saw the mask fall from Carver's face and recognized him! Howard Miller, who will point him out in court and convict him of murder! No, no. I can't release that man."

"But Howard Miller ain't done nothing. There's no legal reason for locking him up. It was just the D.A.'s way of making headlines out of the case, by saying that Miller wouldn't be safe any place but behind bars. Why, he's only a witness. Just release him in the custody of his lawyer. You'd do it quick-like, and it would be all over before anyone knew it."

"All over!" There were deep furrows in Judge Landon's face. "Yes, *all* over. He'd be shot to death in an hour."

"You've been reading books." Gunner Krause's laugh was like a sleigh on dry pavement. "We're friends of his. He's got a wife and kids that need him home. It ain't right to lock him up that way."

"I can't do it." Judge Landon turned his head. "God! I hate myself for even discussing it with you. I know. I know. I'm a crook, just like you're a crook and Johnny Zitto's a crook. But there's one difference. I'm not a murderer. And I won't sign that boy's death warrant."

"You better think on it." Krause's lips curled at one corner. "Them things you said about being a crook!"

"I HAVE THOUGHT on it, day and night. Go back and tell Johnny Zitto just that. It isn't only that I won't do it. I can't do it. It's not strength; it's just weakness. I've seen that boy's face in the night; his wife's face; his children's faces, a boy and a girl, and—and I've seen him too, laying in the gutter riddled with machine gun bullets. No, no. I can't and I won't do it!"

"It's got nothing to do with you once Howard Miller's sprung. Maybe we just want to talk with him. Send him and the wife and kids on a little trip." And coming suddenly to his feet, "Don't stand there making those funny noises at me. You got the office. You know what Zitto wants. What do you say?"

"No!" Judge Landon set his lips tightly.

"You're a fool. You can't play with Zitto. He'll break you. You've done enough to have that black robe dragged off your back. You've taken Zitto's money, and—"

"And done his dirty work." Judge Richard Landon opened up suddenly. "And I'm through. Yes, Zitto can take the robe off my back; bring disgrace to my name; place my body behind bars. But he can't make me a murderer. Ike Carver killed wantonly and ruthlessly, and Ike Carver's going to die."

"Is that all?" Al Krause's words were very low.

"No, that is not quite all. I have been a fool, but not quite the fool Johnny Zitto thought me. Johnny Zitto can't drag me down without taking the fall with me. He can't drag me to prison without going with me. And you might add that from now on I shall watch for Johnny Zitto, and Johnny Zitto's friends."

"I wouldn't have believed that." Krause seemed to smile in appreciation. "It's almost Zitto's very words about you. He read you like a book. I'm one of Zitto's friends. Maybe you thought of that."

Judge Landon looked long and steadily at Gunner Krause.

"I have thought of that," he said. "I have thought a great deal of it, Gunner Krause. There was another man with Ike Carver when the jeweler was murdered. Another man, who fired two shots into the wounded man even as he lay on the floor. The man's face was buried in his coat collar."

"Another man, eh?" Krause's ruddy complexion turned to a dull-white. "Another man! What put that into your head tonight?"

"You, Krause. Your interest in the freeing of Howard Miller. But then, I have prepared somewhat for the coming of this day. The show-down with Johnny Zitto!"

"I see. I see." There was expression in the dull, muddy eyes of Krause now. "You won't spring this Ike Carver witness?"

"No. I won't send this man to his death."

"So that's your last word." Krause stood there, both his hands deep in his coat pockets.

"That," said Judge Landon, "is my last word—for the time being."

Gunner Krause turned his back and walked to the hall door. His shoulders were bent. At the door he turned. Mud-colored eyes flashed, thick lips parted, uneven teeth showed.

"That," he said very slowly, "is your last word for all time, Mr. Justice Richard Landon."

Very slowly Gunner Krause raised his right hand and very deliberately he shot the judge twice through the head. Then, without the least semblance of hurry, he walked to the front door. Very carefully he removed the brass chain and wiped it free of finger prints. Still holding the handkerchief in his right hand he carefully turned the knob and stepped into the night.

Back in the living room the phone rang sharply. A pause, and it rang again. But it remained unanswered. Judge Landon was alone in the house, and Judge Landon was dead—quite dead.

2

THE CLUB VENICE

THE POLICE COMMISSIONER dropped the phone back in its cradle and looked at Detective Satan Hall. The slanting green eyes regarded him steadily from below the V shaped cut of his hair.

"I guess he's gone to bed." The commissioner's voice was easy, but the tips of his fingers came nervously together. "Still, I don't like it after what you've told me, Satan. Judge Landon has been talked about of course, and many of his acts seem irregular; even unethical. Yet, it doesn't seem feasible that Johnny Zitto would be interested in Ike Carver. He's not up Johnny's alley."

"It's not Carver." Satan's green eyes narrowed. "It's the principle of the thing. Johnny Zitto is in a fair way to control the entire criminal interest of the city. At least, that's his ambition. To have Carver sprung is just his way of showing the boys up in the Bronx how he can handle things. How Krause, as his leader up there, can work through him."

"Al Krause. Gunner Krause. He's the worst cut-throat in the city," the commissioner said. "But he's of the old school. Nothing smooth about Krause; he's risen by sheer brute ferocity. Just a killer. If he had Johnny Zitto's brains, why—"

"That's just it," said Satan. "He will have. Zitto has been playing along with Krause for some time. With Zitto backing, Zitto influence, Zitto brains, crime throughout the entire city may become too big to handle."

The commissioner came to his feet and paced the room, his small body swinging with the quick even steps.

"Crime *will* become too big to handle if this Zitto deal goes through, Satan." He looked at the phone again. "Damn it! I'm worried about Judge Landon. The other day he came in to see me. He had a lot to tell me; the man was in a bad way. It was about the Carver case. I sensed something startling, Satan. He's been friendly with Zitto; too friendly." The commissioner's hands came far apart. "But then, bigger men than Landon play golf with Johnny Zitto; entertain him at their chibs."

"Sure!" Satan stretched. "This Landon, now. What did he tell you?"

"Nothing! It was just one of those things. For a moment he was ready to talk—and, I think, plenty. Then the desire was gone. But he promised me something big, something sensational, before the end of the week."

Satan nodded.

"Zitto wants something from Judge Landon. Maybe he got it. Maybe—" He stopped. The phone on the commissioner's desk rang.

Two minutes later the commissioner laid down the phone and looked at Satan.

"Judge Landon was shot to death tonight," he said slowly. "Someone thought he heard a shot and telephoned the police. Doctor Carlton's on his way up now. Inspector Neil is already there. Want to come along up?"

"No," said Satan. "I'll run over to the Club Venice and see Johnny Zitto."

"You think Zitto had a hand in this?"

"I don't know." Satan shrugged. "Zitto and Landon weren't agreeing very well lately, and people who don't agree with Johnny Zitto have a way of dying."

On the sidewalk, the commissioner turned. His car pulled up before the door.

"Remember that, Satan," he said. "You don't exactly agree with Zitto."

"Thanks, Commissioner." Satan grinned. "But Zitto doesn't do his own killing today."

"I wasn't thinking of Zitto. I was thinking of Charlie Devine. He was a big shot in the racket until you jumped on him; pushed him down. He hasn't forgotten."

"He's just a cheap gun. Bouncer at the Club Venice for drunken college boys."

"He doesn't forget, Satan. He hates you."

Satan's shoulders shrugged.

"Don't they all?" he said.

"Well," the commissioner shook his head, "I'd give a year's pay to see this Bronx deal busted up." He paused and looked steadily at Satan. "I don't exaggerate when I say that it's the greatest menace the city has to face. Bust it, Satan—bust it!"

"If I meet Krause tonight I'll bust that Bronx deal." Satan nodded vigorously. "I'll let the hoods along the Avenue know where he belongs. I'll put my mark on him."

"You'll slap down Krause—Gunner Krause?" The commissioner was surprised and showed it.

"I did it to Devine and I'll do it to Krause." Green eyes

narrowed. "Don't worry about him. Krause will have to kill me to make good after tonight, and I don't think it's in the cards that he's the one to do it."

"And, Satan," the commissioner bit his lip, "I hate to tell you this. I'm not criticizing, and certainly not instructing or reprimanding you. But—it's about the girl. Her father's back on the Avenue. The indictment against him was squashed—by Zitto. She's working for Zitto. You know who I mean. Mattie Hern."

"Yes." There was no expression on Satan's face. "What about Mattie Hern?"

"Just a warning. She's spent her life in crime. I've studied it for years, Satan. I know such women."

"And I," said Satan slowly, "know Mattie Hern."

THE BAR AT Club Venice was open to a select few. There were a number of high backed booths along the wall opposite the bar, and at one end a gray door that led to a little rear room.

A huge hulk of a man stood in the semi-darkness; a great hand shot out and rested for a moment on Satan's shoulder, then a throaty voice spoke.

"Back to the dining room, brother. Bar ain't running tonight, and—" Broad shoulders bent forward, beady eyes popped in a round fat face. "Cripes! Hall—Satan Hall." And the hand that rested on Satan's shoulder jumped from it as if an invisible force had jerked it away.

"That's right, Devine." Green eyes flashed. "Now move that carcass of yours out of the way. I've got business in the bar."

"It ain't open." The man's voice was sullen; hate smouldered in his eyes. Here was the man he had sworn to kill; the man who had made him a joke along the Avenue.

"We'll open it up. Fats—now." Satan half raised his right hand, then dropped it to his side as Devine drew back; slunk his huge frame into the corner like a whipped cur. Yes, he hated Satan above all others; but he feared him above all others, too. As Satan passed him, words jarred from between Devine's lips; words that he did not mean to speak aloud.

"I'm going to get you, Satan. Some day I'm going to kill you."

Satan grinned back over his shoulder.

"You fill me with horror, Fats," he said. "But it's a line you've been pulling for close to a year now."

For some time after Satan disappeared into the bar, Devine stood there, his thick fingers clenching and unclenching. For the hundredth time he was killing Satan; beating in his face with a length of pipe. His little eyes glowed as he saw himself strutting again before the boys. It wasn't that he lacked the nerve for it, Devine told himself. It was lack of opportunity, that was all. If Zitto would only give him the chance!

The bartender looked up and said, "What the hell!" as Satan strolled down the length of bar to the rear room. A couple of men throwing dice frowned threateningly, but said nothing. Two men in the corner booth came to their feet and left hurriedly.

"Johnny's busy." The bartender wiped down the bar and called after Satan. "I'll send up word you're here."

"Sure. Sure." Satan nodded. "I'm in no hurry." But he

knew that a button had already been pressed under that bar and that Johnny Zitto knew he was there.

Satan drew up sharp. It was a small room, with a couple of easy chairs and a table. On the table were scattered around the late papers, a few magazines, and a half dozen ash trays. No drinks were ever served there. People who had private business with Zitto came and awaited his pleasure. Those not in the inner circle visited his office on the floor above, by the main staircase in the outer hall.

Close to the door that gave onto the little stairs leading above, sat a girl. Deep, black eyes regarded Satan. It was Mattie Hern.

Satan walked directly to her and stood looking down.

"What are you doing here?" he demanded. "I thought—"

He paused and the girl cut in.

"You thought—what?"

"That the death of Ed Barloff washed you up with the racket."

"So, what?" Black eyes glared up at him. "I was to take in sewing?"

"It wouldn't be hard for a girl of your talents to make a living even in these times; an honest living."

The girl laughed. It was not a pleasant laugh.

"I was born in the racket," she said. "Honesty and dishonesty are simply words, without meaning. I'm washed up with 'honesty.' It means starving for my kind."

"You've changed, Mattie," Satan told her. "You're bitter."

"Bitter! No. I was just a fool. I'd of thrown up the whole thing for you. But you never cared about me in that way."

"Mattie," for a moment Satan's hard face softened, and there was a touch of color in his cheeks, "you mustn't say that. You— Hell! Mattie, I'm just a cop. There's no place for a woman in my life. I tell myself different, but you know and I know that some day I've got to take the dose; take the same dose of lead I'm willing to give."

"Yes," Mattie said slowly, "some day you'll have to take it. Sooner than you expect, if you're set on busting up Zitto's Bronx deal, which he more than suspects. You shot the Barloff brothers; you made a punk out of Fats Devine. He used to be a good man. If Zitto said the word, Fats would go after you like *that*." She snapped her fingers.

"You're working for Zitto; straight from Zitto," Satan said, and when she did not answer, "Is it from choice or—" His eyes flashed. "It's because of your father. Zitto's—"

Satan paused. A door closed, feet beat upon the stairs; hurried feet. Then the door at the foot of those stairs opened. A bent little figure was in the room. He was talking rapidly.

"It's all right, Mattie. You're a fine girl, and—and—" The man stopped dead and looked at Satan. "I didn't know you were in the back room."

The door to the bar swung open and the bartender called in.

"You can go up, Hall."

Satan didn't speak. He just nodded as he pushed by the little man and opened the door to the narrow flight of stairs. The question about Mattie's connection with Zitto had been answered. The man who had hurried down the stairs was Jake Hern, Mattie's father.

3

SATAN'S MARK

THERE WAS A plain wooden door at the top of the stairs. But Satan knew that that door was lined with thin steel. There was a chair beside it in a small recess that was now unoccupied, but Satan knew also that that chair was generally occupied by a quick thinking, quick shooting man. Yet, it was always that way when he came. The air of easy accessibility to Johnny Zitto's private office; the simple faith that Johnny placed in his fellow man. He had nothing to fear; nothing to hide.

The door was open and Satan walked down the narrow hall, by the tiled bathroom, to Zitto's room.

"Come in. Come in." Johnny Zitto called through the partly open door. As Satan entered, he laid down the pack of cards he was shuffling aimlessly. "Take a load off your feet. I see you're using the private entrance now. That's right. What's on your chest?"

Satan didn't sit down. Quick, searching glances he took about that room; the closet, with its closed door, was the only place a man could hide. Johnny Zitto's clear blue eyes followed his darting green ones.

"We're alone, if that's what you mean," he said. "Not needing some jack, are you?"

"No," said Satan; and abruptly, never taking his eyes off Zitto, "Did you hear that Judge Richard Landon was shot to death tonight?"

"Sure. Sure. Bad news travels quickly. What about it?" Zitto's eyes grew slightly cold.

"I was wondering," said Satan, "if you can tell exactly where you were all night."

Thin eyebrows went up; Johnny Zitto's lips curved at the corners, then he laughed.

"Certainly there's nothing subtle about you, Satan. But as a matter of fact I was downstairs all evening." And in mock surprise, "You don't think I had a hand in that?"

"I do," said Satan bluntly. "I'm sure you had him bumped. But that's neither here nor across the street. No one will be able to prove it."

"Now, that's fine." Johnny Zitto laid out the cards in seven piles. "Something new. A cop who admits he can't prove anything!"

"I suppose," said Satan, "you can account for the boys."

"The boys," said Zitto, "can take care of themselves." He flipped a couple of cards above the row. "Two aces in the deal. Not bad."

"All the boys?" Satan's train of thought was not broken. "All of them? Krause?"

Johnny Zitto laid down the remaining cards in his hand. His features seemed to grow sharper.

"I can account for Krause," he said.

"You mean 'you can alibi him?'"

"I mean just that. I can alibi him."

"With whom?"

Johnny Zitto grinned.

"I'll think that up when the time comes. But they'll be big people. So you think Krause might have something to do with it?"

"I don't know." Satan shook his head. "I don't know who did it, but I know who should have done it. I simply put myself in your place, Johnny. I'd of used Krause."

"Why?" Johnny Zitto asked.

"He's a natural. You wanted something from the judge, something to show the boys uptown that you're good. The judge wouldn't perform. Maybe he even kicked over the traces; threatened to talk. You've often said that you don't have enemies; that is, live enemies. Krause is a killer. You promised him a big job uptown! Maybe he just wanted to show his appreciation."

"Maybe he did." Johnny's eyes were very narrow. "Is that what you came here to tell me?"

"No," said Satan. "I came here to tell you that the Bronx deal is off. The commissioner doesn't like it."

"So that's it." Zitto nodded. "There's no secret about that. Since when have you become a Federal dick? There's no law in this State against liquor."

"It's not liquor, Johnny. It's the racket. Building, laundry, garage, stores of all kinds. It's hard for the Department already, without you trying to consolidate the whole thing into one big business. I'm here to tell you it's off, before it starts. In plain words—Krause is out."

"Krause. So that's why you want to lay this shooting of Judge Landon on him."

"No, I can't do that." Satan shook his head. "But the Bronx deal is off."

Johnny Zitto's eyes grew cold and hard for a moment.

"YOU'VE WANTED KRAUSE for a long time," he said. "You've been riding him. You've hated him and he's hated you, Satan. I like you, so I give you a warning. If you step into the Bronx racket you step into trouble. I can control men only so far. Krause hates your nerve. Lay off him, or maybe I won't be able to control him."

"Don't try," said Satan. "I'll let Krause know how I feel about him the moment I meet him."

"Krause may not be as fast with a gun as you are, but he's sure. Lay—" The phone on the desk rang. Zitto listened for a minute and said "yes" twice, then to Satan, "Krause is down in the bar now. I wouldn't tell him how I felt about him if I were you. He's too tough even for you, Satan."

"Maybe. Ask him about that when he comes up." And Satan left the room.

Gunner Krause was at the bar with two other men when Satan stepped from the little back room. Mud-colored eyes spotted the detective the very moment he entered. Satan didn't hesitate. With that slow, even step he walked straight to the bar, jerked a man aside and stood looking at Krause.

Krause laid down his glass.

"Shaking the boss down for a few pennies, flatfoot?" he sneered at Satan.

Satan didn't speak. He just looked at the man for a minute; waited until Krause opened his mouth again, then, suddenly raising his left hand, he smacked Gunner Krause across the side of the face. The blow did not seem a hard one, yet it drove Krause away from the bar.

The crack of that bare hand against the gunner's cheek was sharp and clear, like the distant report of a rifle. Every man in that room looked straight toward the bar; every mouth hung open.

"Cripes! Krause!" were the only words spoken. Hardened criminals, most of those men; yet they were stunned. It was as if Satan had struck Johnny Zitto himself. Johnny Zitto's right-hand man; the man Johnny had chosen to take over the Bronx!

And the man himself just stood there, the red marks of fingers stamped vividly on the sudden white of his cheek. Krause wasn't exactly frightened; he wasn't exactly angry. His sensation, if he had any sensation, was stupefied amazement. And then he knew the truth. Satan was slapping him down; slapping him down before his friends, right in Johnny Zitto's bar.

"Tough guy, Gunner!" Satan sneered, and his right hand came up and rocked Krause back against the bar.

There was a full ten seconds between each blow; plenty of time for Krause to strike back, reach for a gun, even shoot. And Krause's hand did raise; his right hand did shift mechanically toward his left armpit. Then his eyes raised and met Satan's, and he saw what other men had seen in Satan's eyes before they died. And for a moment Krause knew terror.

Someone cried out:

"Don't draw, Krause. He's on the 'kill.' He's marking you for death."

Satan's lips curled; his right hand turned into a fist.

"Just a yellow rat," he said. "Try and laugh this off in the Bronx."

There was a single dull thud. Krause's head jerked back.

He tried to take a step, gave at the knees and crashed to the floor.

Without a word Satan walked to the door and passed into the hall. Back in the bar a man whistled softly; two men helped Krause to his feet. They were all careful to explain how well he had kept his head. But Krause knew, as his head cleared, that each one was wondering who'd take his place in the racket. Satan had slapped him down. The mark was on him. Satan's mark. He'd have to kill; have to kill if he was to hold up his head in the racket. The mark was there; would always be there until— Yes, until Satan was dead.

Five minutes later Johnny Zitto was saying to him:

"I didn't think he'd pull it on you, Krause, but don't worry. I want the Bronx and want you to run it. This time Satan's gone too far."

"I'll kill him. I'll kill him!" Krause was saying, his head buried in his hands. "Cripes! Johnny, I keep telling myself that I would have killed him then only it was in your bar. But don't you see? That's not true. I couldn't. I don't know what came over me. It was his eyes, I think. I couldn't move." Krause came to his feet and paced the private office. "Don't you see what it means? It'll be all over the Avenue by morning. I'll be the laughing stock of the city. Slapped down! The mark on me. Satan's mark. He's got to die."

"Take it easy, Al." Johnny Zitto's words were very calm, but his blue eyes were cold cruel slits, and his mouth was set. "Satan asked for it and he'll get it. By morning he'll be dead. Listen!"

4

THE MURDER CAR

SATAN WAS READY to leave Judge Richard Landon's house. He had not discovered anything there. He wasn't much good in looking for clews anyway. It was just routine with him, and besides, he had wanted to see the commissioner. But the commissioner was already gone when he arrived. Now he was standing by the door when the phone rang, and Lieutenant Dane called him.

"It's a frail," winked the lieutenant. "She's all excited; burnt up over something. I didn't think you went in strong for women. Leastwise, well—" The lieutenant coughed and walked out of the little den where the phone was. A guy didn't get any place kidding Satan, he thought.

It was Mattie Hern. She talked as if she had been running.

"They're going to kill you tonight, Satan. I don't know how it's going to happen. I never thought I'd blow to a cop! You saved my life once. I loved you, I guess. Now, this washes us up."

"Thanks, Mattie. And this doesn't wash us up. Any time you need me; any place, I'll come if I'm able to walk. Just take it easy and tell me, Mattie—" A few clicks of the receiver and Satan said to Central, "No. I guess we finished our talk.

"So things are that bad," Satan thought as he rubbed his pointed chin. "They must be or Mattie wouldn't have called. Good kid!" He smiled and then frowned. For he suddenly realized the chance Mattie must have taken for him.

Satan nodded to the lieutenant by the door, slammed it behind him and went down the stone steps. He walked toward Broadway and was crossing Sixth Avenue when he saw the car. It was a black touring car standing at the curb halfway down the block. He smiled grimly as he thought of Mattie's warning.

He was halfway across when he changed his mind, turned and went back to the sidewalk. He looked at the car again. Just its two curb lights were burning.

With a single swift motion he jerked a gun from his shoulder holster to his coat pocket, then with the gun gripped tightly in his hidden right hand he walked toward that car, keeping almost on the edge of the curb. He recognized the type, of course. Curtains tightly drawn! But he knew that a single flip of a curtain, and the nose of a machine gun could suddenly appear and blaze into the night; into him.

His eyes never left the driver, who was plainly visible behind the wheel. No machine gun could mow him down from the side of that car unless, of course, the operator of the gun stuck his head and shoulders far out over the door. He smiled grimly at that thought. Any gunman who could do that before he popped him off was entitled to his "kill"; certainly he was entitled to a try at it anyway.

Satan liked danger, but he wasn't a fool. He knew the breed of men who slink in the black depths of such a car. Great men to pour lead into an unsuspecting man; a man fleeing along the sidewalk or trying desperately to find refuge in some doorway as the car sped by. He'd walk straight up to that car, climb in with the boys and drive them to Headquarters. Each time that Satan blew up such a "blasting out party" made him that much safer on the city streets. That the boys might fight it out was a possibility, of course. But the night was fairly bright. Satan was willing to shoot at the first sight of a Tommy gun; the men in the car would know that. They would know also that he hit what he shot at.

"Rats!" he parted his thin lips and muttered. "There ain't one of them that would squeeze lead while I'm facing him."

No lead was squeezed from that car. No round-nosed gun flashed suddenly from the heavily curtained interior. The driver sat motionless in his seat.

Satan was abreast of the car; very close to it. He turned suddenly, mounted the step and flashed gun and light through the waving side curtain, into the tonneau, the empty tonneau.

"What the hell?" The man behind the wheel turned and tried to peer into Satan's face.

"Didn't see a guy come out of one of these houses, eh?" Satan flashed his light on the man's face. It was not a good face, nor yet a bad one. Just a face, Satan thought; and a new one on him.

"I didn't see any guy come out of any house." There was more fear than anger in the chauffeur's face, though there was anger in his voice; a crackling, husky voice. "What you want in my car?"

Satan hesitated a long moment, and then he showed his badge.

"Been trouble on this block; robbery a couple of times. Why the drawn curtains?"

The driver grinned.

"It's a cold night," he said. "No law against that. My 'fare' brought a dame home. When he brings a dame home he don't put on a show for every guy on the sidewalk."

"That's right." Satan looked down the street. Most of the houses were in darkness. "Look out you don't lose your watch."

"Okay!" said the chauffeur.

Satan crossed the street and proceeded on his way. Twice he looked back over his shoulder. The black touring was still by the curb.

AT THE CORNER he hailed a cruising taxi; turned once as he swung open the door. The black touring had left the curb. Had he been wrong about that car? Had dark shadows slunk from hidden areaways and furtively slipped behind those drawn curtains? Had one of those shadows toted a Tommy gun beneath his arm? Had the empty touring with the curtains drawn become what Satan first suspected it was a murder car?

If it was, that suited him. He stroked his chin and wondered. Would it be Gunner Krause?

But it didn't matter; not to Satan. Murder cars were duds as far as he was concerned. Krause would have to be a whole lot cleverer than that. Krause couldn't blast him out.

He'd start shooting first, just as soon as he was convinced the gunmen were on his trail.

And Satan was convinced. As his cab swung toward Broadway, the black touring rounded the corner and started in pursuit. When he turned into Seventh Avenue it was close behind him.

Satan watched the touring through the rear window. Of course he could tap his chauffeur on the shoulder, have him pull to the curb, and so escape in one of many dark alleys.

But Satan had no such thoughts. If he spent his time running away from gunmen who wanted his life, he might as well throw away his shield and go into perpetual hiding.

Without a word to his driver, who was unconscious of the danger behind him, Satan turned and knelt carefully on the rear seat. He lifted his gun and with one sharp rap knocked a piece of glass from the rear window. With the nose of his forty-five he smoothed off the jagged edges. The boys wanted gun play! They were going to get it. It would be a simple matter to cop off the driver in the better light of a cross street.

That would end the pursuit.

Satan raised his automatic in the darkness of the cab. The car was drawing closer. He could see the white face of the driver; had even picked out a spot almost between the man's eyes.

And he dropped his aim to the left front tire. Every instinct that was bred in him from years of hunting men told him that this was a death car, but there was the possible chance that it wasn't. No. He'd shoot out a tire and let it go at that.

Lights of a cross street flashed between the taxi and the

suddenly speeding touring. Now was the time; here was his chance. Satan's finger half tightened upon the trigger, and loosened again.

Brakes screeched. The car behind swerved sharply, and to avoid a collision with an on-rushing taxi was obliged to turn to the left and swing down the side street.

Satan grinned. Rotten driving that. The chauffeur was nervous then; didn't relish the idea of sneaking up on Satan Hall and starting fireworks. Well, that ended that. And—

Satan swung. He heard the muffled curse of his own chauffeur. At least, his cry of alarm or fear. And he saw too the blaze of lights on the car that was rushing toward his taxi. But above the roar of the motor of that approaching car, Satan recognized the rat-tat-tat; the sharp, staccato notes of a machine gun. He knew too that he had been fooled; taken in like a child. While he had watched that heavily curtained touring car behind; a car that undoubtedly had been there just for him to watch, the real death car had swept suddenly down on him from the opposite direction.

They hadn't waited to come alongside of him either. They had opened fire the very instant they shot on their headlights, blurring Satan's vision; his driver's vision. And the anxiety to be sure that Satan wouldn't shoot first had saved Satan's life. At least, for the moment it had.

Satan's driver had lost his nerve or his front tire had been riddled, or— But Satan didn't know if the man was dead or not. He still sat stiff and straight, right in the glare of those lights, and his taxi lurched violently just before the crash came.

Satan wasn't sure if he threw himself on the floor or

if he had been thrown there. He knew that the car had come alongside, to pump lead directly into the taxi. Then that crash; the disappearing headlights; the jar as his car mounted the sidewalk and he saw the stone face of a building. After that, the sudden jolt, ripping metal, and the sickening sensation of a car balancing on a cliff before it goes over.

Things were blurred. Satan's body felt stiff and sore, and his mind wouldn't piece things together. In a way, he heard the sound and knew that it was an explosion and not gun-fire. Then the blazing light, as complete blackness gave way to foggy uncertainty.

The night was cold, but Satan was quite warm. "Satan." He said his name several times to himself. That was it. "Satan," and he was in the depths of hell. Fire raged about him; yellow flames licked high toward the sky. The sky! Yes, he could see the sky. He wasn't in hell then. He wasn't—

HE TRIED TO struggle when the truth struck him. The gasoline tank had exploded. That was what he had heard. And he couldn't free his body. Something pressed on his chest; something pressed against his hand. But he could move his hand; even lift it. The thing that gripped his fingers wasn't very heavy. Gripped his fingers? No, that wasn't it. His fingers gripped it. It was his gun. Instinctively, of course, he had held onto that gun. His head wouldn't work right. Flames were very close. There he lay in that burning wreck, clutching his gun, when his hand might be free to try to lift the twisted metal that held him a prisoner. Beneath him was the taxi door. He could feel the broken glass. The door seemed to rock back and forth, as if it hung on broken hinges only. Damn that gun! He'd let go of it and—

He didn't let go. He gripped it tighter. Plainly he heard a voice; a voice he knew. It was very close. It was Devine. Fats Devine. So that was who engineered the knock over! Devine, who he thought a— But Devine was saying to someone:

"There. Hear that!" A moment's pause while Satan, too, heard the distinct screech of a police siren. "Naw, those people running up will simply think I'm trying to drag a man from the flames. That's what I got the wrench for. I'll bash in Satan's head."

Someone answered Devine, but Satan didn't get the words. The flames were hissing now; beginning a dull roar. Then there was the scraping of a huge body over metal; the falling of glass.

And Devine spoke again.

"Hello, Mr. Satan Hall. How do you like your funeral pyre? Who are you going to slap down now? Want to know who killed Judge Landon?" There was gloating in the voice. "Well, it was Krause; Gunner Krause. Take that knowledge to hell!"

Satan opened his eyes wide and stared straight into the fleshy face of Fats Devine; stared, too, at that upraised arm and the ham-like hand and the heavy monkey wrench it held.

Satan laughed. Devine had never heard a laugh like that before. It was a mirthless laugh; as sinister and cruel as those malignant green eyes. Even as Devine raised that wrench to bring it down on the unprotected head, he wondered about that laugh. That Satan could laugh and die! And the hand that held the wrench trembled slightly as it started down.

And Devine knew why Satan laughed. Knew it for a split second only, as his mouth hung open. Surprise, fear, terror, swept over his fat face. Plainly in the glare of the now roaring fire which threatened to engulf both of them, Devine saw Satan's hand raise; saw, too, the black snubbed nose of the police automatic.

That was all. Just the single roar of a gun and a heavy bullet buried itself far back in the open mouth of Fats Devine.

Satan's thin lips set grimly. It was rather nice to take Devine out with him. Then he thought of the commissioner and the Bronx deal, and wished it had been Krause; Gunner Krause.

There was a great spurt of flame that seemed to swallow Devine; an intense heat. Then the huge bulk of Devine collapsed on top of Satan.

Metal groaned, glass tinkled below him, and the door beneath Satan ripped from its broken hinges. The added weight of Devine's body had torn the few remaining screws loose. Satan was free; Satan was falling. But he saw little hope in that. He'd be buried beneath the burning taxi.

He was dropping—dropping. It seemed a long way to the sidewalk. Then his body crashed down on stone. Above him, seemingly quite far above him, was a roaring furnace. And in that burning mass Satan saw the face of Devine; the wide open eyes; glassy, sightless eyes. Then blackness; just dead blackness.

5

JOHNNY ZITTO SPEAKS

SOMEONE SAID:

"I seen it all, Officer. There was the beat of the machine gun, and the taxi side-swiped the big car coming in the opposite direction. Then the taxi jumped the curb, turned sideways, sort of ran up them steps and toppled over the balustrade, almost going into the basement entrance. The chauffeur was thrown right through the windshield and killed like *that*. But I tell you there were two men still in the taxi. I seen one crawl in to help the other. Then there was an explosion; sounded like a shot, and the whole car blazed up and— What's that down there in the court, near the basement entrance?"

"That," said a gruff voice, "is the other man who was in the car. You see, the door of the taxi that held him, broke free, and he dropped the six or eight feet into the areaway. Here, give me that flash you've got and we'll see if he's— God in heaven! It's Detective Hall. Satan Hall."

"Is he alive?"

"Don't you worry about that." Satan's words were hardly a whisper. "I just found out who killed Judge Landon."

"Yeah?" said the patrolman, getting out his notebook and

pencil, for he was a methodical man. "Maybe an antemortem statement," he whispered to his companion.

"That's right." Though there was a confidence in Satan's words, his voice was plainly weaker. "It'll be an antemortem statement for the lad who killed the judge."

A minute of silence; two men with a stretcher; a white coated figure kneeling beside Satan, and the voice of the officer again.

"He was about to tell the name of a murderer, and then couldn't."

"And then wouldn't." Satan's pale lips were grim. And this time when blackness came, he did pass entirely out of the picture.

Two days later the commissioner said:

"I know you hate to stay in the hospital, Satan, and I want you out as much as you want to be out. You were lucky no bones were broken, or your skull wasn't fractured. You can have anything you want."

"Yeah." Satan sat up in the bed. "I never got much use out of my head before, but it came in handy to fall on. I just want my pants. A lad can't do much without his pants."

The commissioner laughed, then seriously:

"You'll stay here a full week, anyway. Glass cuts, you know. You lost a lot of blood before they put those stitches in your neck." And after a moment, "It's all over the Avenue about your slapping Krause down. I guess that's what started the fireworks. I figure that Zitto wanted you out of the way before Krause went after you and you killed him. Krause is not like the others, Satan. He isn't the kind to wait. He's a born killer. Don't try to laugh it off. That's why I want you in shape before you leave here." The commissioner paused a moment and leaned eagerly forward. "Condon, the officer on the beat, said you wanted to make some statement as to who killed Judge Landon. Does that mean you—you know who murdered him?"

"Know!" Satan nodded, and felt his head swim. It was a full minute before he spoke again. "Fats Devine told me before he died. But I guess I always knew."

"The Department will work on it now. Was it Krause?"

"It's my case," Satan cut in, and for a moment his green eyes flashed. "We may never be able to prove it, Commissioner. But if Krause is half the man you think he is and I'm half the man I think I am, we won't need to prove it."

"You mean—?"

"Just that. Krause can't handle any Bronx racket while I live. He's got to do his stuff or quit. Since Devine missed out, Krause will have something to think about, and—"

Satan turned his head. A little white clad nurse had softly opened the door.

"A visitor for Mr. Hall." But it was the commissioner she looked at. "Mr. Zitto."

"Zitto. Johnny Zitto." The commissioner came to his feet. "Why—"

"That's right. Johnny Zitto." The tall, broad man who had made crime a business pushed the nurse aside and stepped into the room. "Howdy, Commissioner!" He was pump-handling the little man's hand almost before the commissioner realized it. Then to Satan, "Damn it! Satan, I'm glad to see you looking yourself; the newspapers have a way of lying so about things. Brought you over a bottle of brandy. Great stuff; too old even for my best customer."

And with his brows knitted, "In a way, I almost feel responsible for your—your trouble."

"Yeah?" Satan grinned as Johnny Zitto, ignoring the standing commissioner, dropped easily into the only rocker.

"Sure. Sure. I kept Devine on at the club. Felt sort of sorry for him. Never for a moment thought he'd turn out a dangerous, homicidal maniac. But then, you're generally able to take care of yourself. How's business with you, Commissioner?"

For a long time the commissioner stood with his hands behind his back, looking at the soft, blue eyes of Johnny Zitto. Then he said:

"I didn't think you'd come here."

"No?" Johnny Zitto's thin eyebrows raised slightly. "I manage to get around. Any reason why I shouldn't?" There was more than a question in his voice; almost a demand for an answer.

TWICE THE COMMISSIONER started to speak and twice he changed what was on his tongue as he looked at the pleased grin on Satan's lips. There was no getting away from it. Johnny Zitto was a big shot in a great city, and Johnny knew it. The commissioner finally said:

"Detective Hall is limited as to visitors."

"Surely not old friends." Johnny Zitto crossed his legs, and then seeing the determined look on the commissioner's face, "I'd like a few words with Satan; private words, if you're going anywhere."

"That's okay." Satan got his words in before the commissioner could speak. "Johnny wants to talk and I want to listen."

"Sure. Sure." Zitto looked up at the commissioner. "A man never did himself any harm by listening."

The commissioner's lips twitched before he turned to the door and said:

"That's true, Zitto. I'll be down the hall a bit."

"Fine!" said Johnny. "Just fine. See you some more."

When the door closed Johnny Zitto came to his feet and walked over to the window. For a minute he stood looking down into the court below.

"It's two stories up," said Satan. "Krause would have to use a ladder if he had any thoughts like that."

"He'd have to use more than that." Zitto nodded. "There's a couple of cops leaning against the wall."

"Yeah?" Satan was surprised.

"Surprise to you, eh?" Johnny Zitto said. "Well, maybe the commissioner hasn't got the same confidence in you that you've got in yourself. There's a couple of quiet-clothes men down stairs, and a flat foot outside your door."

"Too bad, Johnny. But I'll be out next week and give Krause a chance, if he really wants it. You'd like to see Krause knock me over, wouldn't you?"

"Cripes!" Johnny Zitto swung and faced Satan. "That's the last thing in the world I do want. You don't think I'd want a cop killer; a hunted man, working for me!"

"He wouldn't be apt to leave his name and address," Satan said. "I dare say you'd fix up an alibi for him; one that would stick. It would be a big thing for a guy to gun me out and beat the rap; give him standing."

"That's so." Johnny Zitto laughed. "You give a lad ideas, Satan. You'll be taking a vacation for a bit, eh?"

Satan shook his head.

"I'll be back on the Avenue next week. You can tell Krause that."

"Krause is a good egg, Satan. He's quick tempered and got his pride, just like you have. You shouldn't have slapped him down. Now, I like both you boys. I'd like to keep you apart. I thought maybe you'd take a cruise. Mediterranean! Maybe even around the world! It'd do you good."

"On a detective's pay?" Satan laughed.

No." Johnny Zitto dug a hand into a coat pocket and pulled out a huge flat stack of bills. "You see, Satan, it seemed to me I was partly responsible for your being knocked around the way you were. I'd like to make it up some way." He tossed the bills on the bed. "Count it, boy. Twenty grand."

Satan lifted the money and spun it back onto Johnny's knees.

"Nothing doing, Johnny. What next?" There was no anger in Satan's voice. The offer, after all, was flattering.

Johnny Zitto held the money carelessly in his hand.

"It's a nice trip this time of year. And not being well, you might take someone along to nurse you."

"Sure." Satan grinned. "The commissioner, maybe."

"No—" said Johnny slowly, "I wasn't thinking of him. I was thinking of Mattie. Mattie Hern."

The fingers of both Satan's hands closed on the bed. He didn't speak at once. When he did, his words were even—calm.

"I like Mattie a lot, and I know Mattie. Better leave her name out of it, Johnny."

"Sure. Sure." Johnny still held the bills. "Mattie don't run around. She's got ideas. But if I said the word—" His broad shoulders shrugged. "I could roast her father, Jake Hern, by just opening my mouth."

"I never looked on you as that kind of a guy, Johnny. Never." Satan's words were still even, but the softness had gone out of his voice.

Johnny's blue eyes grew hard and cold. He leaned forward now. His words were crisp; sincere.

"I want that Bronx deal to go through," he said simply.

"So it's that bad."

"It's worse than that." Zitto came to his feet. "Krause means business, Satan. He can't get to you now, but he can get to the nearest thing to you. Mattie Hern."

Satan jerked erect in the bed.

"Johnny," the words just shot from his mouth, "you wouldn't lend a hand to anything like that!"

Johnny Zitto's shoulders shrugged again.

"Krause is a hard man to control," he said. A long pause this time, "And I want the Bronx." He moved slowly toward the door, stuffing the bills into his pocket. "Think it over. Mattie does what I say. Maybe I'll talk even bigger money."

"You're talking yourself into a dose of lead."

For a moment the blue eyes of Johnny Zitto met those of Satan Hall, and for a moment Johnny knew what other men had seen there before they died. He didn't exactly feel fear, for Johnny Zitto didn't recognize fear. But he felt something; a nameless something. The presence of death, maybe. Twice he tried to smile, but didn't make a go of it, then he swung suddenly on his heels and jerked open the door. One thing he did know. He saw Satan now as other men had seen him. And he knew that Satan would have to die.

6

SATAN GETS A GUN

SATAN'S ROOM WAS large and comfortable. The window faced on an open court and the sunlight played in the room for a couple of hours each day. The food was good. But he didn't like it all. He didn't like women fooling around him.

The nurse, too, found it rather difficult. She read the papers and told the floor nurse, in a rather awed voice:

"It's not hard to understand what they say about the man. He did talk in the beginning, but now he just lies there, and when I asked him if anything was bothering him he simply said, 'I'm getting well.' To me, he's—"

"Just 'the patient in room 684.'" And as the phone buzzed, the floor nurse lifted the receiver, listened a moment and turned to the little nurse.

"That's for Detective Hall. Take the phone to him."

The nurse carried the phone, with its length of wire, around the corridor. Before room 684 she paused, parted her tightly drawn lips, and after a soft careful tap, entered the room.

Detective Hall took the phone from the nurse, watched her plug the wire into the floor base, set his green eyes on her and waited until she left the room. Then he said into the mouthpiece:

"What now?" It would be Zitto again. Raising the ante, of course.

And it wasn't Zitto. It was Mattie. And her voice was low.

"I wanted to come and see you, Satan, but I didn't dare." She hesitated a long moment, and then, "You said you'd come to me any time I needed you. When will you be out? Zitto said you're just resting now."

"That's right, Mattie. There is no reason why I shouldn't be out now. I'm up and around." He half grinned as he thought of his fifteen minute trip across the room to the chair. "What's the trouble?"

"It's Krause." She hardly breathed the words into the phone. "He wants me to meet him tonight. It's a house in the Bronx; a deserted house. I thought—I hoped— I don't know what to do."

"Don't go," Satan told her sharply. "What's the deal? Where do I fit?"

"It's a scheme to—to trap you. To use me to trap you."

"Don't go!" Satan said again.

"I've got to go. He's got something on me. Something he might—could tell Zitto. He says, if I'll trap you he'll forget it. Krause knows I telephoned you a warning the other night. I didn't think anyone heard me. If I hide out, and he tells Zitto—there's my father. Zitto could—Zitto would roast him if he thought I—I ratted on him."

"Yes," said Satan. "I got you in this jam, Mattie. You want me to come up there to the Bronx and—

"I thought we'd turn the trap against Krause. I'd have you hiding there when he came."

"But he could talk to Zitto later. How would that help?"

"I thought that if you and Krause met, why—why—"

"One of us would never talk again, eh?" Satan's head nodded.

"That Krause would never talk again." Her words were so low that Satan guessed at them rather than heard them.

"That's right. That's right." Satan seemed to think aloud. "I'll be up there, Mattie. What time, and just where is the house?"

"Krause has business with Zitto up until twelve-thirty. Get there by that time." She gave him the address. "Come to the back door, through the lot behind. I'll be watching for you. You're sure you're fit to come?"

"Sure." Satan laughed lightly. "I'm just lying around here because it's an easy life."

Satan clicked down the receiver. Mattie Hern's voice held fear; perhaps terror. But put it any way you liked, whether Mattie meant it so or not, she had asked Satan to come down and kill a man. Well, perhaps a gun in Krause's chest would be sufficient. He shrugged his shoulders. That would work itself out. The thing was—to get out of the damned hospital without making too much of a fuss.

Satan jerked the bedclothes from him, and ignoring the slippers by the side of the bed and the robe over the foot of it, planted both his feet firmly on the floor. It was funny that a guy had to stand erect a minute, waiting for his head to clear before he walked across the floor. But he did walk across the floor, and his feet were even and steady, if slow. It wasn't a time to permit his legs to give at the knees, and he didn't. He held them stiff and straight as he opened the closet door and nodded with satisfaction as he saw his clothes hanging there.

But there was no satisfaction as a thorough search of that closet did not reveal his twin forty-fives. His shoulder holster was there all right, but it was empty. He cursed softly, made sure that he had his entire wardrobe, then he went back to bed. He couldn't get dressed yet. That damned doctor and the hard visaged nurse would be around, pawing him, at nine o'clock. After that, the night was his.

AND THE DOCTOR didn't paw him that night. He just stood by the bed; asked a few simple questions.

"We won't be able to keep you here much longer, Mr. Hall," he said.

"That's right." Satan's eyes were so cold and his lips so tight that the smile froze on the doctor's face as he stepped back from the bed.

"I wouldn't want to meet him in a dark alley at night," the doctor said to Sergeant Michael Callahan, who had night duty on the door.

"He's a killer, if that's what you mean." There was admiration in Callahan's voice. "But as unsociable a fellow as you'd ever want to meet."

And Sergeant Callahan was surprised an hour later when the light flashed above his head and the nurse informed him that Satan would like to have him in the room. And Sergeant Callahan's surprise was increased when Satan spoke.

"There's a bottle of choice stuff in the drawer there. Pour yourself a drink and be sociable."

Sociable? Callahan thought that word over and found that it didn't fit at all. But he took the bottle from the drawer, waved away Satan's suggestion that he send for a cork screw and produced one of his own, on the back of a huge clasp knife.

"The kid's boy scout knife," he explained, as he poured out the liquor, tasted it carefully, then gulped it down. "A little of this wouldn't hurt you."

"Don't touch the stuff," said Satan. "Take another crack at it. Zitto brought it."

Glass half raised, the sergeant set it down again. There was alarm in his face. Satan grinned.

"It'd be too late now, if it was poisoned. But Zitto doesn't work that way."

"No, no." Sergeant Callahan ran the back of his hand across his mouth. Then he tipped up the bottle and poured himself another drink. "It's like the hot seat." He laughed. "Can't kill you more than once."

For close to an hour Satan listened to the sergeant's talk. It had little to do with the Department, outside the small pay, the long hours and the chances a man took. The sergeant spoke of his family; mostly of his eldest daughter.

"It ain't every copper who's got a daughter graduating from college."

"Sergeant," Satan said suddenly, "just what would you do; what are your orders if I decided to walk out of this hospital tonight?"

"Me?" The sergeant was startled. "Why—I don't know."

"You haven't any orders, then, from the commissioner?"

"No. He said to watch you, but that was just for—" And as Detective Hall suddenly threw back the bedclothes and disclosed to the sergeant that he was fully dressed, "You're going out?"

"Yes!" said Satan, swinging himself up from the bed. "I'm

going out tonight. I want you to help me. I don't want to be seen. I want your gun and—"

"God! I couldn't do that." Sergeant Callahan came to his feet and half clutched his hip pocket. "Don't look at me like that. Why do—?"

"To save the life of a girl just about your daughter's age. A girl who didn't have an honest cop for a father, and whose college was the back room of a fence's pawn shop. I've got to save her from a beast of a man." He was on his feet now, staring into the startled eyes of Callahan.

Callahan gasped.

"You can't. Look at them wobbling legs of yours. Your face is white as death now. You couldn't do it."

"No?" Satan held out his right hand. "There isn't much strength in it. But it's fairly steady, and if you let me have your gun—why, I guess I've got enough strength to press one finger."

"You're mad." Callahan stared at those bright green eyes in the dead white face. "Who's the man?"

"Krause," said Satan. "Gunner Krause."

Satan coughed a little; his eyes were very wide. A sudden red came into his face. But he raised a hand and threw off the arm that Callahan placed about his shoulder.

"I've got to go. Got to go, just like you'd go for that daughter of yours."

Callahan took another drink and said:

"You're just like me when I was young. Damn it! Satan, the boys don't dislike you. They—they envy you. You've got nerve. But to give you my gun! Why—"

Satan turned from the closet door with his coat over his arm, his hat thrust on his head.

"Damn it! Callahan, do I have to face Krause with my bare hands, or do I get your gun?"

"Yes," said Callahan, "you get the gun. And me up for my pension in another year!"

It was Callahan who arranged for Satan to leave the hospital unseen. There was a fire escape at the end of the corridor. By calling the man in the court below it off duty and watching that short length of hall, Satan was able to climb out the window unseen.

Satan's head was clear enough when he started down the fire escape. He liked the feel of the gun beneath his left armpit; he liked the final whispered words of Sergeant Callahan that no one had seen him in the short hall, but he didn't like the uncertainty of his feet as he tried to hurry them down the iron steps.

HE HAD TO rest when he reached the court below. But he had plenty of time to reach the house in the Bronx. Plenty of time! And he remembered the detective who had gone above. No, he had to move on. He missed the railing of the fire escape now as he walked across the stone court, reeled slightly, found the gate and was out on the sidewalk.

The fresh air did him good and he had the taxi drive through Central Park. With the ease of long practice he removed the clip from Callahan's gun and tried the trigger. A little tight; not the accustomed free action of his own guns. Or was it, after all, the lack of strength in his finger? But he smiled at that. It didn't matter much. A guy didn't need to be an athlete to squeeze lead.

Two or three times he tried jerking the gun from the holster. Not his usual speed? Maybe not. But then, there was to be nothing expert about tonight's work. He was just going to shove a gun against a man and talk. But maybe talk wouldn't do much good. Was he going to kill a man? That would be up to Gunner Krause. Or would it? Satan wondered.

The house in the Bronx proved a dismal affair. No lights in the front windows; no lights from the side. A vacant lot stood to the left of it, so Satan could see through to the street beyond. He knew his city; knew exactly where he was.

"Where to now?" The driver jerked his head around.

"Turn at this corner," Satan told him. "Then right again at the next corner, and stop."

"Okay, brother." The taxi swung the corner, shot down the block, turned again and came to a stop.

"How much?" Satan stumbled from the cab and staggered across the sidewalk. Regaining his balance, he came back to the taxi.

"Know where you're going?" The driver pocketed the fare. "Know what you're doing?" he added sarcastically, as Satan seemed to sway on his feet.

"Exactly. Exactly what I'm doing."

The driver stuck a cigarette between his teeth and lit a match. For a moment the tiny blaze shot into sudden brightness. Satan was leaning slightly forward; his face was in the light.

The sneering words died on the driver's lips. He looked straight into the white face before him. It was a hard face; a cruel face; a sinister face. For a moment the driver thought that he was looking at the inside of the man, not at the outside of him.

"God a'mighty!" he muttered as the match burned his

fingers and fell to the floor of the cab. Then, as he jerked the car into gear and jolted from the curb, "What a map!" But there was nothing of humor in his voice.

It seemed a long walk to that vacant lot behind the house. Satan could see the outline of the house. Old, dilapidated and deserted, he guessed. He leaned against a street pole and drew in deep breaths. There was a pain in his side; over his heart, he thought. His heart.

That was what was bad. And he grinned and shook his head.

The pain was on his right side. Too high up for his heart, anyway, and those deep breaths hurt him. But he had to have air. It was cool air, yet it seemed to burn.

He jarred himself from the pole and started across the vacant lot. If he rested every minute he'd never get there! But there was nothing to lean against in that lot. He had to keep going or fall down. The ground was rough. Twice he stumbled over cans, pitched forward like a drunken man and with a drunken man's luck regained his balance. He grinned when he reached the house; got his gun into his hand.

He shook his head, in an effort to clear the cobwebs from it. This was the house Gunner Krause was coming to; the house he was going to trap Satan in. Well, there'd be a little surprise for Krause.

Satan tapped three times on the back door, then pushed his back against the torn boards to the left of it. He'd make sure it was Mattie who came to that door. Krause might have arrived ahead of time, suspected Mattie, or— But Satan wouldn't stand before that open door in the half light of a dull moon until he was certain—certain that it was Mattie who answered the knock.

And the door opened. A moment of silence, then a voice; the voice of Mattie.

"Satan. It's you, Satan?"

Her words seemed to stick in her throat. There was fear; even terror in them.

Satan started to speak, coughed once, and wet his lips with his tongue. Funny that. His lips were thick. Finally he got the words out.

"It's all right, Mattie," he said, swinging his body before the door. And, as she stretched out an arm to steady him, he entered the blackness of the house. "I've got it figured out. I'll give Krause a chance to—"

Satan stopped. Mattie had taken his arm; the arm the hand of which held the gun. A shadow had moved beside him; a voice spoke.

"Now, ain't that just too nice."

There was a swish of air, a dull thud, a hoarse laugh as Satan's knees gave. And just before he dropped to the floor Satan had one thought. The commissioner had been right about Mattie Hern. For before that dull thud pounded against his head Satan had recognized the voice of the man who spoke, Mattie had trapped him. It was Krause. Gunner Krause.

7

THE WEAK LINK

SOMEONE WAS BATHING Satan's head with a wet cloth. Someone was running a hand over his forehead and back through his hair. There were sounds, too; queer little gulps. A drop of water fell upon his cheek. Satan opened his eyes and saw Mattie Hern.

He was lying on a dusty couch in a small room. There was a single light burning in the ceiling almost directly above him. For a long moment Satan stared straight into Mattie's dark eyes. They were dim and wet.

"You look terrible, Satan—terrible." The words just forced themselves from between Mattie's lips. They were not at all the ones she wanted to speak.

Satan didn't have to grope around in his head to know what happened. Peculiarly, his head was clear. Nothing foggy or uncertain about his thoughts now, as he gazed straight at Mattie.

"Say something, Satan; say something." Mattie's face was very close to his. Satan closed his eyes and the girl went on; rapidly, stumbling over the words. "I had to do it, Satan. It wasn't because of myself. I didn't care what they did to me. It was my father. Zitto told me to do what Krause said, or they'd burn my father. My father pleaded with me too. It was Krause. He'd of killed him then, I think, if I didn't do it. But they're not going to harm you. You're just going to agree to take a trip; drop out of things for a while, to make Krause right on the Avenue; let it be thought that he scared you off. Then—then—"

Satan's green eyes were open again, still looking straight at the girl. There was nothing of reproach in them; nothing of that cruel, evil glare so many saw there. Just green eyes without expression.

Mattie placed both hands upon his shoulder; shook him, almost violently.

"Say something, Satan; say something. They gave me those few moments with you. I wanted you to understand. Say something!"

Green eyes held hers. And Satan spoke; spoke just what was on his mind.

"The commissioner was right and I was wrong," he said slowly. "You're a rat, Mattie. Just a rat."

She jarred erect, and her black eyes blazed through the fog.

"I loved you," she said. "I gave you your chance to take me away from it all. You wouldn't. You didn't care. Maybe I hated you then. I don't know. They won't harm you."

"They're going to kill me, of course," Satan said. "Krause couldn't do otherwise now."

"No, no." She cried out the words. "They won't. They can't. I won't let them." And as if she recognized the truth, a truth she wouldn't let herself believe before. "He was my father. I had to do it. I—"

The door opened. Mattie jumped to her feet. Satan half turned his head. Gunner Krause stood in the open doorway. Thick lips parted; mud-colored eyes glittered. His heavy shoulders bent forward.

Mattie didn't turn at once. She rubbed her eyes; held a tiny mirror in her hand; daubed her face and studied it in the small glass.

"Come on, kid. Scram!" Krause said. "You've done your stuff, and you done it right. I don't mind telling you flat that I'd of bumped off your old man if there had been a slip—" And with a sneer toward Satan, "How's the boy friend?"

"Bad!" said Mattie. "Zitto lied about the trip then?"

"Not exactly." Krause grinned. "Satan's going to take a trip. A one way trip."

"You're going to kill him?" Mattie's voice was very calm.

"That's right. Deader than hell." Krause nodded vigorously. "Don't kid me that you didn't know."

Mattie walked slowly to the door. She paused once, but didn't look at Satan. She didn't look at Krause either.

"I guess that's true." She directed her words to the blank wall between the two men. "I guess I did know. It won't be here. It'll be the big touring?"

"Sure!" Krause watched her. "That's right. It won't be here; it'll be the big touring."

Without another word Mattie stepped into the hall and closed the door.

"So you're going to kill me, Krause?" Satan said.

"And how!" Krause nodded. His eyes flashed.

"You told Mattie it was just a trip; a talk?"

"Conscience salve! Zitto called it. She didn't believe it, but she could pretend she did. Zitto knows men—and women."

"You think she knew all along, eh?" Krause laughed.

"You never looked on Mattie as dumb, did you?"

"No," said Satan slowly, "I didn't. But then, I never looked on myself as dumb, either. So you can't tell."

"It doesn't matter," Krause said. He walked over to the couch and stood looking down at Satan. "Satan Hall. Tough dick, Satan. Hard guy. Killer. Slaps 'em down and marks 'em. Satan's mark!" His mud-colored eyes closed to twin slits while he talked. He swung his right hand and cracked it across Satan's cheek.

Satan stared up at him and said:

"You know what it means to kill a cop, Krause."

"The cops won't miss you no more than the boys will. I'll have an alibi that will stand up in any court. Zitto's fixing that." He leaned forward now, lips tight, words sneering between them. "And if I didn't have one I'd do for you anyway, any time, any place. I hate your nerve."

His right hand turned into a fist; uncontrolled rage drew his arm back and forward. Blood showed on Satan's lips; trickled down his chin.

"Mark me, will ya?" The hand shot back again—and stayed there. A quiet voice spoke behind Krause.

"Nix, Krause, nix."

Johnny Zitto stood in the doorway. His evening clothes fitted perfectly. He strode easily into the room.

"Why not, Johnny? Why not? The lousy yellow rat! He—"

"It isn't done, Gunner." Johnny's mild blue eyes rested lazily on Krause's angry face. "Might leave finger prints." And as Krause's hand started back again, "Besides, Gunner, I said, 'Nix!'"

Johnny Zitto hadn't raised his voice any. It was still

low, but there was a razor-like edge to it. Gunner Krause mumbled under his breath, but his hand dropped to his side.

"Let's get moving," he said.

"That's right," said Johnny. "Drive the car around. I'll bring Satan down. On your way!"

Krause hesitated; looked at Satan.

"Okay, boss. It's just business with you. But you can't blame a guy like me for having feelings."

"That's right," said Johnny Zitto. Then again, "On your way!"

ALONE WITH JOHNNY Zitto, Satan pulled himself erect on the couch, grinned as Zitto's hand shot into a jacket pocket and a flat nosed gun shoved out cloth. Then he said:

"So Krause is going to push me over?"

"Where did you get such an idea?" Johnny Zitto shook his head very seriously, but his eyes smiled. "I've got a date, and I'm going to let Krause drive you back to the hospital. The night air's pleasant, Satan. Maybe he'll drive you around for a bit."

"It looks bad," Satan admitted aloud. And then, "I was a fool. But I never thought Mattie would—"

"Mattie's of one world and you're of another," Johnny Zitto cut in sharply. "And as Kipling said, 'those two worlds won't jibe.' You're a cop; she's of the night. Damn it, Satan, I hate to see you go! But you made your slip. A guy's only entitled to one slip in the racket."

"And that slip was slapping down Krause, eh?" It was surprising how much clearer Satan's head was. But his legs! He wondered about them as he set them firmly on the floor.

"Hell! no," said Johnny Zitto. "You had a weak link in your chain. That link was Mattie. Tonight it snapped. Don't blame Mattie; blame yourself. When the show-down came she stuck to her own kind. That's why she's working for Johnny Zitto. Come on, Satan. I hate to go through with it, but business is business, and I do want the Bronx."

Satan got slowly to his feet and balanced there. Zitto watched his legs give at the knees; half stepped back as he suspected some ruse. And Satan's legs straightened. His head came up.

"It had to come, I suppose," he said. "I sort of wish it was with a gun in my hand."

"I'd like it that way too," said Johnny Zitto. "But you see how it is. It's a tough racket, Satan. But you gave it, and you've got to take it. It's the same for every guy. You and I both dealt cards to Mattie; one of us had to be wrong."

"That's right," Satan said as he passed slowly into the hall. "One of us had to be wrong." He steadied his swaying body against the wall as he moved before Johnny's prodding gun.

"I'm sorry, Satan," Johnny Zitto said at the door as Satan half stumbled against it, "that it had to come like this. But that's life and death. If there's a racket in hell, remember— women ain't for coppers. Not women like Mattie Hern."

"Mattie's a rat!" Satan said as he staggered down the steps and stumbled toward the dark hulk of a big touring car parked in the driveway.

Gunner Krause was there, standing by the steps. He grabbed Satan roughly; jerked his arms behind his back. There was a sharp click and the feel of iron as his wrists were locked together.

"Coppers ain't the only ones who use bracelets—and guns, too," Krause added significantly as he pushed Satan toward the car. "In the front, flat-foot!" And as Satan tripped and fell on the running board, "Ain't slapping anyone down now, are you?" And to Johnny Zitto, who stood calmly by the side of the car, his sharp blue eyes darting up and down the deserted street, "Won't come along and see the fun, Johnny?"

"No," said Johnny. "I'm driving Mattie down town."

"Not her, you ain't." Krause laughed. "She beat it along." His shoulders shrugged. "She was snooty, too. Like she done something big and expected to cash in on it. A poke in the nose wouldn't do her any harm."

"It's better she's gone," Johnny Zitto said. "She sort of fancied Satan for a bit. Women haven't got the stomach for such things, Krause. Mattie's all head."

"Yeah?" said Krause as he climbed in behind the wheel. "All head! I was kind of thinking different. She's got class. Just needs a little knuckle work. I wish you'd let me handle her, Boss. She ain't so bad."

"We'll see," said Zitto. "We'll see how you handle the Bronx."

"She don't mean nothing to you then?" There was an eagerness in Krause's voice.

"Nothing at all," said Zitto. "Not that way. Well, good luck, Krause. Remember—this is a business trip."

"Sure!" said Krause as he stepped on the starter and the motor purred softly. "And I'm the kind of a guy who likes his business."

"So long, Satan," said Johnny Zitto as Krause threw in the clutch. "Take care of yourself."

Though Johnny Zitto's voice was easy, almost indifferent, there was nothing of sarcasm in it. It was as if he were
performing an unpleasant duty but was resigned to it.

8

THE ONE WAY RIDE

SATAN DIDN'T SPEAK. He turned his head as the car slipped quickly out of the driveway and swung up the street. In a dim way he made out the figure of Zitto, standing there watching. And he thought, too, that Zitto raised his hand in a gesture of farewell. But Satan just sat slumped there in the car, his hands behind him, his feet pressed firmly against the floor of the car.

"Where to?" Satan finally raised his head.

"Up from Van Cortlandt Park; back of Kingsbridge." Krause turned the car to the left and shot across town. "If you make a holler I'll pump your stomach full of lead, open the door and drop you out."

"I won't make a holler," said Satan. "I guess I can take it."

Satan pushed his long body up straighter in the seat. Beneath a passing street light he caught a glimpse of Krause's face. It was white now. White, with a red patch on the cheek that was close to Satan. It was some time before Krause spoke again.

"And you're going to take it right smack in the stomach. All seven shots, Satan. Right in the belly. You're going to feel them; every one of them." Krause's voice rose as he talked, and there was hatred in it. "They'll know. Every one of the boys will know you didn't live long after slapping me down."

"The cops will know, too," said Satan. And then, half aloud, "But somehow it doesn't all seem real."

"It'll seem real when they plant you," Krause sneered. He had hoped to see Satan cringe. Well, he'd beat him to his knees with the nose of his gun before he let him have it. "As for the cops, what they know won't stand up against my witnesses. The bump is in the bag."

"Maybe!" said Satan. It still seemed like a dream to him. He knew the streets well; even recognized an old store or two, the doors of which he used to try some years back, when he was first on the Force. Then his breath whistled in his throat.

And Satan jarred erect in the car. It wasn't a dream any more. It was real now. He was going to his death. Going to be gunned out by a common thug. His green eyes narrowed; he looked at the white face of Krause and his single thought then was: what of the commissioner? The Bronx deal was going through. And he was going to die.

Krause was driving slowly now; out around a lonely stretch of road. There was the grassy bank; matted yellow grass, and in the distance the dull glare of city lights.

The cold hand of death was on him. Funny, that thought. It was so real, as if icy fingers touched the back of his neck. He shivered slightly. His head was clear, but his arms ached; and his back too. He tried forcing his back-tighter against the cushion. Damn it, he must be weak as a woman! The cushion felt as if it had lead in it; hard metal that bored into his back. And Satan moved slightly forward as Krause spoke.

"Here's the spot," Krause said as he turned the car quickly off the road, ran it partly onto the grass and stopped it with a jerk. "Well, do you get out yourself; or do I plug you here, open the door and let you drop out?"

Viciousness was now in Krause's voice, but Satan wasn't listening. When he moved forward, something had jarred down his back, thudded on his hands—hard and cold. No icy fingers of death, this; no imaginary weakness of his body. His fingers crept around that cold surface, clutched it familiarly. Satan could not be mistaken. His manacled right hand now held a gun. A small one, to be sure; a thirty-two. He didn't have to look at a gun to know the caliber.

Was he delirious? Where had the gun come from? Was it lying there on the seat behind him, and had it worked its way out with his moving body? And—with a gulp deep down in his throat—*was it loaded?*

"Well?" Krause leaned over, his face close to Satan's. "You're turning yellow when the time comes, eh? Slap a guy down. Mark me! Satan's mark! How do you like that one?"

Gunner Krause pounded his gun down on Satan's forehead. It knocked his head back; dazed him for a bit, then he felt the blood running down his face. Things weren't all clear now. Only one thing was clear. His right hand was clutching a gun behind his back. How to use it!

Satan heard a door slam closed; then another one open. Krause had gotten out of the car, walked around it and was standing on the grass. Reaching in, he grabbed Satan roughly by the arm.

He was laughing. At least, there a queer sort of grating noise in his throat. Words came huskily from between his lips.

"Come out and take it. Take it on your knees. On your knees, Satan. Tough dick. Killer! That's how they'll find you. Begging for your life. Begging—"

Desperately Satan tried to stay upon his feet as he was dragged from the car. Desperately he gripped the gun in his right hand behind his back, his finger on the trigger, his mind trying to piece things together.

He would have fallen, but Krause held him up. A white face; glaring, mud-colored eyes on either side of a flat nose. And Krause's gun came up and down again. This time, as Krause half supported him, Satan sank slowly to his knees.

What the hell! It wasn't so bad to die. It was easy and restful. Satan wanted desperately to lie down—lie down there, right in the grass. His head dropped forward on his chest.

Words were coming from a distance. At least they seemed a long way off.

"Can't take it. Can't take it."

Maybe Krause said the words only once; maybe he said them a dozen times. They raced through Satan's head; echoed and re-echoed in his ears. He didn't know if they came from outside his head or inside it.

BUT HE'D TAKE it. He'd— He tried to raise his head. At first he couldn't, and then he did. His head came up; his green eyes locked with Krause's before he knew the truth. Krause was holding his chin in his left hand, glaring down into the face. His lips were twisted; brutal. His eyes narrowed to two thin slits. And—and his gun was held in his right hand, close to Satan's stomach.

"And that's the end, Satan. They'll know who has the Bronx when they find you up here. Don't want to look, eh?" This as Satan turned his head away. "Don't want to take the dose of lead!" This as Satan swung his whole body, from the knees; swung it so that his back turned toward Krause; his right hand pushed well over to his left side, and the small black nose of the thing that right hand held slanting upwards.

But Krause didn't see Satan's hands. He was looking at Satan's face; trying to force those green eyes back to his.

"All right," Krause said at length. "Beg your prettiest. I'll count three. One—two—"

There was a sharp report of a gun. Krause paused; straightened. His right hand dropped to his side.

"What's that? What's—" He started, and stopped. There was surprise in his voice.

There was another shot. Krause's whole body trembled, but he didn't move. Both his hands went to his stomach. He tried to look into Satan's face. And suddenly he knew. He saw the gun as his eyes dropped to Satan's hands; the black nose of it.

"You dirty, yellow rat!" he shrieked, and there was fear in his voice now; terror, as he jerked up his gun. He fired wildly; blindly, his eyes riveted on that right hand of Satan's; on the thing in it, that belched flame again even as his own finger closed upon the trigger.

There was blood in Satan's eyes now. He couldn't see very well, but he held the back of his right hand firmly against his left side and twice more squeezed lead up at Krause's body.

There was no answering shot. Satan turned his head; his whole body. Through a mist he saw Krause. His mouth was hanging wide open, as Devine's had hung; both his hands were pressed against his stomach. And Satan nodded. Krause sank slowly to his knees; then collapsed upon the matted, yellow grass.

"He wanted it that way," Satan thought, half aloud, as he staggered to his feet. "A bellyful of lead." That was what Krause had said.

In the dull light of the moon Satan looked down at the dead gunman. And his laugh was neither pleasant nor hysterical.

"I always sort of knew that it wasn't in the cards," he muttered, as he nodded his head in stupid gravity. "I—" He stopped and blinked. His laugh was sort of hollow as he thought to rub a hand across his forehead before he realized that he was still handcuffed. Then he turned, and in slow measured steps, like a drunken man's, walked toward the car. It was a lonely spot, of course, and the shots might not have been heard. Well, he'd lean on that horn until some one came. He'd—

He staggered; straightened. Someone was in the back of that car. Someone was climbing from it; some one was coming toward him, flinging arms about him, clinging to him. Of course it couldn't be, yet it was—a girl—the girl. Mattie Hern. She was saying:

"It's you—you, Satan. I didn't know. I thought perhaps— He's dead? Krause is dead?"

"That's right." Satan nodded very gravely as he leaned against the side of the car. "Krause is dead; very dead. You—you—"

"I hid in the car," she said. "When the show-down came I couldn't let you die. I meant to shoot Krause. Twice I knelt up in the back of the car that covered him. And I couldn't do it. I couldn't kill. I didn't have the nerve for it, Satan. Then I was afraid. I tried to let you know, and—and the gun just slipped down behind you. After that, things happened."

"Yes, things happened." Satan tried to laugh as he sank slowly onto the step of the car. Those icy fingers on his neck had been real then.

Satan knew that somehow Mattie got the key to the handcuffs from the body of Krause, and helped him into the car. He knew that she talked as she drove; that she said Zitto must never know she was there. Satan nodded, but it was very hard to stay awake. But he did tell her about Sergeant Callahan.

Satan never knew how Callahan got him into the hospital, but he did remember that Callahan whispered to him:

"My gun! Where's my gun?"

And Satan knew that he answered: "You won't need the gun, Callahan. Krause won't be coming for me now."

After that his sleep was very peaceful and his dreams pleasant. The Bronx racket was as dead as Krause—or maybe Krause was as dead as the Bronx racket. Take it any way you wish, Satan's dreams were pleasant. He was built that way.

IF IT IS MURDER

*As Five Rapid Shots Rang Through
That Half-Darkened Room, Satan Hall
Threw Back the Curtain and Sprang in
on a Maelstrom of Mystery and Death*

1

THE BIG RACKET

MORRIS METZ LOOKED long and steadily at Johnny Zitto; opened his mouth to speak, then thought better of it. Leaning forward, he lifted the bottle and poured himself a drink. Over the edge of the glass he saw Johnny's eyes; the soft blue of them was hard and steely now. The thin eyebrows had lifted slightly.

Johnny shuffled the cards, dealt them out in seven neat piles for Canfield, and very slowly placed a red six on a black seven. The silence got heavy. Metz shifted in his chair, reached again for the bottle—when Johnny Zitto's hand went out and moved it across the desk.

"Cripes! Johnny." Metz could keep silent no longer. "Why not go yourself a hooker? It'll do you good."

"Not me," said Johnny. "Varnish makes a lad think he's a better man than he is. I'm big enough now." And suddenly, the subject Metz was waiting for. "They couldn't mistake my truck. They couldn't a been coppers on a night off?"

"Not them!" said Metz. "Buck looked right at them. No masks; no disguise. Just the chain across the road. It was over like *that*."

"Buck's getting soft," said Johnny.

"Nix, Boss. Nix." Metz shook his head. "I'd 'a' done the

same thing myself. A guy gets the habit of knowing he's safe on a Zitto route. Every gun knows that Long Island run is yours."

Johnny Zitto flipped the ace of diamonds above the row of seven and said:

"Strangers, eh?"

"That's it. Strangers! But they worked like old timers, Buck says. Like they done it every night."

Zitto looked at the figures on the paper beside him.

"Six grand!" he said. Then lifting a pencil and pointing it at Metz, "As good in my pocket as in the other fellow's. Who'd have the nerve for it?"

"Something screwy about the whole business." Morris Metz puckered up his mouth into a grotesque caricature. "Something damn screwy."

"Yeah." Johnny Zitto came to his feet and walked across the room. For a long minute he stared at Metz. Then, "Yeah," again, just as the phone rang.

Zitto went to his desk, lifted the receiver and snapped:

"Let's have it!" Listened a moment, and then, "H-m. Well, send him up." Replacing the receiver he said to Metz:

"It's that hood, Joe de Grassie. Thought I had seen the last of him in town five years ago."

"Joe's been doing good." Metz squinted rat-like eyes. "Damn good! He's fixer for that Combine. Big shot in it. Better listen to him, Johnny."

"That's right." Johnny Zitto stood looking down at the cards on the desk. "Beat it along, Morris."

Morris Metz left the room, closed the door softly behind him. Johnny Zitto still stood by the desk, but his eyes drifted from the cards to a partly open drawer. Then he quickly ran his hand inside of it, and his fingers fastened on the cold surface of a heavy automatic.

Joe de Grassie was a short man whose waist-line was beginning to protrude. His eyes were a yellowish brown and his face florid, with prominent blue veins running through it. He carried a cane and wore yellow gloves. He took the chair Johnny jerked a thumb at, and removing one glove leaned forward on his cane.

"Nice place," he said. "It wasn't like this a few years back."

"Five!" said Zitto. "When you ran out."

"Retired." De Grassie's eyes blinked. "But you never get out of the business entirely, Zitto. I've sort of advised the boys from one end of the country to the other." And after a pause, "I was a big man before, Johnny. I'm a bigger one now."

"You were a hood to me then, and you're a hood to me now." De Grassie was not offended, or if he was he didn't show it.

"I was always one to organize," he said. "Always one to make the boys see it my way."

"Your way!" Zitto's eyebrows elevated.

"Sure! My way. I've always been in touch with things. You understand my business here, Zitto. The Combine never heard from you. I remembered the old days and I wanted to see you personally before—before you were shoved out."

"Shoved out!" Johnny Zitto's laugh was mirthless, his blue eyes glared dangerously.

"A guy never did himself any harm by listening." Brownish yellow eyes opened wide. "You always said that yourself."

"That's right," said Zitto. "Talk!"

And Joe de Grassie did talk.

"I'VE BEEN AT this thing ever since the repeal of prohibition became a certainty. Look at the boys who were caught unprepared now that beer is legal. But they won't catch me on the repeal of hard liquor. You were felt out on it, Zitto, so I won't go into the details again. But we've organized the entire country. Prices are going up. When repeal goes through we'll be in a position to take over the legitimate liquor trade; we'll be bigger than the liquor interests. In the meantime we jack up hard liquor prices. It's a perfect system. The organization greases all the wheels. Rights are rated on the traffic up to half a million. The wholesaler comes in for twenty-five thousand; the retailer, from five grand up. I've forgotten the past, Johnny; everything personal. I just remember you're a good man. I want you to have the big plum of the organization—New York City. The fee is half a million, just put up to show good will. We've got to have financial control, you know. Something to hold the Combine firmly together."

"Yeah," said Zitto. "Well, I've got New York, or most of it. I let your people know before that I wasn't interested."

"I know. I know. But you don't fully understand, Johnny. It's big. You'd be like a State trying to secede from the Union. For old times sake I want to let you know, Johnny. You'd be wiped out just like *that*," A thick finger and thumb snapped together.

"Rough stuff, eh?"

"No, no. Hardly that. Just organization, except in rare instances."

"And I'm a rare instance?"

"I hope not, Johnny. I hope not. You see, you're growing soft in the racket. The name, Johnny Zitto, means a lot. It means money for the right boys; it means death for the wrong boys. But these would be different boys. Strangers."

"Strangers!" Johnny Zitto jarred erect. He looked down at the figures on the paper. "Strangers," he said again, half aloud. "So that was it."

Joe de Grassie nodded his understanding.

"That was it." He stared over at the paper, dug a hand in his pocket and tossed a flat package of bills across to Zitto. "Seven grand. This time the organization is buying that liquor. Seven grand."

"The price was six." Johnny Zitto looked down at the money.

"We're raising the price, you know. That's what it will bring now. Want to treat you right." And very low, "You'll make millions, Johnny, with organization behind you. We'll be running in canned goods when things get working."

"Going in for dope too." Johnny stroked his chin. "Then women, I suppose. You always were one for women, De Grassie. I always said a woman would finish you."

"Even business men got to have recreation." De Grassie grinned. "Our biggest bankers and industrial leaders have their moments. I saw Mattie Hern down stairs in the dining room. She's a beautiful girl, Johnny. And you don't care for beautiful girls."

"She's a smooth worker," said Johnny Zitto. "Best in the racket." And scowling, "Remember she works for me. I use brains; not sex."

"I'll always remember that, Johnny." De Grassie licked his lips. "If you were to let her come over to me, why—well,

Satan watched an instant. He didn't speak

I could let you in the Combine for—say, four hundred grand, and—"

"I don't sell women," Zitto snapped. "You always were a louse, De Grassie."

JOE DE GRASSIE grinned again. His stock in trade was never losing his temper. He said, pleasantly enough:

"A louse is an industrious animal, Johnny. He can bite, too. I saw a lot of Mattie when she was in Chi, doing a bit of work for her father, Jake Hern. I grew quite fond of her. After all, Johnny, a hundred grand is a pile to save."

"Yeah? Well, this racket of yours isn't costing me a cent, so I can't save a thing. Wait!" when De Grassie would have cut in. "I've got a warning for you; for the men behind you. I've got seven truck loads of stuff coming through tonight. Same road; same time. One man to a truck. You

*"What did he want?
What did he say? By
God! you'll tell me or—"*

can get those trucks, De Grassie, if you have the nerve for
it. Then—"

"Then—" De Grassie leaned forward when Johnny did
not finish.

"Then I'll come after you, Joe. Put the thumb down on
the louse."

"That's a challenge, eh?"

"That's more than a challenge, Joe. That's gospel."

De Grassie shook his head.

"You're making a mistake, Johnny. You want to be taught
a lesson. Next time, you lose the trucks." He leaned forward
on the cane. "You're a small time racketeer from now on,
Johnny. The Combine's got organization. We wouldn't

strike unless we were ready. It's a big thing, Johnny. If I open my mouth I can cut your booze off at its source."

"You can't open your mouth if you're dead, Joe," Johnny Zitto said.

Brownish yellow eyes narrowed and regarded Zitto steadily. There was nothing of fear or of anger in them; just speculation.

"So that's how it is," De Grassie said at length.

"That," said Johnny Zitto, "is just how it is."

De Grassie came slowly to his feet, slowly put on the yellow glove, coughed once behind his hand and said:

"Of course, to make the others see it our way, we've got to have New York. I'm sorry, Johnny; very sorry. You're still a young man, and had promise of a brilliant future. Had promise, Johnny. Understand that. What will I tell the boys; the big boys of the country, who are behind the Combine?"

Johnny Zitto watched De Grassie back to the door, then he followed him.

"Tell them you saw me." Johnny Zitto threw back his coat, disclosing a shoulder holster and the heavy automatic protruding from it. "And tell them that Johnny Zitto is packing a gun again."

Joe de Grassie's eyes rested for a moment on the gun, then dropped quickly to Zitto's right hand; the right hand that was moving slowly up toward the left armpit. Blue veins grew heavy; yellowish brown eyes widened. Thick lips parted but no words came. De Grassie's feet seemed frozen to the floor.

And again the phone rang.

"Don't go yet," said Johnny Zitto as he lifted the phone.

There was no threat in his voice or in his words; only perhaps in that right hand which was very close to his gun. A right hand that De Grassie knew, or had heard, hadn't lost any of its quickness in the last five years.

"Let's have it!" Johnny said into the mouthpiece. And then, "Hell! he's on his way up now."

He dropped the phone quickly back in its cradle; listened a minute. Heavy, steady feet beat upon the stairs beyond the open door. Lips parted and Johnny grinned. His voice was loud.

"Thanks for dropping in, Joe. Goodnight!" And as De Grassie backed out the door, "It's Satan Hall. Detective Satan Hall. You remember him."

De Grassie did. He grinned slightly and nodded to Zitto as he backed into the hall that led to the stairs. For the moment he thought that he had read death in the eyes of Johnny Zitto, and for the first time the name of Detective Satan Hall rang pleasantly in his ears. But he did get in the last words.

"I may accept that challenge about the trucks, Johnny, as long as you want a demonstration."

2

TO KILL A RAT

THE COMMISSIONER OF police was a little man with sharp, alert eyes; and quick soft speech. Now his movements were jerky as he walked up and down the room and regarded Detective Satan Hall. More and more he saw in those slanting green eyes, the thin lips, the pointed chin and the V shaped cut of his hair, the likeness that had given the man his name. He turned, drummed the ends of his fingers together and looked at the long, lean, muscular body stretched unconcernedly in the chair.

Satan was the first to speak. He said, continuing a previous conversation:

"We have no State laws to control liquor. The people want it. If you wanted to put a stop to it—well, it just couldn't be done."

"It's not that—not that," the commissioner snapped. "It's no secret that liquor comes along that road. And it's no secret, even if we never could prove it, that Johnny Zitto's back of it. But," he pointed, a finger smack at Satan, "it is our business when seven men are shot and left dead along that road. Seven men. Seven strangers."

"They won't he strangers long," said Satan. "The bureau

at Washington will pick up the fingerprints. If you were to ask me, it's a good job."

"Makes nice reading in the newspapers." The commissioner almost hurled himself into the chair. "Hijackers. Hijackers that were expected. We've got an eye witness to the holocaust. The truck came down the road; a big covered truck, with just one man on the front seat. Seven men jumped out on the road; jerked up a chain between two trees. The men in the road leveled revolvers; called out something threatening, and then it happened. The whole side of that truck just belched lead. The witness said they went down like flies. Not a moan, not a cry. Just the roar of machine gun fire, and it was over. Seven dead. Seven strangers."

"Did this witness get the license number of the truck?"

"Sure! for all the good it will do us. It turned out to be the plates of a Ford delivery wagon, that was stolen from the Judson-Raines wet wash laundry early last night. What do you think, Satan?"

"I know," said Satan. "I should have suspected something like it. Johnny Zitto took such pains to tell me where he'd be last night. It was built for an alibi. The boys muscled in on Johnny's racket, and you see the result."

"Yes," said the commissioner. "And everyone else will see it in the afternoon papers. I've asked Zitto to come in. He's outside now, I want you to listen."

Satan shook his head.

"I think that's a mistake, Commissioner. There's nothing against Johnny Zitto. If you leave him alone, maybe De Grassie will work things out to suit the Department."

"Sit back and wait for public enemy number one to kill

public enemy number two, eh?" The commissioner stroked his chin. "That isn't my way, Satan. Besides, this Combine; this organization of all the public enemies, rival rackets, under one racket! It's a danger to the city, to the State, to the whole country."

Satan shook his head.

"I don't think so, Commissioner. Racketeers are like kids at play. Murderers suffer from an overdose of ego. They'll all want to be leaders. Imagine anyone bossing Johnny Zitto!" And with a smile, "Crooks can't work on the level for long."

"I don't know," said the commissioner. "Rackets, big or small, there's got to be a leader."

"Sure!" said Satan. "And it's because of that we're able to keep crime from running the country entirely."

"Maybe." The commissioner shook his head doubtfully. And then, "Maybe you're right, Satan," And crossing the room he threw open the door to his outer office and told the man by the desk to send in Johnny Zitto.

Johnny Zitto swaggered into the room, nodded and smiled at Satan Hall, dropped easily into the most comfortable chair, and looking at the commissioner, said:

"Well, what's on your chest? I was in the neighborhood, anyway, and I dropped in," It was like Zitto never to submit, at least openly, to authority. He didn't have to.

"Johnny"—the commissioner stood before him—"seven men were shot to death last night—or rather, early this morning. You're going to have trouble covering this, even with the big friends you've got behind you."

"Seven men." Johnny Zitto grinned. "Think of that! Now, where was I last night?" And suddenly, slapping his knee, "There was that dinner to Judge Airington. I was at the speakers' table. After that"—stroking his chin—"several of us played poker until five o'clock this morning. The judge was one of the party."

"I didn't doubt you'd establish an alibi," the commissioner said. "I didn't bring you in for that. I—"

Johnny Zitto was on his feet. His mild blue eyes flashed. **"YOU DIDN'T BRING** me in at all," he said. "I came in. I came in because I knew why you wanted to talk with me. I came because—well, there's never been any rough stuff in my racket. It's good, clean work. No fuss, no ballyhoo. No killings. You've liked it that way. No trouble for the Department. Now, there's a blow up on the Long Island road, and the Department needs a fall guy!"

The commissioner patiently waited until Johnny Zitto had finished.

"That's your route, Johnny," he said slowly. "We know the men who drive it; all of them. You won't be able to fix them on a murder charge, and when the electric chair looms up they'll talk. And when they talk—"

Johnny Zitto laughed and shook his head.

"You and me have never exactly crossed, Commissioner. You keep the city clean. I like that. Now, I'll tip you off. I'm not saying, you understand, that I have any interest in booze running. But you think I have, and I'll tell you this. The men you think work for me; the men you think run booze trucks on Long Island, ran them last night on a different road: They were all through with their routes and home in bed when the shooting took place. Hell! don't try to laugh that off. You can easily prove it."

The commissioner looked at Satan, and Satan grinned.

"Pretty smooth," said Satan.

"Smooth as glass," said Johnny Zitto. "Why all the fuss? When the record begins to turn up on those stiffs, the cops should celebrate. They ain't lads you'd want about the city."

"Nor you," said Satan. And suddenly, "Joe de Grassie threatened you yesterday, didn't he? Threatened your trucks."

"Joe!" said Zitto, and his laugh was real. "He's just a hood."

"A hood that controls millions." And when Zitto did not answer, "He came to offer you a job in the Combine. He came to threaten you; threaten your trucks if you refused."

"Did he?" said Zitto. "Well, maybe he did. He was always one for talking big things into his hat."

"He's a big man, Zitto," said Satan. "Maybe you're right and the Department won't ever be able to pin that Long Island knock-over on you. Maybe you won't live long enough."

"All men got to die." Johnny Zitto came to his feet and walked toward the door.

"I suppose," said the commissioner slowly, "even you won't have the front to run those trucks along that road now."

"Hell!" said Johnny Zitto. "Didn't I tell you that route was changed last night?"

"Why?" the commissioner snapped.

"Just a hunch." Johnny shrugged broad shoulders. "A hunch that it might be dangerous. Funny that. Hunches are right sometimes. Good day, Commissioner. Good day, Satan. Give me a jingle any time I can help the Department out."

The commissioner scowled as Johnny Zitto left the

room. But Satan smiled. In a way he admired Johnny, even though more than once Johnny Zitto had tried to have him murdered.

"Satan," the commissioner said slowly after Johnny Zitto had left, "you think Zitto's a pretty big man; bigger even than the Department."

"That's right," Satan nodded. "I can check half a dozen murders directly responsible to him. And yet"—broad shoulders shrugged—"they'd be laughed out of court. He's the biggest danger to the city today."

"I don't think so." Heavy lines appeared in the commissioner's forehead. "At least the Department has been able to hold him in check. Liquor running is a necessary evil. Now that beer is legal the gangsters' income is cut. Today we have a new and greater evil. Far greater than Johnny Zitto. I mean Joe de Grassie. It's known to the police departments of every big city in the country. It's been building up ever since De Grassie left New York five years ago." The commissioner paused and pointed a finger at Satan. "And it's not hard liquor alone. That's only a blind. It's dope. It's murder. It's a single racket to control the entire nation. Just as Johnny Zitto wanted all of the city and failed to get the Bronx, so does Joe de Grassie want the entire country and so far has failed to get New York."

"That's right," said Satan. "Johnny won't go in."

"But he'll have to," the commissioner insisted.

"Maybe." Satan stroked his chin. "But I doubt it. Zitto isn't the kind to play ball unless he can make the rules. You think De Grassie is the head of this Combine, and that it's serious?"

The commissioner fingered some papers on his desk.

"HE PRETENDS NOT to be, but I know he is. You know his record from years back. De Grassie built up this new nationwide underworld while the country was struggling with the greatest problems in its history. Now, with New York, he's ready to strike—perhaps at the very foundation of the government itself. Liquor and dope and women. Johnny Zitto is a murderer and a racketeer. De Grassie is a national menace." The commissioner lifted a pen and pointed it at Satan. "I tell you, Satan, with the unrest in the country today, Joe de Grassie is in a fair way to spread a reign of terror through the country that has not been equaled in our national history."

"And only Zitto stands in the way?" Satan asked.

"Zitto!" The commissioner shook his head. "No, it isn't Zitto that stands in his way." And suddenly, "It's you, Satan. You!"

"Me!" Satan jerked erect in his chair, the commissioner's eyes were so bright, his lips so tight. Satan never had seen him so thoroughly in earnest. "Why, I haven't got a thing on him." The commissioner didn't talk for a long time, then he said slowly:

"De Grassie has a weakness. It's women."

"Yeah," said Satan. "I know."

"Well," said the commissioner, "undercover men have given me a lot of information. De Grassie came to New York personally because of a woman. Mattie Hern."

And Satan jarred to his feet. His hands clenched at his side. Mattie Hern. Mattie, who was born in the racket. Mattie, whose father was a well known fence and whom Zitto could roast with a single word. Mattie, who was controlled by Zitto. Mattie Hern, who had saved his life.

The commissioner said:

"Joe de Grassie gets what he wants."

The red disappeared from Satan's face, his thin lips parted and his fingers unclenched. And then, his eyes narrowing to thin slits of green:

"By God! Commissioner, you're suggesting that I—that I kill this man."

For a full minute the two men regarded each other. Then the commissioner turned, and walking to the window looked out at the teeming city below. Young girls passing; young men wandering aimlessly about the streets. Prey for Joe de Grassie. Haunted, hungry looks. Fearful looks in other gaunt faces. A new generation of criminals, maybe. A maelstrom of discontent; of poverty and fear.

Five minutes passed and still the two men did not speak. Then Satan walked to the commissioner and stood behind him. Green eyes burnt; lips were a single red gash.

"They've called me a killer, and I have killed. But you— you've always understood, and now—He took the commissioner by the shoulder and swung him around; leaned forward, his face very close to the smaller man's. "I've never gone in for murder. But now—"

And Satan raised his head and drew back a step. What he saw in the commissioner's face thrust the words back in his throat. For a moment it was as if he looked into a man's soul and saw—saw—well, just the agony of it.

"Hell!" said Satan. "So it's that bad."

"It's that bad." The commissioner hardly breathed the words. "I haven't slept for nights. It's rotten, Satan. I've even thought to frame De Grassie, but I know the truth. He'd be out again in an hour. I've been tempted to throw up the job, and then—"He waved a hand down toward the crowded street. "We've sworn to protect them, Satan—you and me, and—"

"I never want to murder," Satan said very slowly.

"No, no." And suddenly taking Satan's hand, "Forget what I said; forget what was in my mind—if it's murder to kill a rat. I've never thought of you as the others thought of you. Forget it. It was just the talk of a tired man; a very tired man, Satan."

Satan pulled back the curtain and looked down at the street. The commissioner shook his head.

"They're your people and my people, Satan, and they don't understand. They condemn us and they ridicule us, but they count on us and trust us. We—"

But Satan wasn't listening. He was saying very slowly:

"If it's murder to kill a rat."

3

JOE DE GRASSIE SPEAKS

JOHNNY ZITTO CLIMBED into the long, expensive roadster and shoved his big body behind the wheel. As he stepped on the starter and sixteen cylinders purred softly, he looked long and searchingly at Morris Metz half slumped in the seat beside him.

Johnny Zitto's eyes narrowed slightly. There was no doubt in his mind that Morris Metz was the cleverest man who ever worked for him. Not that he was any good at the actual execution of a knock-over, but to plan it! Metz could think up more sure-fire schemes than any ten men in the racket put together.

But Metz lacked nerve. Johnny had long known that. In that ride uptown, Johnny Zitto was going to decide whether he'd shoot Metz to death or not. The thing was worrying him. He wanted Metz's brains, but he feared that streak of yellow. Now, the police in general and Satan in particular would be interested in the activities of Johnny Zitto. If the police dragged Metz in; if Satan went to work on him, Metz would squawk. And Metz had planned the knock-over of the seven strangers just as it had taken place, except for one thing. The thing that would silence Metz's tongue. Metz was to have been in that truck.

Metz twisted nervously in the far corner of the seat, under Johnny Zitto's scrutiny, before the car gathered speed on the way uptown. Johnny was the first to speak.

"So you weren't with the boys last night?" he said.

"Cripes!" Metz half whined. "I told you, Johnny. I was sick. Damn good and sick. I wouldn't be around today only you sent for me. Hell! it worked out, didn't it?"

"Yeah." Johnny nodded. "It worked out. You were sick— sick in the stomach, Metz. A yellow streak running up and down your spine." And suddenly, "What did Joe de Grassie want to see you about? Don't lie. I know. He called at your apartment this morning."

"Same old baloney." Morris Metz tried to shrug his shoulders indifferently, but his attempted smile was a ghastly failure. "Wanted me to talk you into joining the Combine. After all, Johnny, it isn't a bad racket. Joe de Grassie is big; big people behind him. A chance to rake it in by the hundred grand. And no trouble; just brains."

"Just brains!" Johnny Zitto swung by a truck, straightened out again and let his sharp blue eyes rest for a moment on the pale left cheek of Morris Metz. Then, "What did you tell him?"

Metz laughed. And it grated like finger nails along a wall.

"I told him that it was up to you, Johnny." A moment's pause, and when Zitto did not say anything, "He *went* after that; right after that."

"Right after that. With seven of his men dead; men that you planned to kill; that you—"

"Cripes!" said Metz. "He didn't know that. Only you and me know that. Only—"

"Only you and me know a lot," Johnny said slowly. Then he nodded vigorously as he suddenly turned into a side street. "We've got to have a talk, Morris."

"Where you going?" Morris Metz was alarmed and made no attempt to hide it.

"To 116," said Johnny. "We'll talk there; find a way to get rid of dangers—like Joe de Grassie."

Metz's tongue came out and licked at dry lips. He knew No. 116; knew that those who went there to meet Johnny never came out again. At least, never came out alive. He turned his head and looked back down the street. A big blue sedan had turned the corner in their wake. Up to that moment Morris Metz had not made up his mind whether he'd do it or not. Now he had no choice. He didn't wait; he didn't speak. He just jerked out a gun and shoved it against Johnny Zitto's side.

HIS VOICE TREMBLED and his hand shook.

"Pull to the curb," he said, and as blue eyes narrowed and the car stopped, "I mean it, Johnny. It's you or me."

"You or me, Punk." Johnny's voice did not tremble. "You're taking a runout powder, eh?" It never once entered Johnny's head that Morris Metz would have the nerve to bump him over there on the quiet street. "So No. 116 got you. I wanted it to get you. I wanted to see if you'd be afraid to go. So you squawked all over your face to Joe de Grassie. Now—"

And the door of the car alongside Johnny opened; something hard clamped into his other side.

Johnny Zitto swung slowly and looked into bloodshot eyes beneath a tightly drawn gray cap. The man with the gun did not speak. He didn't need to. Johnny had never seen that face before, but he had seen the same thing in men's eyes before. The man was a killer.

And Johnny understood. He turned his head back just as the door slammed and Morris Metz crossed the street and went hurriedly down it toward the corner. Then Johnny swung his head back to the killer again. But now his eyes rested on the man who stood behind him. It was Joe de Grassie.

"Come! Hop out, Johnny." De Grassie's voice was low and soft. "It isn't as bad as you think, if you've got any sense. Only Metz thinks you're through." And with a shrug of his shoulders as Johnny climbed from the car, "Don't be foolish, Johnny. This boy with the gun lost his brother early this morning."

The gun had gone into the killer's pocket now. Johnny could feel it, though, close to his back. He looked up and down the street. People were passing. A man and a woman turned and looked at the trio beside the big car. It was broad daylight; four o'clock in the afternoon. At the corner was a cop; another one talking to him. A cop that turned suddenly and came slowly down the street. And Johnny was quick with a gun. His lips set tightly; just a single jerk of his right hand to his left armpit and Joe de Grassie would go out like *that*. But what of it? He thought of the man behind him; the thing he had seen in his eyes. And the man behind him spoke to De Grassie.

"Harness bull, Boss," he said in a throaty, perhaps eager voice. "Will I let this lad have it?"

Yellowish brown eyes blinked. De Grassie shrugged his shoulders, opened his mouth to speak—when Johnny Zitto moved suddenly toward the sedan.

"You're a sensible man, Johnny," De Grassie said when he was seated beside Johnny, the gunman on the other side. "And I like sensible men. If you continue to be sensible, you and me will get along nicely."

"Morris Metz, eh?" Johnny's laugh was not pleasant. "I didn't think he'd have the nerve for it. Fear, eh? Fear of the Combine."

"Not altogether." De Grassie shook his head. "Maybe fear and greed. Fifty grand cash, and the promise of the New York end of the Combine."

"You'd give that punk a job that big?"

"Hardly, Johnny; hardly. That is, if *you* want it."

"You'd give it to me after—" Johnny half glanced at the man who had lost his brother and finished. "The Combine must want me a lot."

"They do, Johnny. They do. Dead or alive. And I—I like Mattie Hern."

The blue sedan pulled from the curb as the heavy feet of the policeman pounded almost beside it. All unconscious of the little drama being played within ten feet of him, Patrolman Hunt paused for a moment to admire the lines of the sixteen cylinder roadster. Perhaps, after all, Patrolman Hunt's lack of knowledge was a good thing, for a dead policeman would be of very little use to the citizens who pay him. Nor did Patrolman Hunt notice, as the blue sedan turned the corner, that a taxi followed it. Or if he noticed it, he would not have been aware that Morris Metz, nerve or no nerve, wanted to know where Johnny Zitto was taken.

JOHNNY ZITTO THREW himself back in the easy chair, looked at the tightly closed door and the heavily curtained window. Joe de Grassie played with the gun in his hand, started to put it in his pocket, noted the broad shoulders, muscular arms and hard fingered hands of Zitto and thought better of it. Putting the table between himself and the younger man, he finally said:

"There are a couple of men outside that door. It's a safe place to talk and a safe place to die. You'd like to leave here alive, Johnny, wouldn't you?"

"Sure! Who wouldn't?" said Johnny Zitto. "Let's have it."

"Well," yellowish brown eyes got to blinking, a huge head to bobbing, "four hundred grand lets you into the racket. We can forget the seven men in the road." He dismissed that with a wave of his hand. "It simply shows them I was right in suggesting you."

"I've agreed to that." Johnny nodded. "I want to live. I can get the money here without much trouble."

"Four hundred grand." De Grassie stroked his chin. "That's the cut rate, Johnny. That's for letting Mattie work for me; turning Mattie over to me. I could work it out myself, or through Metz, but I want it open and above board; straight from you. You're to send for her."

Johnny Zitto sneered.

"I'm not that kind, Joe. That's out. I don't sell women."

Joe de Grassie leaned heavily on the table, the gun grasped in his right hand. When he spoke, his words were carefully chosen, as if he only intended to say them once.

"It's not your choice, Johnny. It's mine." He pointed to the phone. "You've known me a long time, Johnny. My word is good, and—"

"Your word!" Johnny cut in. "Who'd take that?"

"My threat, then. Threat." He flipped the watch from his vest pocket and laid it on the table. "You've got five minutes to telephone her. Think of it! You walk out of here a free man, the New York representative of the strongest organization that ever dominated a country. And you walk out of here with the opportunity of meeting Morris Metz again."

Johnny Zitto's lips smacked. His blue eyes sparkled. He would very much like to meet Morris Metz; meet him just once more before he died. But his eyes hardened and his lips set.

"I don't sell women," he said again. "Those that know Johnny Zitto, know that."

"Four minutes more," said Joe de Grassie. "Then, if you haven't telephoned Mattie; made arrangements for her to come here and work for me, directly for me, I'll kill you, Johnny."

And Johnny Zitto looked at Joe de Grassie. He studied the man. And what he saw there didn't help him any. One thing Johnny read in that face; one thing Johnny knew to be the truth. In four minutes; less now, Joe de Grassie was going to kill him. Kill him, unless—

And as Johnny watched those brown yellowish eyes he didn't think as other men might think. He thought simply one thing. It was his life or Mattie. There was no other way. He simply lifted the receiver and called a number.

When he got Mattie on the phone, he said:

"Go to the corner of Ninety-sixth Street and Broadway. Joe de Grassie will pick you up in a car and—" A moment's pause and then, "I don't care whether you like that grease ball or not, do what I tell you." And just before he jammed up the receiver, "I've got another message for Charlie."

Joe de Grassie rubbed his hands and said:

"That's fine, Johnny. Just fine." And bringing ink and

pen and Johnny's check book, which had been taken from his pocket with his gun when he was first brought to the house, "Make the check payable to me. You're good for that amount?"

"Yeah," said Johnny. "On four different banks. I've got money scattered around."

"And you understand it's just security, Johnny. Just shows your good faith. If you ever have any personal animosity for me—why, just think if four hundred thousand dollars is worth it."

"Yeah," said Johnny slowly, "I'll think of that. I can trot along now?"

"Well—no. No." De Grassie grinned pleasantly as he blotted the checks and slipped them in his pocket. "If it was just me I'd say, 'Go ahead.' But the Combine, Johnny. If your banks certify the checks, you can leave in the morning. I want you to tell Mattie how it is with me anyway. I'll want the Avenue to know how you feel about me."

"Okay," said Johnny. "Okay!"

After all, the Combine seemed an easy way to make money. They just wanted his name—and with a scowl, his money. As for Mattie! He dismissed her with a shrug of his shoulders. He wanted to live.

4

THE MESSAGE OF DEATH

MATTIE HERN WAS at the Club Venice, in a small booth at the rear of the bar. It was almost directly under Johnny Zitto's private room. Charlie, the bartender, wiped down the bar and nodded to her in warning as the steady feet beat down the room. Mattie Hern smiled back. She knew those feet and didn't need the warning. It was Satan Hall, of course. She shrugged her shoulders. Mattie didn't know if she loved or hated Satan; or perhaps it was both, as her moods changed. But she did know that they were of different worlds, and that her interests and her father's interests lay with Johnny Zitto. Johnny, who knew how to treat her as a cog, an important cog, in the well-oiled Zitto machine.

"Hello, Flat-foot." Mattie's dark eyes brightened despite the slight quickening of her pulse.

Satan didn't smile back. He pushed his wiry body along the seat opposite Mattie and said:

"You've got to get out of town for a bit. It's De Grassie. Perhaps you know."

"Sure!" She nodded. "I know. Somehow I attract such men. It isn't very flattering, is it?"

Satan looked at her for a long time, and not understanding women gave the wrong answer.

"No, it isn't."

Mattie ran a hand through soft black hair, shrugged slender shoulders and said:

"You forget I'm working for Zitto. Everyone knows that. I don't have to fear any man now. Not even Joe de Grassie."

Satan shook his head.

"Johnny Zitto will think only of Zitto. De Grassie's big, Mattie, he could squeeze Johnny like *that*." Satan's thumb went down on the table.

"Not Johnny," said Mattie, and with a little touch of pride, "He knows all about the Combine, Satan. They may be big enough to walk all over your Department, but not over Johnny Zitto. Anyway, why tell me?"

"It might be because you saved my life, but it isn't. I never really thanked you, Mattie, and I've often wondered why you did it."

"Don't ask me." Shoulders moved again. "I've wondered too. But it washed us up, Satan. I had a foolish idea once." Black eyes stayed on him for a long minute. "You'll always be a cop and I'll always be a crook."

"You won't, Mattie, if—"

"Don't, Satan. Preaching doesn't fit you. You're just a killer that fate put on the other side of the fence. Others fry for it, but you carry a writ in your left hand. Legal murder!"

Legal murder. An hour ago Satan would have smiled, but now he didn't. Legal murder! He thought of Joe de Grassie and half nodded.

"Joe de Grassie," he said very slowly, "is a slimy rat who's suddenly pushed his way to great power. Zitto will finally have to see things his way, and De Grassie's way is your way, Mattie. That's why I'm telling you to run-out before it's too late. When the show-down comes, Johnny Zitto will sacrifice you to his own interest."

"Johnny's got too much pride. His strength is his own pride. Just strength, not weakness."

"All men have a weakness." Satan nodded. "De Grassie's is women; maybe one woman. Johnny Zitto's is men; maybe one man."

"One man!" Mattie Hern knitted her eyes and looked down the length of the bar, where a single figure stood drinking. Satan half turned his head and followed her eyes.

"That's right, Mattie. That's the man. If I was ever in need of information; desperately in need of information, that's the man I'd go to. The master mind of crime. The master mind, with the yellow streak running up his spine. Morris Metz."

"Morris Metz." Mattie repeated the name half aloud, as if she had given it thought before. "No. Not even Metz would dare double-cross Johnny. As for Johnny taking orders from De Grassie!" She laughed. "I know what he thinks about anyone, even De Grassie, telling him where he heads in."

The bartender, Charlie, called across the room to Mattie.

"A jingle for you, sweetheart. Want to take it in the back room?"

Mattie hesitated, and started to shake her head when the bartender cut in.

"Better take it, Mattie. It's a guy that won't take 'no.'"

Mattie came to her feet.

"BACK IN A couple of minutes," she said, and left the room. The eyes of Satan and Morris Metz followed her. Both were speculative. The eyes of Morris Metz were filled with fear. A vague sort of fear to be sure, but fear just the same. Those mean little eyes were riveted on the door which led to the private room behind the bar. Then, without so much as a glance at Satan Hall, he strode quickly the length of the bar and flung open that door. Satan was on his feet at once, moving to that door; his hand against it before it fully closed.

He paused, holding the door so, listening. Metz's voice was rasping:

"I tell you it wasn't Johnny. Someone was giving you a stall." And when the girl answered something in a low voice that Satan did not get, "It's a lie. I tell you it couldn't be Johnny. He—he—" And suddenly, "What did he want? What did he say? By God! you will tell, or—"

There was the shuffling of feet, the quick intake of breath, then Mattie's words.

"Take your hands off of me, you fool. Morris! What's the matter? You're mad. You're—" A sudden gasp; a half stifled scream and Satan swung open the door.

The room behind the bar was a well appointed waiting room for visitors "in on the know," who wanted to see Johnny Zitto. There were easy chairs, magazines, smoking stands, and a long table behind a low couch. To the left of the stairs which led above, to Johnny's private office, was a telephone. It was to this corner of the room that Satan's attention was drawn.

Mattie stood by the phone, as if she had just replaced the receiver. Both her hands were raised, tearing at the two wrists of Morris Metz; frantically, trying to pull the fingers from her throat.

Satan watched an instant. He didn't speak. Even from

where he stood he got a glimpse of Morris' face. The burning eyes and the quivering movement of colorless lips. Satan simply stepped across the room, clutched Metz by the shoulder and nearly lifted him from his feet as he dragged him from the girl. Then, as Metz turned; a snarling animal, Satan raised his right hand and with his open palm struck Metz once. Metz staggered; his foot caught against a chair. He tried to straighten himself and half stumbled, half collapsed on the soft low couch.

The door opened and Charlie, the bartender, walked into the room. He had on a white apron and a white jacket, and carried a cloth in his hand. He stopped, stood by the table, but didn't speak.

Mattie shook her head several times, moved her neck a bit, cleared her throat and said:

"He—the man on the wire, had a message for you, Charlie. Did you get it?"

"Yeah," Charlie answered.

"He had a message for me too," said Mattie in a listless voice. "And—and I'll be going along."

Mattie moved quickly toward the door to the stairs, shook her head when Satan called to her and passed hurriedly through the room when he would have stopped her.

Satan followed quickly, was on the stairs, could see silk clad legs disappearing at the top and was about to follow them when the cry came from the room below.

"Satan—Hall—Hall! I'm coming with you." It was Metz, and there was fear in his words; a deadly terror in his voice.

SATAN HESITATED, TURNED and retraced the few steps

he had taken up the stairs. Morris Metz calling for his natural enemy; calling for the man who had just struck him! As Satan opened the door and stepped into the room he heard Charlie say:

"No, you're not going any place, Morris. Not ever going any place Johnny said." And seeing Satan, he stopped suddenly; his lower lip slipped beneath his upper teeth, his narrowing eyes opened.

But Satan had seen things in Charlie's face. Charlie, who had twice beaten the rap for murder and was now tending bar because his activities in the outside world were attracting too much police attention.

Morris Metz was on his feet, half walking, half stumbling toward Satan.

"I'm going with you, Hall." He mouthed the words, laid a hand on Satan's sleeve almost timidly, screwed up his eyes; made queer ingratiating movements with his mouth. A different man than the self assured, sneering Morris Metz, the advisor of Johnny Zitto, with the power of Zitto behind him and fully aware of it. Now— And Charlie spoke.

"Metz stays here," he said. Then seeing that hard look creep into those slanting green eyes of Satan Hall, "Cripes! Satan, can't you see he's got a snootful? He took his drinking in strange places last night, almost got the rams and—" Charlie's hand came out and clutched Metz's arm.

The gesture was a friendly enough one, but the strong fingers of Charlie bit into the thinness of Metz's flesh. Yet Metz's twisted, contorted face; his trembling knees, were all out of proportion to the offense; at least, the outward offense of Charlie's simple movement.

"I'm going with you, Satan. Don't let him keep me here. He'll—he'll—" And his voice raised to a shriek. "Johnny told him to—to— I tell you he'll kill me."

"See!" Charlie shook his head and screwed up his mouth in concern. "What'd I tell you? Talking about his friend, Johnny, that way! But don't worry about him none, Satan. I'll take care of him." Charlie's fingers tightened; muscles bulged, and he drew the trembling man toward him.

The expression on Satan Hall's face never changed. Green eyes glared searchingly into the terror stricken ones of Morris Metz. Then Satan moved his right arm suddenly. His hand that was white, showed black, and crashed straight down on the stiffened arm of Charlie.

Charlie's arm dropped to his side, the redness left his fat cheeks. White showed for a moment, and then almost mechanically his other hand shot toward his armpit beneath the white coat. But only toward it. His big eyes grew larger; his mouth hung open. He had suddenly seen the hard black thing with which Satan had so suddenly paralyzed the muscles of his arm.

"What the hell! Satan?" he said, and remembering Satan's reputation with a rod and his easy indifference in using it, "What's on your chest, anyway?" And he backed toward the door.

"It's a free country." Satan's gun disappeared as quickly as it had appeared. "If Metz wants to take the air he can take it." And as he took Metz by the arm and led him toward the bar, "About that gun of yours, Charlie! It's caused you lots of trouble. Jerk it out now, and your troubles are over." Then to the man he had by the arm, "Stand up, Metz. We're going places."

Several pairs of eyes followed Satan as he left the bar, pushed through the door at the front, nodded at the door-man of the Club Venice and reached the street. That no one tried to stop him was not surprising. Satan had a way of moving as he pleased. Gentlemen of the racket were familiar with that way.

Satan hailed a passing taxi and pushing Metz into it, climbed in after him.

"Uptown!" he told the driver. And then turning to Metz, "Johnny wants to give you the bumps, eh? How come? Isn't he using that fertile brain of yours any more, or did he use it once too often?"

Rat-like eyes looked at Satan, a tongue moistened dry lips, a trembling hand shoved a cigarette into his mouth and spent a block and a half setting fire to the end of it, Then Metz spoke.

"Me? Johnny wants to give me the bumps? Did I say that?" And his laugh was hollow. "I must have been screwy, like Charlie said. I was drinking."

"So Charlie was right!" Satan nodded innocently; then shaking his head, "You were bad though, Morris, pretty bad. You're a nice boy, but I haven't got the time for it."

"Time for what?" Metz didn't get the humor in Satan's words.

"To watch you. You might get violent again. You should be with your friends; with Charlie." He leaned forward and raised a hand toward the glass behind the driver. "I'll tell him to go back."

"No, no." Metz grabbed at his arm. "I was telling the truth. Johnny wants to put the finger on me."

"Why?" Satan snapped the single word.

"He—I—" The words stuck in Metz's throat. "He just don't like me any more."

"Now," said Satan, tapping on the window, "ain't that just too bad?"

5

JOHNNY ZITTO TAKES ORDERS

THREE DAYS LATER Satan sat in Johnny Zitto's private room above the bar and watched Johnny flip red cards on black ones; black ones on red. Finally he said:

"Where's Mattie?"

"Search me." Johnny Zitto leaned back and let his unlighted cigar slip across his mouth. "You sure have an interest in that jane, Satan. Women are bad for guys in the racket; for coppers too."

"That's right." Satan nodded slowly. And then, "I'd do a hell of a lot for Mattie."

"I've been thinking that for some time," Johnny Zitto said. "So—I let Mattie out. She's not working for me any more."

"No?" Green eyes held Johnny's mild blue ones. "I always thought you liked—felt that my interest in Mattie was a good thing for you."

Johnny Zitto pushed all the cards together, carefully sorted them into a neat pile, shuffled them, started a deal for a new game of Canfield, and thinking better of it, laid the cards down on the table beside him.

"Mattie's a free agent," he told Satan. "She's left me. With my permission, of course."

"For Joe de Grassie?" Satan asked.

Johnny Zitto hesitated a moment, and then:

"For Joe de Grassie." And as Satan's lips curved and thin eyebrows arched above green eyes, "Take a tip from me, Satan. Your days of strutting the Avenue are over. You've had your swing; the commissioner has sat squarely behind you. Now, things have changed in the city. I'm working with people who have only to lift the phone to place you out on Staten Island; to lift the phone and send a commissioner back to private life. And we can do it!"

" 'We,' Johnny?" Satan's lips parted and his teeth showed. "So you've been gobbled up by the Combine. Johnny Zitto, the man too big to touch. They just swept down and took you in. Joe de Grassie, the hood! You strutted your stuff; sat back in your chair and had seven of De Grassie's men knocked over. Then De Grassie put the thumb down on you; shoved a gun against your chest, and you sold out."

"That's a lie; a damn lie." Johnny came to his feet and paced the room. And suddenly, "You got it from that rat, Morris Metz."

"Rat, eh?" Satan sneered. "Well, you oughta know a rat when you see one, Johnny. I always contended that every lad in the racket was yellow at heart. You gave me doubts, Johnny. Somehow, you seemed different. And when the big moment came, you were just like the rest—another rat."

Johnny Zitto swung suddenly as Satan came to his feet. Johnny's right moved toward his left armpit. Soft blue eyes were two points of steel that flashed up and down from Satan's green eyes to his empty hands.

"Careful, Satan." The words came through the side of

Zitto's mouth. "You can't pull that stuff on me; not on Johnny Zitto. Everyone that knows me, knows different."

"Yes, they'll know, Johnny. I'll see that they know. Johnny Zitto, who sticks to his own; who can fix a rap even up to murder! Sure, you're a big guy when you can lay the finger on some trembling, crooked politician and make him pull the strings in court. You're a big guy when you dish out a roll to buy a lad's freedom or another's death. But as soon as a hood shoves a gun in your belly you turn yellow. Morris Metz a rat? You should know. You sold out every bit of decency and every bit of fear you inspire in the underworld. The boys will know the truth; know that if the show-down comes, they may be next. You did more than simply double cross Mattie when you ratted out on her to save your own hide. You ratted out on yourself, Johnny. The boys will wonder and—"

"You can't talk that way to me." Johnny Zitto's face was livid. His fingers twitched at his side. "By God! Satan, there's a limit even to your— I could kill you for that."

"You've got a gun, Johnny," Satan said slowly. "You've got a permit to carry it. All you haven't got, is the nerve to use it."

"You'd like to get me, eh? You've always wanted to get me, Satan. Maybe you'd go to murder."

And very slowly Satan said:

"If it is murder, Johnny. Murder, to kill a rat."

JOHNNY ZITTO LOOKED toward the closed door that led to the stairs; to the other closed door behind him. Then he stepped slowly back to his desk. The threat to kill, or the words he took as a threat to kill, were very real to him. His hand was very close to his gun, and Satan's hands were empty. He'd chance it if he had to. Johnny Zitto could aim and fire in just one second, but he wondered would he be just one half second too late. Yet—yet he didn't think Satan would shoot him down like that. He watched those green eyes, and what he saw there didn't help him any.

"You like Mattie and so do I," he said. "She's got a chance to do big things. Joe de Grassie took—well, I guess they took a fancy to each other." He tried shrugging his shoulders but did not make much of a go of it. "The boys will see them together, and—and that wild story of yours won't stick."

Johnny Zitto nodded at that thought. The damn little tart! Didn't she have any gratitude? He only had to open his mouth to roast her father, and now— Hell! Bigger women than Mattie, in the racket, would be glad to be seen with Joe de Grassie. De Grassie had talked to Johnny for hours, and Johnny had listened; listened, amazed. De Grassie had an organization that made his own look like the old Gas House gang. De Grassie had names on his list; influences behind him that made Johnny's contacts seem very small indeed. De Grassie—

But Satan was talking.

"That's right," Satan said. "I guess you can square that rat-out with the boys; with the Avenue, Johnny. But can you square it with yourself?"

"What do you mean?" Johnny was puzzled. And with a grin, "Good God! Satan, you don't mean—can't mean conscience."

"Hardly!" Satan shook his head. "I guess I just mean pride. I guess I just mean— Well, you'll know fear, Johnny.

You've always feared rats; you'll fear yourself. Worst of all, Johnny. You've always hated rats; you'll hate yourself."

Johnny Zitto laughed gruffly when Satan was gone. He dealt out the cards, twisted his lips tightly when he saw three aces face up, and then with a single motion of his hands swept the cards onto the floor. The phone rang. It was Johnson, who had an eye on the coast guard.

Zitto scowled as Johnson talked. That was the third call that day. De Grassie was making use of the information he had given him.

"I wasn't sure," Johnson was saying, and the "respect," as Johnny liked to call it, seemed to have gone out of his voice. "But De Grassie spoke like he meant it. Of course I knew, but I thought orders were to come only from you. What!" And then, "I'll tell him to call you first?"

"Well—no." Johnny Zitto hesitated and the hesitancy was something new to him. "I'm busy as hell for a bit. Er— you can take orders from De Grassie for a while." And Zitto jammed the phone back in the cradle with a force that cracked the instrument.

Ten minutes later, at exactly ten p.m., Joe de Grassie called him on the phone.

"I've got that damned woman locked up in a room here, Johnny." He started right in without preliminaries. "She's putting on the front that you don't know. Trot around here and tell her what's what. Busy? Hell! You're busy working for me." And very softly, "You've got a lot of money involved in this thing, Johnny. The Combine demands service."

And the crack widened when the phone crashed back this time. Johnny wondered. It was so long since he had taken orders from anyone that—that— And he thought of Satan. Oh, not his threat to kill. Maybe just the twist of his mouth and the mockery in his voice. But he grabbed up his coat and hat. He was taking orders. De Grassie had convinced him that the Combine was big; far bigger than Johnny had ever conceived things for himself, and Johnny was ambitious. Besides, Mattie kicking up a row, and him mixed up in this thing to the tune of four hundred grand!

Johnny Zitto paused before the mirror to straighten his coat. Fingers on the lapel, he paused. The face that looked back at him from that glass seemed different. How, he could not tell. But *it* did seem different. It lacked maybe the same confidence; the same self assurance. Then he shrugged his shoulders and went down the stairs.

THE MAN WHO let Johnny Zitto into De Grassie's hideout in the city had a flat nose, a big mouth, and sucked in his breath when he talked. He didn't seem impressed as he followed Johnny into the room, watched him drop into a seat. Then he went to a bookcase and took out a big volume. *Who's Who*. He fumbled through the pages and finally asked Johnny how to spell a certain name.

"The senator?" Johnny's eyes went wide. "You're not asking something from him, are you?"

The flat faced man regarded Johnny from sunken eyes, his thin lips parted:

"You'll learn, feller," he said slowly. "No. Joe de Grassie ain't asking him. He's telling him. You ain't used to dealing with big names, eh?"

Johnny Zitto came very slowly to his feet. His lips were a cruel, even line. Blue eyes had gray in them; cold gray, like the winter dawn.

"Maybe not," he said slowly. "Nor am I used to dealing with small fry. Tell De Grassie I'm here." And before the other could speak, "He wanted to see me—right away."

"Yeah?" The man grinned and nodded. "If he does, he will. Keep your vest on and sit down. You've got to learn to warm chairs. Better start now, Zitto. I come from Chi and ain't impressed by your breed. I'll tell De Grassie when I—" The man mumbled some words as he turned back to the bookcase and started to replace the book. Then he swung suddenly. He saw the shadow cross the light and sensed the danger as he turned back to face Johnny Zitto.

Johnny made a single movement of his right hand to his left armpit. The flat faced man turned back as the nose of the gun beat down across his face. The quick flash of anger turned to one of surprise, and then fear, as the blood ran into his eyes and his knees gave slightly beneath him.

Johnny Zitto said:

"Hop now, and tell De Grassie I'm here." And as the man rubbed at his face and moved toward the door, "And remember I'm in this racket because I don't take lip from punks like you. Cripes!" Johnny twirled his gun a couple of times, then jarred it back into its shoulder holster, "I should a put lead in your stomach." And as the man left the room, "That senator's name begins with a C, not a K, hard guy."

For a moment after the man left, Johnny felt pretty good. Then, as the minutes passed, he grew nervous. After all, he had knocked over seven men of the Combine on the Long Island road. De Grassie would have no doubts about that. It must rankle in his mind. But, above everything else, De Grassie wanted New York. And without Zitto; without the

Zitto influence and organization, he couldn't get very far. At least, not until Johnny was through and—

Johnny Zitto stroked his chin. Hell! What were seven men compared to the Zitto name? As for Johnny! He'd make more money than he ever made in his life. Easy money too. He couldn't have punks like flat-face giving him lip. But what would De Grassie think about gun swiping his man? What—

Flat-face walked in and jerked his right thumb over his shoulder.

"The boss'll see you upstairs," he said sulkily, and stood aside for Johnny to pass into the hall.

"You first," said Johnny. "And don't look so mad. I don't like guys around that look mad."

Johnny swaggered a bit as he climbed the stairs and went down the long narrow hall to the room in the back. But he was conscious of his swagger; conscious that it was "put on" to—to impress Joe de Grassie? No. To give Johnny more confidence in himself. Confidence! A few days ago Johnny Zitto would have laughed at the suggestion that he needed confidence.

6

FOUR HUNDRED GRAND

JOHNNY ZITTO PASSED through an outer room, between heavy curtains and into a room beyond.

Joe de Grassie sat behind a big desk and rested his elbows on it. He held his heavy jowls in two thick hands, which twisted up his face so that the blue veins looked like moving rivers, beneath the lamp. There was nothing to read in his yellow-brown eyes, and certainly no anger distinguishable in his placid face. He just regarded Johnny steadily, his thick lips slightly parted.

The flat-faced man gone, Johnny was the first to speak.

"That mutt was mussy." Johnny moved his hands apart. "I didn't like the way he acted."

Joe de Grassie came slowly to his feet, rubbed a thick chin, then held his jowls in his hand a moment before he spoke.

"You'll have to get used to a lot of things you don't like, Johnny. I'm going to make a big man out of you, but only because you're working for a big man. They'll fear you, Johnny, only because they fear the power behind you; the brains behind you—Joe de Grassie. Make up your mind to that. Now, it's Mattie Hern." Joe de Grassie let his lips slip back. "I want you to have a talk with her. I'm leaving for Chicago tonight and want to take her with me."

"You can't handle her, eh?" Zitto grinned. "Well, that's your hard luck, De Grassie. My agreement was only to bring her here."

"Agreement!" De Grassie's bushy eyebrows went up. "There's no such thing as agreements between us now, Johnny. I order, and you obey. As to Mattie! I can handle anyone, or any situation. But it's brains now. My days of cave man stuff are over."

"You made a mistake in locking her up here." Johnny shook his head. "Mattie's class; she's high strung. She isn't just for the first lad who takes a fancy to her."

Joe de Grassie looked down at Johnny Zitto with almost child-like surprise in his eyes.

"The first lad!" he echoed the words incredulously. "Why, I'm paying her the biggest compliment that has been paid to any woman in the racket, or out of it for that matter. I don't rule a district or a town or a big city. I rule the country. Joe de Grassie's woman will be— But never mind that. I've kept her here because of her mouth and her way of wanting to use it. I don't want it around the Avenue that you sold her over to me. That's because of you, Johnny. I don't want to hurt your standing. Now, run in and talk to her. You've got the stuff on her father; let her know how it feels to burn."

"Cripes!" Johnny started, and then stopped. The words just came to him suddenly; more, a spoken thought. "De Grassie," he said, "you stuck a gun in my stomach and got me to— Well, you painted up a big thing for me and I came in. Now," blue eyes narrowed, "I come here armed, you know. Don't you ever think of that?"

De Grassie laughed.

"You wouldn't live very long," he said, and then shaking his head, "I know men, Johnny. I know you. Four hundred thousand is a lot of money to lose. Greed, Johnny! You've made a good investment. It may be hard for you in the beginning, but you might as well learn right now who's boss." He walked to the big safe in the corner, swung it open, took out a typewritten sheet and carelessly thrust it across the desk. "Read that list of names. They're men you'll control through me. Men who'll have to do as I say."

Johnny Zitto sucked in a deep breath. Many of the names he recognized as powerful influences in politics. Men he could never reach; men he never thought of reaching. His blue eyes flashed. Mechanically his hands rubbed together.

"What will I tell them, Joe?" Johnny's voice was whispered awe. "Just what have you got on them?"

Joe de Grassie grinned.

"You'll simply tell them that you come from De Grassie."

"That'll be enough to put them in line for—"

"For anything." De Grassie nodded. "Put it in your pocket. They're just names, that don't mean anything alone. My evidence is in Chicago; my home there."

"The judge, here." Johnny put his finger down on the third on the list. "He'll be a— If I'd known of him a month ago—"

De Grassie shook his head, took a pencil, and leaning over crossed that name off the list.

"I forgot," he said. "I saw him only three days ago and told him where he stood and what I'd like from him."

"And he wouldn't—wouldn't stand in?"

"They've got to stand in or die," said De Grassie.

"You—"

"No. I got word half an hour ago that he killed himself. But, there! You'll read all about it in the morning papers." And as if he just thought of it, "It would make a nasty scandal, Johnny. There might be some money in it from the family. I understand his brother's a rich man. But trot in and talk to Mattie." Out came the heavy gold watch. "You've got five minutes for the job."

De Grassie crossed to the door, opened it and pointed to a door across the narrow hall.

"She's in there," he said. "Tell her she's got five minutes to decide. Tell her about her father, and if she thinks more of herself—"

"If she thinks more of herself—" Johnny repeated the words.

"Well, that's up to her. She knows."

THE DOOR CLOSED and Johnny Zitto was alone in the hall. There was a key in the outside of the lock and Johnny turned it and stepped into the room. Mattie sat in a big chair under the light. There were books and magazines on a table behind her, a smashed glass at her feet; feet that were chained tightly together. Johnny whistled softly to himself. Beneath that glass he saw the cracked, torn photograph and thought that he recognized it as a likeness of De Grassie.

Mattie regarded him with her big dark eyes. Zitto was prepared to see her spring to her feet and plead with him to help her; take her away. He was surprised and perplexed when she didn't. There was something in her eyes that he didn't understand. It couldn't be disgust, but it certainly wasn't the assurance that Mattie always had; the assurance that was instilled in people who—who—and Zitto gulped. In people who worked for him.

"Mattie," he started in after a moment, "what's this Joe tells me? Be sensible." He tried to laugh. "It's just like working for me. Why, De Grassie's big enough even to take me in."

"Big enough!" She stared steadily at Zitto. "Why, anyone big enough to stick a gun in your stomach is big enough to take you in."

"It was you or me, Mattie," Johnny said simply, and when she didn't answer him, "I've put a lot of money into De Grassie's racket. You better stand in with De Grassie and me."

"And you!" She laughed far back in her throat. "That's funny."

"Funny!" Johnny went closer to her and stared into her white face. "Don't give me that look. I know too much about your father. I still give orders to you, Mattie. What do you mean—that's funny?"

"Funny? Well, maybe it isn't. I didn't believe what De Grassie told me. I thought you were just leaving me here until you worked things out. I thought I knew you, Johnny. I thought— Well, I was ready to appeal to you the moment you came in the door. Then I saw your face; your eyes. And I knew the truth. You're through. You're washed up."

"None of that stuff!" Johnny leaned forward and shot the words through the side of his mouth.

Mattie laughed again. Shrilly, hysterically.

"Your mouth too, Johnny. Your— Don't be a fool alto-gether. There's a glass behind me. Look at yourself! Why, it stands out all over you. You're just yellow." And her eyes widening, and surprise for a moment dominating her fear, "God! Johnny, you're a rat. When the time came, you turned out just a rat."

She came to her feet when she'd finished and stood facing him, both her hands against her cheeks. And Johnny did it. He raised his right hand and struck her across the mouth.

"Your father will burn for this," he said, and swung toward the door.

"That's not for you to say," she cried out at him, a tiny bit of blood forming on her lower lip. "That's for De Grassie. I'll kill him some day if he touches me. And if he doesn't— well, I'll never reach South America alive."

"South America!" Johnny Zitto turned back from the door.

"Yes, South America," she nodded her head up and down. "At first De Grassie painted a glorious picture for me in the racket. He paid a good price for me; a hundred grand to you. When I couldn't see things his way he wants some of his money back. He talked fast, Johnny, and he talked well. Girls out of work by the hundred thousand. Well—I'm going to South America, I suppose, but I'll never reach there alive. I—I— Damn your rotten soul, Johnny Zitto. Get out! And see how a crook; yes, a crook, born in the racket, can take it when the time comes."

Johnny's hand went up again. It turned into a fist, started toward the girl and stopped. Mattie had moved her head suddenly, and Johnny's eyes were fastened on the mirror behind her. He was startled at his own reflection in the glass. It was a brutal, beast-like face. A weak face, too, he thought. Things in it that he had seen in the face of Morris Metz.

And Johnny Zitto turned and suddenly left the room. The door closed behind him, but no key turned in the lock.

Johnny Zitto walked slowly across that hall, opened the door to the smaller room, which led to De Grassie's temporary office, beyond the heavy curtains. He could hear De Grassie moving papers on the desk inside.

JUST BEFORE HE reached the curtains, Johnny paused, stretched out his right hand and looked at it. The room was dimly lighted, but Johnny could see that his fingers trembled violently. He looked back toward the door. The stairs beyond that door would lead to the hall below; to the big front door that would let him out on the street. Let him out! That was it. He wanted to run out—yep, take a run-out powder.

Quick flashes went through his mind. De Grassie giving orders to his boys! Satan saying he'd ratted out on himself! Mattie marking him as yellow! Mattie, who— But he wasn't thinking of Mattie now; he was thinking of Johnny Zitto. Zitto, who controlled a city. Zitto, who only had to wave a hand, and— And he looked at the hand again. The fingers were not trembling so much now. Johnny Zitto jerked himself erect and walked into De Grassie's room. He said suddenly:

"I don't like this South America stuff, Joe."

"No?" De Grassie blinked yellow eyes and parted thick lips. "I won't trouble you for your opinion, Johnny; only your services. So you couldn't even handle Mattie, eh?" He shook his head. "You'll have to take a grip on yourself, Johnny. When things don't go right, and easy for you, you—you—"

"Turn yellow, eh?" Johnny Zitto leaned forward. "I don't like your giving orders to the boys. Trying to—to squeeze me out."

"Yellow!" De Grassie made chuckling sounds in his throat. "Johnny Zitto!" And as if dismissing the subject, "You'll have to get used to liking things, Johnny; and don't begin to lose confidence in yourself. I've done a lot for you, Johnny. I had my mind set on Mattie. I overlooked that bit of shooting on Long Island."

"Did you overlook that?" Johnny stood very still and straight. "Or did you just take my money, Mattie, and—" Then suddenly, "Aren't you trying to take my prestige in the city and then—"

"And then—" said De Grassie slowly.

"And then— Aren't you a bit afraid of me, De Grassie?"

De Grassie laughed, unfolded his hands from before his stomach and came to his feet. Very slowly he turned his back on Johnny Zitto and went to the wall safe.

"I'm leaving for Chicago in an hour, Johnny," he said, without looking back over his shoulder. "I've got some money here for you, and instructions. We can't have Mattie talking along the Avenue, and she's too valuable to dispose of. You may be short of cash. Four hundred thousand was a lot of money, and—"

Four hundred thousand dollars. Four hundred grand. The words chased themselves through Johnny Zitto's brain. There, leaning before the safe, De Grassie talked on. But

Johnny Zitto didn't hear him. Four hundred grand was a lot of jack, even to Johnny Zitto. De Grassie was a great power, with many killers behind him. De Grassie was— And Johnny stiffened. His hand didn't tremble now; not his right hand. It moved with a single swift and silent movement to his left armpit. Four hundred grand to kill a man! Then do the job himself.

A voice spoke.

"You're not a bit afraid of me, Joe; not a bit afraid, eh?"

And De Grassie knew that it was the voice of Johnny Zitto before Johnny Zitto fully realized it himself. And De Grassie paused, a hand in the safe. He wasn't certain; he wasn't sure, but he thought it was not the voice of the man he had broken. The man— And when Johnny spoke again, De Grassie knew the truth. He had made a mistake in judging men. His first mistake! And he knew, too, that in his business, your first mistake is very likely to be your last. Yes, he knew, as his hand slipped slowly around his own gun, that he or Johnny Zitto was going to die.

He tried talking—talking before he swung quickly, with a blazing gun.

"Four hundred thousand dollars! A lot of money, Johnny. No, I'm not afraid of you, Johnny. I—"

And Johnny broke in. And this time his words were crystal clear to him. He meant every one of them. There was a confidence in his voice. It was the old Johnny Zitto; the Johnny Zitto the Avenue knew and feared. But most of all, the Johnny Zitto that Johnny Zitto knew.

"It's the best money I ever spent," he said slowly. "I always said a woman would get you some day. And she did, Joe. She called the trick. She let me see myself as she saw me, as you saw me, as the Avenue will see me. And you're all wrong; all wrong about Johnny Zitto. Turn around, you big punk, and take it in the stomach."

And Joe de Grassie swung, a heavy forty-four in his hand.

7

BEYOND THE CURTAIN

JOHNNY ZITTO GONE, Mattie looked down at her chained feet. She tried walking toward that door, tumbled to her knees, came to her feet again and thought of the guard downstairs. Then she swung quickly. Glass tinkled on the floor; the window was thrown up.

She clapped a hand across her mouth to keep from screaming at the face she saw framed in that window. A deadly, sinister, cruel face. And then her hand left her mouth and a glad little cry came.

"Satan," she whispered. "Satan Hall."

"That's right." Satan climbed into the room and caught her in his arms just before she fell. "Morris Metz, you know, was the weak link in the chain. He told me where De Grassie was, and—"

"Take me away. Take me away!" Mattie cried over and over. For the first time in her life she felt that she was going to faint. Blindly, wildly she tried to keep her head from swimming. Over and over she said to herself, "I can't take it. I can't take it."

Satan carried her to the bed and laid her on it.

"Easy does it, Mattie." And in answer to her plea, "I'll

be taking you away all right." And lips setting in a single straight line, "I've got a job to do. Where's Joe de Grassie?"

"Satan, Satan." She clung to him desperately. "I can't let you. I can't let you do this for me."

Satan gulped. Words stuck in his throat as he moved her hands from about his neck.

"It isn't you, Mattie, not just you. It's others. Thousands of others just—just like you."

He backed from the bed and swung the gun into his hand. Mattie's eyes met his, and neither spoke. But both were of the night, and both knew that Satan was going to kill a man.

Satan Hall crossed the hallway and his green eyes narrowed as he found the door give easily beneath the turn of the knob. A dead silence greeted him as he entered the dimly lit room and saw the heavy curtains at the end of it. He was listening, a gun clutched in his hand, murder perhaps in his heart—when he heard the laugh.

It froze his feet to the floor for a split second. Then he was moving quickly toward those curtains again.

Five shots rang out in quick succession, with almost the speed of a machine gun. But Satan knew that it was not a machine gun, and he knew also that the finger that had closed that trigger was steady and sure, and perhaps as fast as he himself was. Then a sudden thump, as if a heavy body fell to the floor.

Satan was at those curtains, stretched out a hand to draw them violently apart, hesitated, then carefully parting them peered into that room.

A man was crumpling to the floor, another stood above him. And the man who stood was the man who had laughed. He laughed again now, and pushed the body over with his foot. An arm flopped grotesquely. Dead fingers twisted and lay on the rug.

Satan sucked in a deep breath. The man who stood above the dead man had broad shoulders. He whistled softly as he moved toward the window. He was shoving a smoking gun back into its holster. At the window he turned, and Satan saw his face. It was a strong face, a determined face. The face of the city's public enemy, the ace of racketeers, the face of Johnny Zitto. But the blue eyes were mild and pleasant as he threw up the window and slung a foot over the sill.

Satan's eyes dropped quickly from Johnny Zitto to the man on the floor. Sightless eyes stared unblinkingly up at the light. It was Joe de Grassie.

Then Satan raised his eyes and his gun together. Both settled upon the all unconscious Johnny Zitto. Satan had wanted Johnny for a long time. Now he had him red handed. Caught just as he had shot a man to death; brutally murdered a man.

And Satan's hand dropped to his side as the huge bulk of Johnny Zitto disappeared in the darkness. He just couldn't shoot a man, even his worst enemy, for doing the very thing he had—had perhaps planned to do himself.

"Murder!" Satan thought, half aloud. "If it is murder to kill a rat."

SATAN STRIKES

*With a Perilous Glint in His Green Eyes,
Satan Hall Walks into a Three-Way Trap
That Is Baited with Mattie Hern's Body*

1

THE BUSINESS OF CRIME

THE SIX MEN who sat at the long table might have been members of a directors' meeting of any big legitimate organization. They might have been, but they were *not*. Certainly they represented big business; the vultures who were tearing at a distracted nation. The master racketeers who made the listed public enemies sink to insignificance before their activities.

There was Tonti Marcco, the beer baron, who had watched millions flow in and out of his hands. Now it was flowing out. Since the legalization of beer, Marcco had a problem to face. And in the beginning he faced it as he had any other problem. More muscle men went out with his beer trucks; machine gunners not only made threats, but acted upon them; pineapples were hurled into former "Speaks" that now wanted to do an honest business. Yes, they bought his beer as they had always bought it—that is, in the beginning. Marcco struck hard and swiftly; for years he had been known as the Snake.

Then the great mass of American people stepped in and put Marcco on the spot, just as he had put many another. They didn't shoot him to death; they ripped open his purse strings and let his great resources drain out of it. It was not

*Johnny Zitto licked his dry lips and the hand that
clutched the gun in the drawer, trembled*

the law; at least, the *officers* of the law. It was just that the
people refused to patronize the places that Marcco supplied
with his inferior beer. They closed up by the hundreds, by
the thousands. And where he could still force those who
fought desperately to stay open to take his beer, he could
not force them to pay for it. They did not have the money;
you can't get blood out of a stone. And Marcco found out
for once that murder was not always good business. If a
customer couldn't pay and died, it did not make others pay.
Doors simply closed, shutters went up, and TO RENT
signs filled windows.

Marcco, like the others at that table, was used to facing
trouble. He looked under shaggy brows at Concillio. Yes,
Marcco had been thinking of muscling in on the hard
liquor racket, but he knew now that that business was not
lucrative. He might lose less of course, but Marcco was not

"If she stays herem" Satan said, "I'll drag you
downstairs and slap you down before them all"

in business to lose money. If his English was a little broken
at times, and he was given in moments of passion to being
a bit foul-mouthed even in his home, he did remember
that he had a beautiful mansion on the South Side. That
his daughter attended one of the swankiest seminaries in
the East he put down to his own rise in the world, not to
the depression and the sudden financial difficulties of that
socially snobbish institution.

In his heart Marcco had not come so far out of the
gutter as he believed. He was ruthless in his dealings with
men. Now the wolf was stalking at his door. Not the wolf
of hunger—at least, not personal hunger—but the money
hunger of those he had built up; the great organization he
had raised against the law of his country. He was still the
master, of course. He wouldn't believe otherwise. Yet hate

and suspicion and the lust to kill was burning in the eyes
of the men he had made. Not one or two; nothing he could
wipe out with a single quick order. It was burning in all
men's eyes. Greed! They wanted money.

Now he sipped champagne as if he liked it and toyed
with the gold watch chain across his vest as he looked at
Concillio. Five other men beside himself—five other men
as big as himself—and had he betrayed them? But that
would depend on how things worked out. The great syndicate; the Combine that Joe de Grassie had talked about
and which had brought these men together, had fallen
like a house of cards. Or had it? Well, if things worked out
as he planned it, those two questions would be answered
together. The betrayal would turn to a clever move; the
house of cards to one of stone.

He didn't look on himself as a rat. This move was for
his own interest. Rats, to Marcco, were only those who
betrayed *him*.

MARCCO STIFFENED AND sat erect. Concillio was on
his feet. He was talking. It was funny how he looked like
a waiter; an old time Coney Island waiter, in his stiff shirt.

Concillio was saying:

"We meet for a purpose. Joe de Grassie had brains. He
foresaw the repeal of prohibition long before anyone else
did. He wanted to form a syndicate that controlled all—"
He coughed, and hesitated. The word "crime" did not suit
him. Then, almost apologetically he continued: "—a syndicate that controlled all *rackets*. He worked on it for some
years; he got the goods on some of the biggest men in the
country. Then what? We needed New York. He went there
to line up Johnny Zitto. Wonderful reports came in. He

had Johnny under his thumb. He took him to a place and stuck a gun in his chest and made Johnny buy the rights to operate in New York."

Concillio paused a moment, and then went on:

"I don't know if you know the facts. But he wanted Johnny's girl, as well as Johnny's four hundred grand. De Grassie sent on the four hundred grand and sent word that he had Johnny right; that Johnny had to obey his every order. Then what? You know the rest. Johnny Zitto put six shots into De Grassie's body and left him dead. Zitto wasn't so smart. The money is here, and we are here to abandon all idea of the syndicate and split that money six ways. We can all use it."

Concillio turned and beckoned to one of the men who stood by the door. A suitcase was brought in. The man had difficulty lifting it onto the table. Concillio opened it and tossed out the tightly bound packages of new bills.

Marcco cleared his throat and spoke.

"We've gone a long way in this thing. De Grassie had a brilliant mind, but he and Zitto were enemies from a long way back. He threatened where he should have pleaded; he cursed where he should have flattered. I think we should go on with the thing. De Grassie had a lot of personal information; names in this country that would let the syndicate control courts, legislatures. Political influences that we all thought impossible. Legal beer ruined my business; it has hurt yours. The repeal of prohibition will wipe us all out unless we take steps now to control liquor when repeal is finally established. I tell you, we have created a system that will ruin us all; kill us all. Men must have money or they will have blood. I see it now, Concillio; you will see it shortly. We must have other fields to work in." He leaned forward and his slit-like eyes were almost hidden by rising pink flesh. "The milk racket, the laundry racket, the garage racket. Small time stuff! We must have one single racket that will cover them all. Building: railroads; in fact, we must have labor."

Concillio nodded and sneered.

"You forget that we must have New York, and to have New York we must have Zitto," he said. "And to have Zitto we needed De Grassie, and De Grassie—" He shrugged his shoulders expressively. "He had a brilliant mind, but he died just the same. No—we have all decided. We have met here to divide the money. Let us be thankful that Johnny Zitto left us a little memento of the death of De Grassie, and remember that—that—"

Concillio stopped; his large mouth fell open. The men about the table were staring wide-eyed toward the door. Slowly their hands were rising; going above their heads.

Concillio turned and faced the door. He thought of the four men who were stationed there. All good shots; all trusted men, and he gulped. All Marcco's men. But what he saw and what he thought were two different things. Three strange men stood in that doorway; one leaned with his back against the wall. There was a cigarette dangling from his lips. He saw, too, the object that man swung easily under his arm. He had seen such an object often; handled it just a few years back. It was a Thompson sub-machine gun, and the man who held it had handled such a gun before. Concillio had no doubt of that.

HIS BIG ROUND eyes took in the other man with the twin guns in his hands. But mostly he looked at the tall,

broad shouldered man with the blue eyes that were smiling despite the tightness of his lips. And he knew the man,
of course. Knew him even before his own hands shot into
the air.

"Johnny Zitto!" he said, and after a moment when no
one else spoke, "Johnny Zitto, from New York."

"That's right." Johnny Zitto nodded as he motioned
with a long blue German Luger toward the money on the
table. "I've come for the jack—my jack. No one is going to
dispute my right to it."

Concillio said very softly:

"You couldn't know we'd be here; you couldn't get up to
this room. So it was a frame-up. It was Marcco."

"That's right," said Zitto. "But there's nothing to do
about it now. The building is closed for the night. We're
on the fourteenth floor; no one would hear a sound on the
street. They wouldn't find anything until morning. I *could*
gun you all out."

"Could!" breathed Concillio. "But won't, eh? Why?"

"Well," said Johnny Zitto, "De Grassie and I had long
talks and I liked his syndicate idea," his shoulders moved
slightly, "but I didn't like him. The syndicate needs New
York. The syndicate is going to have it. That's why Marcco
brought me here."

"So that's why Marcco brought you here!" Concillio's big
eyes rested on Marcco. "And what do you intend to give
the syndicate for the New York interest that you will run?"

"Everything," said Johnny Zitto, and his eyes brightened. "Everything. For, you see, I intend to head the syndicate. Marcco thought of it that way. Marcco has more
brains than De Grassie. I'm here to talk business."

And they did talk business for the best part of two hours, and all the time they talked Concillio never took his eyes off Marcco. Marcco had been the first one to want to break up the syndicate when Concillio seemed in a fair way to head it. Then when that decision was reached and they had met in that room for the express purpose of dividing the Zitto money, Marcco changed. Marcco hated him, of course. He knew that. And his eyes widened; even brightened. He guessed he hated Marcco, too. And Marcco! His end of it was simple enough. He had been very close to De Grassie. He hoped now to control the syndicate through Zitto. That was it.

And the men talked and came to an understanding, and Concillio listened and nodded his head and kept his wide eyes on Marcco. He was thinking that one of his men, Sam Hertz, had been out in the hall. His closest man; his right hand man in the racket, and he wondered was he dead or—or—

The other men had left and only Marcco, Concillio and Johnny Zitto remained in the room. Johnny said:

"I've heard about you, Concillio, and I like your work. I hope you feel right about this thing now. After all, I couldn't let De Grassie get clean away with that cash."

"Bah!" said Concillio, his shoulders moving. "The money was nothing. I just didn't like your way of doing business. There'll be killing of course."

Johnny Zitto frowned.

"There'll be some. There'll be boys who want it that way. Good night!"

He had just turned to the door when he heard the gun roar. When he swung back Concillio was crashing forward, shot through the back of the head. There was a smoking gun in Marcco's hand.

"What the hell!" said Johnny Zitto huskily.

Marcco looked at Johnny Zitto for a long moment; his eyes were thin and cruel. He said:

"If it wasn't for me you wouldn't run this racket. Sam Hertz will take Concillio's place with his boys. Sam's a good man."

"Sure. Sure!" Johnny looked down at the dead man. "But what did you shoot him for?" Then looking up at Marcco, "By God! You were afraid of him."

"That's right," said Marcco softly.

"And what I fear, I kill."

"So—" Johnny Zitto stroked his chin. "What you fear, you kill." And for ten full seconds he kept his steady blue eyes on the shifty ones of Tonti Marcco.

2

A WITNESS OF MURDER

THE POLICE COMMISSIONER jerked his small, wiry body across the library rug of his home in short, quick steps. Occasionally he turned sharply and stared at the man who sat in the low chair by the table. The green, slanting eyes, with the thin eyebrows, regarded him fixedly. The thin, red lips never moved. Finally the commissioner said:

"Well, why don't you say something? I've given you the facts, Satan."

Detective Satan Hall crossed his legs, and his lips parted.

"Should a dick tell the commissioner where he gets off?"

The commissioner smiled without mirth.

"All right, then. I'll tell you. I was wrong and you were right. I thought Joe de Grassie the greatest danger the city faced; the country faced. I thought he had Johnny Zitto just like *that*." The commissioner's right thumb pressed tightly down on his left palm. "But De Grassie is dead, and Zitto has taken over the syndicate. You see, De Grassie was a far seeing man. For five years he spent a fortune planning for this syndicate; the corruption of trusted men. You know all that! But he had a weakness, when the time came to act. Perhaps two weaknesses. Hate and women! He hated Johnny Zitto and he tried to break him. He took—" the commissioner paused, remembering the interest Satan had in Mattie Hern. "Well, De Grassie tried to take over Mattie Hern, and Zitto killed him. You never told me just what happened that night, Satan, and I think you can."

Satan shook his head.

"Mattie Hern had nothing to do with the death of De Grassie. Zitto was done out of his money, but most of all he was done out of his pride. He killed De Grassie and let the money go. Now he's got back his pride; and from what you tell me, his money. Yep," Satan nodded vigorously, "Johnny Zitto was always a great danger. He's a man of action. But now," long arms moved apart, "he's got a man behind him who'll cater to his ambition and greed. Johnny was always satisfied to run his own rackets here. Now he's ambitious, and with the encouragement of this single man, who'll control him by flattery, well—we'd be far better off if De Grassie had lived."

"You mean Marcco; Tonti Marcco, of course."

Satan nodded and said nothing.

The commissioner said, after a bit:

"They've started action already in the city. Ed Fowler, who headed the dry cleaning racket, wouldn't come in line and he and three of his men were shot to death. George Pierce, who's young and coming and working the garages in a small way, has seen the light and already extended his activities. They're working the docks now, and where one or two of the bigger companies have complained, we have nothing to go on. Marcco knows his stuff."

"He knows how to handle Zitto and Zitto knows how to handle men—and he knows New York." He leaned forward suddenly. "And he knows how to *fix* men."

The commissioner said:

"And I know how to fix Zitto." And when Satan's green eyes merely blinked, the commissioner said: "That's why I asked you here. You remember Morris Metz?"

Satan jarred to his feet.

"Sure!" Green eyes were alive now. "Zitto's right-hand man. Metz, who ratted out on him and trapped him for De Grassie. I've been looking for him. You—you haven't found him?"

"Not exactly." The commissioner laughed. "But he found me. And what's more, he's going to talk; wants to talk. He says he's got facts, dates; he's a witness that'll burn Zitto a dozen times. He's coming here tonight. He's a very much frightened man; his voice on the phone trembled so that I could hardly understand him. Funny, he made me promise to lock him up. That's why the police are out front."

Satan dropped into the chair again, relieved. Morris Metz had cause to fear Zitto. But Satan had a trick of his own that he felt would end forever the activities of Mr. Johnny Zitto, although he didn't want to *use* that trick. He had never told the commissioner exactly what had happened the night De Grassie died. He had gone to De Grassie's house through the information furnished him by this same Metz. He had saved Mattie Hern, and he had stood in a doorway and seen Johnny Zitto shoot De Grassie to death. Yes, stood there and raised his gun as the huge figure of Zitto showed up in the open window before he dropped into the darkness. And for once Satan couldn't pull the trigger and shoot a man to death. Now, perhaps, he wished he had. But at the time he couldn't, and the reason was very simple. He, himself, had gone to that house for the single purpose of killing De Grassie, and he couldn't shoot down the man who did—well, who did the job for him.

But Satan sat and waited for the coming of Morris Metz. And Metz came.

There was the screeching of brakes, the roar of a racing engine, a sudden cry of men in the night. Then a half dozen shots in quick succession.

Though the commissioner was on his feet and nearer to the hall, Satan was the first in that hall, had jerked the chain from the big front door and was pounding down the stone steps. Far up the block a man in uniform was running; somewhere, distant, a police whistle blew. A single man with a gun in his hand still stood by the steps; another was returning from the corner. Satan knew both of the detectives, but he gave his attention to the thing that lay on the sidewalk, grotesquely close to the iron fence. The man was dead all right. His white shirt was torn open and ripped down almost to his waist. There were deep cuts across his body; burns, too.

SATAN NODDED AS he bent to one knee, swung the man's face slightly into the light of the street lamp. Even before he saw those contorted features, the agony still in the glassy eyes and the twisted grimace of the lips, he knew that the man had been tortured before he died.

Satan came to his feet.

"No use to look, Commissioner," he said. "It's the man you expected tonight. It's Metz."

A young detective was saying:

"I was standing right by them steps, Ed was by the fence, Freddy in the areaway. We saw the car of course. It came down the street, swerved, almost hit the curb and—God!

the body just came hurtling through the air. Missed me by inches; the flying legs, I mean. But I got the number. It was 7Y28—"

"Put it down in your book," Satan interrupted. "It's a stolen car, of course." And taking the commissioner by the arm as they went up the steps and back into the house, he said: "Poor guy. He sneaked from his hide-out to telephone you and they put the finger on him."

"But how?" said the commissioner, after he had quieted his servants and sent his wife and daughter back upstairs. "How did they know where—where—"

"To deliver the body?" Satan cut in. "If you'd seen his chest you'd know the answer to that. He told them. He had to. Maybe he was glad to."

"Johnny Zitto." The commissioner nodded solemnly.

"Sure. Sure!" said Satan. "Zitto was behind it, all right. Metz ratted out on him and was marked for death.

That's right and natural and the code of the night. But," and Satan's long bony fingers pulled at the point of his ear, "the mutilation isn't up Zitto's alley. It's more—well, when I was out in Chi I heard a lot about Tonti Marcco. It's more like his work."

"It's Zitto's job. Metz would have nothing on Marcco. Unless," the commissioner hesitated, "Marcco and Zitto are one now. Zitto's danger would be his danger. By God! Satan, we've got to get Johnny Zitto. Tossing that body at my door! The head of the police department. It's not personal except in the way the newspapers will take it. It's a defiance to all the people; the millions of the city. A man who rates himself above the law."

Satan nodded grimly. It might of course be an attempt

to undermine the confidence of the people, of the officials, in the commissioner. But Satan knew that many had tried to discredit the commissioner, and all had failed.

Satan finally said:

"I think I'll go and see Johnny Zitto. I think he'll leave the city. It'll be a break for him."

The commissioner's hand left the telephone he was about to use.

"What do you mean?" he asked.

"I mean, there was a witness to his killing of De Grassie. A witness he doesn't know about. A witness who won't appear against him if he gets out and stays out. It'll be a surprise to Mr. Zitto."

"He'll buy off that witness. He'll—he'll—" The commissioner paused and looked at Satan. "You're a peculiar man, Satan, but you've always done your duty—for me and for the people." He took Satan's hand and held it for a moment. "Go and do your duty now. I think I know who that witness is."

Satan smiled. At least the commissioner took it for a smile when thin lips parted and green eyes narrowed.

"You don't think that witness can be bought?"

"No," said the commissioner. "But—he can be killed."

"Sure!" Satan shrugged his shoulders. "If it's in the cards."

3

AT THE CLUB VENICE

SEATED IN HIS private office above the Club Venice, Johnny Zitto was feeling pretty good. The world was treating him well. Marcco was a great little guy. Why, he made monkeys out of such scum as De Grassie and Metz. Marcco knew how to take orders. Besides which, there was that list of names De Grassie had given him and which he still had. Names that meant something today, and on every one of those names De Grassie had collected some evidence. What that evidence was, Zitto didn't know. Some of them could be smacked right into line by mentioning De Grassie's name. Others—well, that was where Marcco stepped into the picture. Zitto just put a finger on a likely bit of influence and Marcco went to work. How he worked, Zitto didn't care. But he got results; turned up their past. It was funny how pompous, big frogs in big ponds had slipped up at times. After all, Zitto reflected, it isn't the crime itself that sends a man to jail or puts him on the police list. Crime and honesty! They were just words. There was no meaning to "crime," unless a guy was found out. Funny, too, how there were times when he suspected Marcco of wanting to take his place. But he dismissed that thought.

Yes, he felt pretty good. Twice now, in the same night, at least, in the same day—for Johnny always carried a pack of cards around with him—he made the game Canfield. Now he shuffled the cards, started to deal them out again. If he could make "game" three times! But he shook his head, laid the cards on the table. That was forcing his luck. Then there was a slight buzz and a light burned brilliant red above his partly open door.

He had just come upstairs. A dozen well-known people had seen him in the dining room, less than five minutes before. But the red light meant the police, and that brilliant red meant it was no simple shake-down. Well, he'd deal the cards out for appearance sake now. He knew what had happened. They had found the body of Morris Metz and wanted to raise a stink about it.

Johnny Zitto's blue eyes widened slightly as the door opened and Detective Satan Hall walked in. He hadn't seen him for some time.

Satan kicked the door closed and looked straight at Johnny Zitto.

"Metz was found tonight," Satan said.

"Found?" Johnny's eyes knitted.

"Yeah. Found dead."

"Well—why tell me?"

"I thought," said Satan, "you'd like to know. He used to be around here a lot. Thought maybe you'd give him a swell funeral. That's the custom, isn't it?"

Johnny Zitto smiled, then frowned.

"It's no secret on the Avenue how I felt about Metz. I'm no cheap gangster. I don't put on any weeping act. If he hasn't got the jack, the city will have to bury him."

"Of course you can account for your time; every minute of it this evening." Satan's words were more of a statement than a question.

"What do you think?" said Johnny Zitto.

Satan ignored the question.

"Someone had dug holes in Metz's chest with a hot knife."

"Jeez!" Even though Satan knew Johnny Zitto was prepared and used to simulating emotions, he believed that it was a surprise to Zitto. It was a full minute before Zitto spoke. Then he said:

"You oughta know me, Satan; you sit on my tail enough. I could have kicked Metz over with pleasure—but not the knifing." He knitted his brows. "You know that."

"I saw Marcco, Tonti Marcco, downstairs."

"Yeah?" Zitto was interested and showed it. "Where did they find the body?"

"Chucked from a speeding car onto the police commissioner's front steps."

Zitto's mouth hung open in amazement, then he leaned back in his chair and laughed. After a while the laugh died away and his mild blue eyes focused unseeingly on the ceiling. When he jerked his head down, those eyes were twin flares of fire.

"I'm busy," he said. "I can't be clowning around with a cop. I've got someone to see." Zitto got to his feet.

Satan lounged easily back in the chair.

"So you didn't like that one after you had your laugh. I didn't think you would. You've got to see a man about a dog. Well, the dog was Metz—and the man is Marcco, eh? The torture is up his alley."

"The dirty dago," Zitto said under his breath. Then aloud: "Beat it along, Flat-foot." He went to the door and threw it open.

Satan said, without moving from his chair:

"Wait!"

It was just a single word, but Zitto turned and looked at Satan's face. He hesitated, and Satan waved a hand toward the door. Then Satan said:

"You're leaving the city, Zitto—in twenty-four hours. I've got something that for once you can't cover. Close the door."

Mechanically Zitto closed the door and came back and stood above Satan.

"I'm interested," he said.

"I know who killed De Grassie."

Johnny Zitto laughed.

"**EVERY GUN ON** the Avenue thinks he knows that; every rookie on the Force. But they're all afraid of the law. Even the papers don't like libel suits."

Satan shook his head.

"I've got a witness who saw the killing; saw you shoot him."

Zitto whistled.

"That's a hot one. A frame, eh? Well, it won't work."

"It'll work," said Satan. "This witness can't be bought, can't be intimidated, and"—Satan tapped his left armpit—"can't be killed."

"So I leave the city on that. Good old Satan, with a murder charge that he won't pin on his old friend, Johnny Zitto; won't produce the witness against me if I scram and get off the commissioner's toes. What a laugh!"

"No laugh," said Satan seriously. "It's true. This witness won't talk if you get out."

"Why?" Zitto snapped. He was amused, and puzzled. It wasn't like Satan to crack wise.

"Because," Satan said very slowly, "this witness went there himself for the purpose of killing De Grassie. That's why he don't like to see you take the rap for it. That's why he didn't raise his own gun an inch higher and shoot you to death."

"Cripes!" said Johnny. "It was you, then."

"Well," Satan leaned back very comfortably, "I thought I'd plug you some day, Johnny, but I guess it isn't in the cards. Here's your out. Now get!"

And Johnny laughed. He leaned against the wall and his huge frame shook.

"By God! Satan, I didn't think you had it in you. An honest cop! One who can't be bribed or scared. Now— you'd do a frame."

Satan shook his head.

"I'm sorry, Johnny. But the city's too big for you."

"For you and me, eh?" Johnny sneered.

"No. For you and six million other people. I know what you're planning to do and I see the danger of it. I'm going on the stand and put the finger on you. It's no frame. You stood over the body after De Grassie fell. Then you walked to the window and put your left foot over the sill first. The gun was dangling in your hand when you turned your head and looked straight into my eyes. But I was in the blackness by the door. Then you dropped into the night. You'll have hard work getting an alibi to that. I've got a reputation for honesty."

"God!" said Zitto. "I really think you mean it. You're a funny guy, Satan. I guess you thought you saw me." And with a grin: "It must have been two other fellows. It shows what imagination will do for a guy." Satan's lips parted, but Zitto spoke first. "If I wasn't so busy these days I'd let you make the pinch. I could prove it was a frame; give both you and the commissioner a black eye. Don't sneer. I've got an alibi. That night I was with," he hesitated, leaned forward and whispered a name in Satan's ear.

Satan straightened slightly, then jerked erect.

"Got you, eh?" said Johnny Zitto.

And it did. For the name Zitto mentioned was a big one. Not just a big one in the city, but well known and respected in the national capitol itself.

"Well," said Zitto, "where's the warrant? How about the pinch?"

And Satan knew there would be no pinch. Not that Johnny couldn't always grab off an alibi, but Satan had thought that his testimony would break it this time, and that Zitto would know that he would break it. Now It was the same old story. He shrugged his broad shoulders and came to his feet. Johnny Zitto might be lying, but Satan didn't think he was. However, he would visit the "name" Zitto had whispered.

"I'm sort of sorry, Johnny," he said, "I didn't shoot you to death that night, when I had the chance—and the right."

"Now, now," said Johnny Zitto, "don't spoil it. But I wouldn't go around telling guys all I know! If another lad had told me what you told me," his hands came far apart, "well—I'd miss having you dogging me. But there are times, Satan, when you get in my hair."

"There's only one reason you don't go after me, Zitto," Satan said slowly. "You're afraid."

Johnny Zitto shook his head.

"No, I'm not afraid." Then suddenly, "I'm not afraid of you, Satan. But maybe Marcco is."

"Marcco! Why do you tell me that?"

"Because," said Zitto very slowly, "Marcco kills what he fears. Good night, Satan!"

Satan nodded grimly. He knew Marcco; knew enough about him, too. And the stories were not pleasant ones. He didn't have the nerve of Zitto; the push that Zitto had; the same secret of handling men. But in his way he was far more deadly. He didn't let hatred for him smolder long in a man's heart. He struck quickly. As for fear! Well, Marcco knew it and recognized it, and eliminated it from his emotions quickly. That's why for years he was known as the Snake.

4

___

SUGGESTION OF DEATH

TONTI MARCCO SAT in the booth in the far corner of the Club Venice dining room, and in the seclusion of the shaded lamp and the high-backed seats, leaned across the table and patted Mattie Hern's slender arm. Her black eyes regarded him fixedly; she tried to keep the loathing out of them. Killers, rats, stool-pigeons, crooked politicians, and even crooked cops she had associated with for years, but this man—why, even the dead De Grassie had been a high minded gentleman beside him.

Marcco's voice was low and soft, his great white teeth showed when he talked, and despite the freshness of a face that had just been heavily powdered by the barber, the oiliness of his skin crept through.

"You're a beautiful young girl, Mattie. I don't like to see you in this sort of work." He sighed, ran fat fingers around her wrist. "I have a daughter of my own, you know. She's been abroad. The place to forget, Mattie. The sun-swept waters of the Mediterranean, and—" Then suddenly: "Why don't you break with Johnny Zitto, after that De Grassie affair?"

"It's no secret why I don't." Mattie met his narrow, cruel eyes.

"To be sure. To be sure." Marcco nodded. "Your father. He could do things to your father, send him to the chair. A terrible thing to hold over a young girl's head. Horrible! I shall have to speak to him, Mattie. But first, I thought that I would speak to you. You would be very grateful to anyone who—who relieved you from Zitto's influence?" And as her black eyes flashed, "You hate him, don't you?"

"I hate him and fear him," said Mattie simply, but her lips were set very tightly.

"Fear him!" Marcco shook his head very gravely. "That is a bad emotion to entertain for long. Fear kills men, unless they conquer it, kill it. I have just come from talking with Zitto. He is ungrateful after all I've done to build him up."

"He—" Mattie started. "What—what do you offer me? What do you want in return?"

"I offer you," said Marcco very slowly, "freedom from Zitto's power. I promise you that."

"Why?" she demanded.

"Because," he said, "Johnny Zitto needs me now." Fat, greasy hands came far apart. "But in a little while Zitto will need me no longer."

"What does he need you for now?" Mattie asked.

Marcco leaned far over the table.

"The list De Grassie gave him. They are just names. But De Grassie had another list, with the evidence of each one's wrong beside each name. Zitto does not know that I have such a list; he believes I raise the information myself. If it was as easy as that, my dear, a thousand jackals would command these people. And I have one name he has never seen. But enough of that!"

"You intend to kill Zitto?" she asked.

"Me!" Marcco shook his head. "No. To head this syndicate one must control New York. Zitto is very strongly entrenched. His boys follow him, not in fear of quick and sure vengeance, but because they like him." He gulped once. "They would tear me to pieces if I killed Zitto. But it is the same with Zitto. If he killed me he would lose the West."

"Then what can you do while Zitto lives?"

"Nothing," he said, and when she looked perplexed: "Nothing, while he lives."

"But if he is not to die—"

"But he is to die. Another must kill him."

Mattie thought she understood, and shuddered.

"You want me to—"

He laughed easily and cut in on her as he patted her hand.

"One would not soil those pretty hands with blood," he said. "Nor would I have you torn to pieces by these idol-worshiping boys of Zitto's. We must find someone who will be—just a natural."

She nodded and said:

"What do you want me to do?"

"I want to know how much time I have. I want to know what Zitto said; what this Satan Hall said to him; what Zitto thinks of me."

Mattie Hern drank deeply from a tall glass.

"Well," she said, "you made your second big mistake tonight. Not so much the—the torture of Metz, but putting his body on the commissioner's front steps."

"Ah! That—" Marcco stroked his chin. "That was a good move; a brilliant move, almost. The power of the syndicate, the defiance of the syndicate, the indifference of it to the police system must be instilled deeply in the hearts of the timid. It is fear, my dear. Fear they cannot kill. I told Johnny that."

She shook her head.

"He did not believe you. Metz was his enemy. Metz ratted out on him. The death of Metz is laid to him. And such a display of bravado amounts to foolhardy reckless-ness in the eyes of the men he must impress with the syndi-cate."

"I see." Marcco leaned forward. "And what does he believe?"

"He believes," said Mattie, "that you did it for the purpose of undermining confidence in him, so that you might take his place. At least his thoughts run that way."

"His thoughts run that way!" Marcco seemed to think aloud, and then, "And the first mistake?"

"THE FIRST MISTAKE," said Mattie, "was not a mistake until this second one was made. The first mistake, which he thinks of now for the first time, was the shooting of Concillio." And when those narrow eyes of Marcco almost closed, "Oh, he didn't tell me that. But I know—I know. It was in his eyes."

Tonti Marcco's head bobbed slowly.

"There is not much time, Mattie. You have worked for Zitto; he pays you well enough, yet he looks on you as simply a machine. You are beautiful, Mattie. You should have cars and chauffeurs and jewelry, and my daughter to take around. Take you around, my dear." He leered over at her. "I have hopes that if things are right—things go right—my daughter may even be presented at court.

Maybe shortly, very shortly." He squeezed her hand tightly; cruel eyes became two slits. "There's everything in it for you a woman wants, Mattie. Zitto sold you to De Grassie. There's vengeance in it for you, Mattie. Vengeance!"

Mattie's dark eyes glistened.

"Can you—are you big enough to manage the syndicate?"

"There's been millions run in and out of my hands," he said simply and truthfully. "It'll be billions now. Almost impossible to conceive, Mattie. The list of names I've got is—"

And Mattie cut in.

"I've got to be sure you're not lying to me. Zitto said the information about each man was burned by De Grassie as soon as he memorized it. De Grassie wanted to be sure to lead, alone."

"I know," said Marcco. "I told Zitto that." And as if he read the doubt in her eyes: "I'll show you that information; pages of it. I'll show it to you tonight."

They both came to their feet, prepared to leave the booth. Her hand was resting on the table when Marcco grabbed her wrist. And this time there was no caress in that fat hand. It gripped her wrist like a steel vise. The soft tones of Marcco had gone. His face now was an ugly sneering thing. When he spoke, his words were deep and hard in his throat. The thin veneer of what his daughter called "culture" had slipped from him as if the years went with it, driving him back twenty years, to the time when he stalked his prey through the dirty streets of Cicero. But Mattie knew what he meant when he said:

"It's a big chance for you, Mattie Hern. If—if you double

on me I'll slit your pretty white throat for you, with pleasure."

And the "with pleasure" did not sound like melodrama. It sounded just like a simple truth, and she believed it.

She didn't speak as they turned from the booth and almost directly bumped into Johnny Zitto.

"Hello!" said Johnny. And to Marcco: "You and the girl friend going places again?"

Marcco shrugged and grinned.

"A few night clubs, Johnny. There ain't so many now, but you might as well have first hand information on all of them, you'll own them so soon."

"That's right." Johnny nodded. "And Mattie's the girl for it. Take care of yourself, Marcco. You're too valuable a man for me to lose."

Marcco smiled his appreciation.

"I hope I didn't make a mistake about Metz." He lowered his voice. "I hope you see how it is, but after this I'll see things your way."

Johnny Zitto patted Marcco on the back.

"Forget it!" he said. "Satan asking about you put ideas into my head. Take care of Mattie. She's the finest bit of dress goods in the racket. Loyal, straight as a die. By God! a credit even to Johnny Zitto."

Mild blue eyes turned and flashed on Mattie Hern's. Her black ones met them steadily. Inside his head Marcco nodded approval. Both Johnny and Mattie had been long in the racket.

"Take care of yourself," Johnny Zitto said again.

"Why?" This time there was a direct question in Marcco's voice. The easy indifference was gone.

"Oh," Johnny's big shoulders moved, "Satan's been talking about you. Somehow it didn't strike him as being up my alley. He's a killer, you know. But you *do* know."

"All men have to die," said Marcco. "Even Satan, I suppose."

"Sure. Sure!" said Zitto. "If you fear them enough." And now his lips tightened, and his eyes, set rather far apart, were brighter. That is, brighter in the center, for there was not so much of them to see.

But Zitto watched them, the man and the girl, as they walked the length of the dining room and passed into the hall at the end and disappeared. He stroked his chin, too. Mattie was loyal; Mattie would stick. After all, Marcco only knew that he turned her over to De Grassie. He didn't know that at the end it was because of Mattie that De Grassie died. And what's more, Zitto didn't know *that* either. He only thought that he did. De Grassie did not die because Zitto thought so well of Mattie, but because, after all, Zitto thought so well of—of Johnny Zitto.

5

A VISITOR IN THE NIGHT

IT WAS POSSIBLE, of course, that Johnny Zitto was riding him. Yet Satan didn't believe that. But it was possible, also, that this alibi of Johnny's might break down. Satan grinned. Here was a nationally known political figure who was not apt to break under any pressure. Yet, he had broken under pressure from Johnny Zitto. Why?

But Satan knew there were few lives, few families that were free from the rattling of the skeleton in the closet. He went back over his own life and shook his head. Certainly there was plenty that he wouldn't want to be public property—yet, he set his lips grimly. He'd of done it all again. Now he looked at his watch. It was twenty minutes to twelve. Not a time to make a call on such a man. But he dismissed that thought. He was investigating a murder case. Or was he? Down inside of him he knew that he was investigating the character of a man that people thought beyond reproach.

The front door was open almost the moment Satan pressed the bell by the man who was in a long dressing gown, gray trousers and soft felt slippers. Satan recognized him at once from pictures in the papers.

"I wanted to see you, Mr. Creighton." Satan pushed

brusquely by him and into the great hall, and when the man just stared at him and held the front door partly open, Satan said: "I'm Detective Hall." A moment's pause as he turned that satanic face of his upon the owner of the house. "They call me Satan Hall. Maybe you were expecting me." For it struck Satan at that moment that Johnny Zitto might have phoned a warning. Why was the man fully dressed and ready to open the door almost the moment he pressed the bell?

Creighton was tall, stood very erect. His hair was graying slightly at the temples and his eyes were capable of a direct, almost penetrating scrutiny. Satan knew that he was being sized up, quickly and perhaps accurately.

"Detective Hall, to be sure," said Creighton. "It must be important, that you come so late and so suddenly. I know the commissioner, of course." The last was spoken apparently as a simple conversational statement, yet the significance of the suggestion was not lost on Satan. He nodded grimly, followed his host across the huge hall and into a comfortable library. Creighton indicated a chair to Satan, dropped easily into another and waited.

Satan spoke directly.

"Mr. Creighton, I'm not much at fancy words so I won't try to use them. A notorious character, Joseph de Grassie, was shot to death by Johnny Zitto. The evidence would be conclusive but for one thing. Johnny Zitto states that he was with you at the time of the murder." And Satan, very careful as to detail, stated the time and the place of the killing. "I've come to hear you deny that statement of Zitto's."

Mr. Creighton cleared his throat.

"I am sorry," he said, "to break up your case. Mr. Zitto was with me at the time of this—this affair."

"And the nature of his visit?"

Mr. Creighton smiled crookedly.

"The nature of his visit was private."

"Too private to state, if you were questioned about it on the witness stand in Johnny Zitto's trial for murder?"

"No. I would under oath disclose the reason of his visit. I can assure you it was nothing detrimental to the welfare of the community. You feel, after my statement, that you have enough evidence to even warrant an indictment?"

"I feel," said Satan very slowly, "that you have lied." And when the red shot into Mr. Creighton's face and he came suddenly to his feet, Satan flung out: "Let's have no dramatics. I was there at the house and saw Zitto shoot this man to death."

"You!" Creighton's eyes bulged, a hand went to his chest. "You have taken your good time, Mr. Detective Hall. Might I ask why this information of yours has been kept secret, or at least kept from the public for such a length of time?"

Satan bit his lip. That was a mistake, of course. But he said:

"Police business. There are others back of Zitto. I wished to complete the case against a gigantic criminal organization that is in a fair way to over-run the country, through such people as you."

Mr. Creighton stiffened and came more erect.

"I think," he said, "the interview is over. Mr. Zitto was with me that night. And I would so swear on a witness stand if it is necessary."

Satan stood up, too.

"Mr. Creighton," he said, "you're protecting a murderer, and I don't know why.

"But it's possible that if one man can find a secret in your life, another man might be able to find it."

"That is possible," said Mr. Creighton, "if there is such a secret. It is, of course, possible that you were mistaken about this—this death. I shall not warn you that I am in a position to break you, for I believe you are doing your duty as you see it tonight. Er—" he turned to the desk, "to show my confidence in you and in the fine system behind you, I would like to give to your benevolent association, or your police pension fund, a check for ten thousand dollars."

Satan grinned.

"I am afraid," he said, "you misjudge the police as a whole. The fund you mention contains no dirty money." And suddenly: "Did you ever wonder, Mr. Creighton, how a man without money eases his conscience for a wrong? Good night!"

SATAN TURNED AND left the house. There was no use to stay longer. Mr. Creighton was an honest man, with an honorable name. He would do everything to protect that name, even to the extent of perjuring himself so that a murderer might go free.

When Satan walked down those steps and turned left, his right hand mechanically slipped beneath his left armpit. He had made a mistake when he let Zitto live. Influence, politics, corruption and blackmail, no matter how powerful, can't take a lead bullet out of a man's head and put it back in the gun that fired it.

Altogether, it was nothing new to Satan. He had been a cop for a good many years. Hundreds of men, little and big criminals, were walking the city streets free men today. It was all part of the system.

Satan turned his steps toward home. That is, the little apartment he occupied.

This thing was big; terribly big. He'd have to wait his chance, until someone made a mistake; until Johnny Zitto made a mistake, and then the State would have justice; justice through the nose of a gun held in the hand of one of its employees. Maybe he'd better work on the Metz angle. If it didn't lead to Zitto, it might lead to Marcco. And any way you look at it, Zitto had certainly taken on power, great power, since Marcco came into the picture.

Satan let himself into his walk-up apartment house, climbed the dimly lit stairs. At his own floor he walked to his door, stuck the key in the lock and turned it gently. He wasn't sure, of course; he didn't see a light suddenly die. But he did hear, or thought that he heard, the dull click of an electric button. He closed the door softly and stood for a moment with his back against it, his head raised, his ears strained—listening, his nostrils dilated like an animal's.

Funny, that. Instinct, living close to death. Give it any name; Satan never tried to explain it. But he always sensed danger; sensed an alien presence. And now— The thing hit him as it always hit him. He was not alone in his apartment. Nothing menacing, nothing fearful, that brought the cold sweat out on his forehead. Just a sense of danger that brought a grin to Satan's lips, a nod to his head, and most of all a heavy forty-five automatic into his right hand. Traps had been laid for him many times, but this was the first time anyone had ever entered his apartment and waited for his return.

His apartment was small. There was the narrow hall, the living room and the bedroom, and the bath beyond. The lock on the specially constructed steel door was good and had, Satan was sure from his own entrance, not been tampered with. But entrance was easy. There were no bars on his windows, a fire-escape gave easy access to his bedroom; a jimmy properly handled would open that window. No, Satan did not avoid contact with his enemies. A lad with nerve enough to enter his home was entitled to find his way in.

Satan moved quickly, silently down the hall; stopped by the curtains to the living room, listened a moment and tried to tell himself that he heard quick, sharp breathing. He liked that. Whoever it was, was feeling that big moment he had planned. Marcco? No, that wouldn't be his way. Zitto? Well, he might come himself; whatever Zitto lacked, it was not nerve. Others! Well, it wasn't exactly pride that made him rake his brain in split-second thoughts for a possible gunman. It was simply an assurance, a confidence in himself, that left him without a likely candidate for the office of killing him there, alone in his own apartment.

His hand, with those long, strong fingers, slipped through the curtain, skirted the woodwork, felt of the wall and finally found the light button. Satan's finger hesitated a moment; he would be shooting from darkness into light and—

His finger pressed upon the button, his gun shot between the curtains, and a low voice spoke.

"It's me, Satan. Mattie."

Satan looked into the room and saw Mattie Hern

crouched there in a big chair; his big chair, her feet drawn up under her.

"Oh, Mattie," he said. "Are you alone?"

"Yes." She let her feet slip from under her and anchor firmly on the floor. "I came by the bedroom window."

"Of course." Satan parted the curtains and stepped into the room. His green eyes surveyed every corner of it and then he pushed through to his bedroom beyond, looked in the closet, under the bed, had a slant into the bathroom and came back to the living room, to find Mattie standing, her black eyes on him slightly questioning, slightly defiant. He tapped her cheek, and walking to the wall, turned out the light. Then he crossed to the windows that faced on the alley, flung one open and cautiously looked out. The fire-escape, to the left, gave off his bedroom. Green eyes searched it in the darkness; flashed up and down. He closed and locked the window, pulled the shade down and snapped on the light again.

"What is it, Mattie?" he said.

She didn't speak for a moment. Then she said:

"That's the trust you have in me?"

He grinned and pushed her into a chair.

"I'm not a fool, Mattie," he said simply. "Now, what's on your chest?"

She hesitated a long moment.

"I'll never understand you, Satan; nor you me. I've a chance to get out of the racket. I'm going to take it."

GREEN EYES BRIGHTENED. Satan leaned down, placed both hands upon her shoulders.

"God! Mattie," he said, "I wish you meant it."

"I do. I do." She bobbed her head up and down. "That's

why I'm here now, that's why I chanced seeing you. You
wanted me out of it. Now I've got the chance." She came
to her feet and laid both her hands upon his shoulders.
"Satan, they hate you. Hate you because you're straight
and good and fine, and now—" She pushed him from her,
but clutched his shoulders; her black eyes studied his green
ones. "I'm not a squealer, Satan. I'm not a stoolie. But I'm
going to tell you things; things you already know, and see
what you say." White teeth bit into a red lip. "But I want
to know I'm talking to a man, not a cop."

Satan caught the panic in her voice.

"I never let you down, Mattie," he said simply. "I won't
let you down now. But I promise nothing."

Mattie Hern looked at him.

"You're just a cop, Satan," she said, and she could not
keep the sneer out of her voice.

"That's right," said Satan. "And I always will be—just
a cop."

"And I loved you," she flamed up. "I came here tonight
to let you know—let you know," she hesitated, then flashed
quickly, "that De Grassie collected information—but you
know about that. Marcco has it, and I'm going to have it.
It would buy my freedom from Zitto." She shook him by
the shoulders. "Understand that. Also it would make me
rich; make us rich."

"So that's how it is. Marcco has it." Satan stroked his
chin.

"It's big, isn't it, Satan?" She was very close to him now.
Black eyes grew soft. She said, and her voice was low:
"You're ugly, Satan. Men fear you and women hate you,
and I—I love you, Satan. You've done a lot for me; you

saved my life. You must care. I'm beautiful, Satan; at least, men think so. There was De Grassie, there's Marcco, there were many others. But," she shook her head, "I've kept myself for you."

She looked up at him now. Her body snuggled against his, the arms that had been upon his shoulders creeping about his neck. Her head was raised; her chin pressed tightly against his chest; black eyes shone up at him.

"There must be some reason, Satan; some reason why you've watched over me and protected me and— After all, you're flesh and blood, just as I am, Satan. Satan! Don't you see? I'm going to risk my life for you; for us. That list of names; that information. Marcco wants me to double-cross Johnny Zitto. Johnny wants me to double-cross Marcco. Both of them would like me to put you on the spot. Well, I know where that list of names is. I've seen it. I saw it tonight And I'll get it for you, for me—for us. There's thousands in it; millions maybe. Then, Satan, just you and me— and the world to see."

Black eyes swam alluringly just below Satan's green ones, red lips were slightly parted, soft white skin was tinged with red on the cheeks as slender hands pushed at the back of Satan's head.

"Mattie," Satan just breathed the words, "you don't know what you're saying. I like you; maybe I love you. I don't know. I never did know. But I've hunted criminals and hated crime. Now you're offering me, suggesting to me the rottenest of all crimes—blackmail."

"Why—why is it rotten?" she cut in quickly. "If Marcco has the information he will use it to help him prey on others; use it to control people, politics, whole cities—even murder. Zitto! It would be just the same. But you and me, Satan.

"We'd free these men from such influences, at a price. I'm a criminal and I must pay for my crime when I'm caught. Why shouldn't they? It's cheaper, for they only pay with money.

"If you're respected and sit in high places, then all bad is good. That's it. That's what you're trying to tell me. I—"

"Mattie," Satan watched those black eyes that had become burning things, "you're thinking backwards."

"All right, all right," she said quickly. "I've got no shame in this thing. I love you. Now, if I live I'll bring that list to you. You can go ahead and burn it or jail them or fry them or—

"Don't you see, Satan, I'm offering you—"

She clung suddenly to him. Exerting all her strength she jerked down his head. Arms clutched him tightly. His hands raised, rested on her shoulders; great long fingers went far apart and—

6

A THREAT TO KILL

SATAN PUSHED THE girl suddenly from him. His face was blanched, his lips grim and tight. Someone had pounded heavily upon the apartment door.

A moment of silence, and Mattie breathed:

"Don't answer it. It's—it might be Zitto."

Satan shrugged his shoulders and looked long and earnestly at the girl. No emotion in his green steady eyes; they just studied her unblinkingly.

"I've got to answer it," he said. "It might be police business. You go in the bedroom." And as she turned he took her by the arm and swung her back. "I'm stupid about some things in life, Mattie; maybe, after all, the biggest thing. But," he hesitated. "I guess what you said was good and fine, and I like you, Mattie; like you a lot. Further, I can't—or maybe, just don't know how to go."

She jerked her arm free of his grasp, raised on her toes suddenly and kissed him full upon the lips. Then she turned and was gone, disappearing into the darkness of the bedroom. And the knock upon the door came again; louder, and this time followed by the sharp ringing of the doorbell.

Satan turned and walked into the hall. His right hand

rested easily in his jacket pocket, his index finger caressed the trigger of his gun. Passing to the right of the door he clutched the knob, and without removing the chain opened the thick steel door.

"All right," he said slowly, "what do you—"

And that was as far as Satan got. If a cannon had exploded in that small hall there could hardly have been more noise, but this was not a cannon! The shots came in too rapid succession. Satan understood and his head nodded, but his mouth hung open slightly. A machine gun had been let loose at that door. Lead sprayed against solid steel and did no harm, but other lead found the partly opened door and riddled a picture to pieces as it tore plaster from the wall.

It was Satan's boast that he was never surprised at anything and that nothing was unexpected, because he refused to recognize the unexpected. But this time he was both surprised and certainly the staccato notes of the machine gun were unexpected. He grinned evilly as he waited behind the thick steel barrier and made a mental note to thank the commissioner for his insistence; emphatic orders that his apartment door be made of several thicknesses of steel. And he thought, too. There were some things that Johnny Zitto didn't like, and one was that a man lived who saw him shoot another to death.

Then Satan saw Mattie, shouted to her above the din to stay back. And the din stopped; feet beat in the hall without. Running feet, that echoed clearly on hard stairs.

Satan's guns were out, his hand was on the chain. And Mattie was on him, clinging to him despite the menacing guns, begging him not to go.

"It's a trap. They'll be out there in the hall. I tell you, Satan, your last threat to Zitto was a bad one. The De Grassie killing! Though he smiled, it shook him and—and—"

Satan tossed her from him, closed the door, shot the chain free and jerked it open.

Only silence now. No running feet, no roar of guns. Just smoke that dimmed the vision and burned deep into his nostrils. And then pandemonium.

Windows went up and voices screamed. A door opened and someone shouted "Fire!" and Satan stepped into the hall. Feet running on the stairs now; a police whistle shrilled from a window above. People in various stages of dress and undress were shouting to each other, and Mattie straightened from the wall and stepped into the hall.

"I'll get away in the excitement," she said. "Good night!"

"If Zitto thought you were—" Satan started, and stopped. It was too late. Mattie had run quickly to the stairs and disappeared.

Hysterical women; frightened men! Satan spent time quieting them. Then a cop pounded up the stairs. Satan explained, and the cop grinned.

"The landlord will be asking you to leave again." He looked at the condition of the door, the lead in the wall—and the smile left his face. "The Zitto outfit." He nodded.

And Satan smiled. That was law and order. Even the cop on the beat understood the menace that overhung the city, the police department, and he, too, must wonder why nothing was done.

Satan had put on his hat and was leaving just as the fire engines pulled up in response to the call of several excited tenants. He nodded to an inspector of police who jumped from a police car, then he turned toward Broadway. He had one rule in life, and a very important one, he thought. After an attempt upon his life, especially such an attempt, that would be all over the city in a short time, he always turned up among those most suspected, by the underworld, of the attack.

This was far from mere bravado on Satan's part. He had spent a busy day and wanted sleep, and he could have curled up right now with the hum of machine gun bullets still whistling in his ears.

But there was a duty; self protection. He must let the killers of the night see how lightly he took it and how willing he was to come back for more. It wouldn't do to have every cheap gun in the big city, who hated him, willing to take a shot at him. This "gun-out" had been a big one; a sure thing from Johnny Zitto's point of view. Now he'd let Johnny know what he thought about it.

THE CLUB VENICE was in full swing when Satan shook his head at the hat check girl, kept his hat planted firmly on his head, and turned down the narrow hall which led to the bar. He grinned, too, as he saw the man stationed before the door of that bar. It meant but one thing. The bar was closed tonight except to a chosen few of Zitto's friends. A celebration perhaps was intended. Maybe they were to bury him with honors, Satan thought.

The man at the door raised his hand as Satan approached. The hard words, ready to shoot through the side of his mouth, died. Twice he opened his mouth before he finally spoke. Then his voice was low and almost ingratiating.

"Sorry, Sa—Detective Hall. The bar's closed tonight."

"It's open to me," said Satan as he thrust the man roughly aside, and then his hard green eyes glittered. "Well, do you want to stand there on your feet or have me step over your body?"

The man didn't speak. He stood back against the wall and watched Satan open the door and walk in. He knew Satan of course, and knew, too, that he didn't talk to hear the sound of his voice; that in another moment he might be clubbed to the ground with Satan's gun. As for his own gun! Such a thought never entered his head. Those who drew guns on Detective Satan Hall met a quick and violent death. That was not simply hearsay; that was gospel.

The buzz of voices in the bar stopped the moment Satan entered. Charlie, the bartender, looked quickly up and quickly down again. He was ready to drop to the floor if things commenced. Charlie was worried. There were strangers at that bar; at least, strangers as to the accurate knowledge of Satan's activities. The strangers were Tonti Marcco and the former lieutenant of Concillio and now close to Marcco, Sam Hertz.

Tonti Marcco, who like Satan prided himself on never being surprised, coughed as his drink went the wrong way. Plainly in the clear, polished glass behind the bar he saw that evil, pointed face. Men he knew didn't act that way. Satan could easily or should easily have suspected where the attack on him came from; everybody else knew. Now he was walking smack into danger; smack into— And Tonti Marcco wiped his handkerchief across his mouth and his eyes narrowed. After all, Satan was safe. The Club Venice was the last place in the world in which Zitto would want him to die.

Half a dozen men stood open-mouthed at that bar, a couple of others stretched slightly out of booths that lined the wall in the back.

Satan went straight to the little room in the back, where the flight of stairs led to Zitto's private office above. Charlie, the bartender, called to him hoarsely.

"The boss is busy, Satan. Better take a load off your feet for a minute."

Satan never paused in his stride. He just flung his answer back over his shoulder.

"He won't be too busy to see me."

Charlie had just time to drop the bar rag on the counter and press the warning button; the brilliant red one. There was murder, he thought, in Satan's eyes. But then he shrugged his shoulders philosophically. There was always murder in those devilish green eyes. And he wondered, too. There wasn't another dick he knew—any outsider, for that matter—who'd quietly walk by those "boys" at the bar, and turning his back on them make his way to Zitto's office. Yet—

Charlie nodded his understanding. He was a tough guy in his line; none tougher. And while he had a gun bellow that bar he made no attempt to reach for it, nor did he even think of doing so. He had done all he could for Zitto. If that door wasn't locked, which it probably wouldn't be with the bar supposedly closed to outsiders, then that was Johnny Zitto's affair.

But all Charlie said, which was simply a spoken thought, but quite audible to those at the bar, was:

"Cripes! Who'd of thought he'd show up here tonight?"

The door at the foot of the stairs was open and Satan

heard the voice of Johnny Zitto. It was raised in anger, and it wasn't often that Zitto grew angry.

"You've got a beating coming to you anyway," Zitto was saying. "Close the door and—" A pause as Satan turned onto the stairs. Then, "Damn it! Get on your feet! It can't be anyone else."

Satan's feet pounded evenly up the stairs; they did not hurry. He reached the top, walked the few steps down the hall, saw Zitto's door partly open, and kicking it the rest of the way, walked in.

ZITTO STOOD BEHIND the desk, leaning on it with his left hand. His right hand was in a partly open drawer and it stayed there. Mattie Hern was leaning against a bookcase, breathing heavily, straightening her hair, dabbing at her face with a powder puff. There were marks of fingers upon her throat.

All this Satan took in with quick sharp glances. But his eyes rested on Zitto. The whiteness of Zitto's face, the hardness that had crept into those usually mild blue eyes, and the arm of the right hand that was hidden in the drawer.

A second or two of silence that was deadly long, like a missed cue in the height of a dramatic play. Then Satan said:

"Get out, Mattie."

Mattie tugged at her throat, moved toward the door. Then she spoke, and her voice was husky.

"Don't do anything you'll be sorry for, Satan."

Satan said again:

"Get out!"

Zitto spoke suddenly for the first time, but he didn't change his position over that desk. Satan's hands were empty; both of them. Zitto could see that, yet Satan's right hand tugged at the left lapel of his jacket. And Zitto knew what that meant. Satan was paying him a compliment; a compliment to his quickness with a gun. For mostly Satan stood with his hands at his sides, empty—empty for the split second before he made his kill.

Zitto said:

"You can't give orders here, Satan." And his lips curled in a sneer. "Stay here, Mattie."

Satan spoke very clearly.

"If she stays here, Zitto, I'll drag you from behind that desk, take you downstairs and slap you down before them all." And as feet beat on the stairs behind: "If anyone else enters this room I'll put a bullet between those two eyes of yours; there's plenty of space." Then, more quietly: "I want to talk to you."

Johnny Zitto licked at his lips. They were dry, very dry. He had never exactly feared Satan before, never exactly understood the fear Satan inspired in others; always wondered how Satan could reach, draw and kill before the other man got his shot in. Now, in a way he understood. He wasn't afraid; not as *he* knew the meaning of fear yet his hand that clutched the gun in that drawer trembled; the hand that had only to jerk back and up and—and— Sweat broke out on his forehead. There was something in those green eyes; something far back, deep and hateful and—yes, and hellish. That was it. It wasn't just the features that gave Satan his name; it was more than that. It was—

And a voice was speaking. It said:

"All right, Mattie. Go on down stairs. Satan wants to talk to me."

And Mattie was out the door and had closed it behind her before Johnny Zitto realized that the voice was his.

"That's sensible, Johnny." Satan nodded very gravely. "Very sensible. Now I'll tell you what's on your mind. You wonder if you could shoot first and if you could alibi it later, but most of all you wonder if you could shoot first. Personally, I don't know. You're rated fast with a gun; none quicker on the Avenue. Well," and Satan's voice rose slightly, "there's no gun in my hand yet. Why not pull yours from that drawer and we'll find out-—or one of us will find out."

Johnny Zitto said nothing and did nothing. He just stared at those eyes and looked for a moment into the fires of hell. Then the eyes seemed to change. They were still green and malignant! It wasn't the eyes themselves that changed, it was what Johnny Zitto had seen behind them, or thought that he saw.

Satan's right hand moved suddenly. Johnny Zitto's eyes bulged, his mouth hung open, his fingers tightened about the gun in the drawer, but stayed there. He was looking down the nose of a heavy automatic. And Satan spoke.

"NOT THIS TIME, Johnny," he said. "Take your hand out and take it out empty." And when both Johnny's hands were on the desk and he sank slowly back into the chair behind it: "I know just what you were thinking tonight. You were thinking that if anything happened to Creighton—well, if he died, you'd burn." A moment's pause as Satan's gun disappeared and he leaned forward. "That is, if I lived."

Johnny said:

"I don't know what you mean." He was feeling a bit better now. He even felt for the cards upon his desk, and when no warning came from Satan he shuffled them mechanically.

"No?" Satan nodded. "So you've come to beating women!"

"That's it, eh?" Johnny was recovering now, but he felt that his breathing was heavy, labored, and he hoped that Satan did not hear it.

"No," said Satan, "that's not it. Some of your hoods tried to smoke me out tonight. They even brought a 'typewriter' along."

"Mine?" Johnny Zitto jerked up his head and smiled, but it was not a pleasant smile. A guy never knew what this Satan might do. He wasn't like other cops. He had pull, too. The commissioner stood directly behind him, and he worked straight from the commissioner. Johnny was ready to say more; deny it, then he didn't say anything. He caught a sound outside the door. The boys were close at hand. They—

And Satan heard it, too.

"I wouldn't encourage them to come in, Johnny. They'd have something to talk about for a week, as to how your body lay. I'm not going to—to shoot you tonight."

Johnny leaned back and laughed. It sounded hollow; peculiar, like a man gargling through a horn. He killed it at once. He tried to wise crack, but the best thing he could get off was:

"Not tonight, eh?"

"I tell you, Johnny," Satan's voice wasn't tense any longer; it was low and natural, just conversational. "I might have been killed tonight but for the fact that my door contains several sheets of steel," he said. "That was the commissioner's idea—not mine. Now, I never kicked when a lad went gunning for me. It was him or me. So far, *him*. And I have no objections any time you want to take a gun in your hand and try your luck at putting a bullet in my back. But I work alone. I haven't any boys to slip a few grand to and tell them to come and get you, Johnny. I'm tired of it!" Satan paused a moment. He was glad to see that Johnny was getting back in shape. His grin was more natural. "So I want you to understand how I feel."

"Sure. Sure!" said Johnny Zitto. "I know how you feel. I don't know anything about tonight, but I guess you want to make a deal. You lay off me and I'll lay off you!"

"No, it's not exactly that." Satan shook his head. "It's like this; just like this, Johnny. And believe me, the next time you send boys out after me be sure they make good. If they don't, then I'm coming right here to the Club Venice, walk up those stairs like I did tonight and put a bullet right between your eyes."

Johnny Zitto started to laugh and then didn't. It suddenly struck him that Satan was speaking the truth.

"You!" Johnny said, and his amazement was real. "You, a copper. Why, that would be murder."

"You can call it what you want, Johnny, but you'll be deader than hell." And Satan turned on his heels, jerked open the door, and elbowing his way through the half dozen men who stood in the narrow hall, went down the stairs that led to the bar.

Not one of those men tried to stop him; not one raised a hand against him.

Satan reached the bar, walked slowly through it, conscious of the steady, narrow eyes of Tonti Marcco that followed him. But he didn't look at the man as he pushed open the door and walked toward the street.

7

A QUESTION OF TIME

MATTIE HERN WENT directly down the stairs, through a little door in the room behind the bar, down the long hall and out into the night. She didn't hesitate then. She took a taxi and went straight to her own apartment. Mattie had been many things in her day. Shoplifter, pickpocket, and then she had gay-catted jobs for professional burglars who later fenced the stuff through her father, Jake Hern. She was born a crook, lived a crook, and hoped— hoped to die out of the racket. The racket! Everyone was in it, from the cop on the beat to the politician who drank his wine, rolled his eyes and suggested "delightful" sea trips. Yes—everyone but Satan, she thought.

But she knew that her strongest asset was those slender, beautiful fingers. Whether it was lifting important letters from the inside pocket of an influential man, or— But she was above the days when she could take a "ticker" from even a trouser watch pocket without others, let alone the victim, noticing the movement of those quick, alert fingers.

Magic fingers, they called them. Now—she was going to work on her own. She felt sure she could open that tiny safe behind the picture and slip out of it the thick sheets of typewritten paper that Marcco had shown her a few hours before.

A fool, Marcco. What did he offer but promises? She laughed, but it was a hollow laugh.

Above her father's shop she selected a small glass cutter, pushed it into her handbag, and leaving by the rear door of the closed shop and not disturbing her sleeping father, passed through the alley to the street behind. She was going to burglarize the house in the Seventies, where Marcco stored his treasure; those sheets of paper that held a fortune.

As for Zitto! Well, Mattie had seen things in his eyes just a few hours before, when he took her by the throat and forced her to her knees. And she hadn't double-crossed him. She had never thought of playing Zitto into Marcco's hands. But Zitto had sold her out and she was through with him. Through with him, if she *could* be through with him. Those type-written sheets were the property of Marcco. If she wanted to give them to Satan, that was her business. She hadn't decided just what she'd do with them. They would, presented to Zitto, wipe all distrust from his mind. They would gain freedom from Zitto; from the racket. Her father's freedom. Why not? They were worth a fortune; several fortunes, in the hands of a man like Zitto.

Mattie did not approach the house from the front. She came through from the block behind, slipped down the narrow alley, into the court, and swinging easily over the high, wooden fence dropped without a sound on the hard stone of the rear yard.

Her close-fitting, dark, knitted suit merged with the darkness and became one with the shadows. There were servants in the house, she guessed, though she had not seen them earlier in the evening when Marcco had opened the safe. Opened it while she watched every movement with those alert black eyes, her magic fingers closing and unclosing at her sides. He was a fool, this Marcco, with his assurance and—

The house was in darkness. She picked a kitchen window, for the cellar ones were barred, and upended a barrel, reached up and pulled her slim body onto the sill. She pasted a bit of fly-paper on the glass, close to the lock, and went to work with the diamond-pointed cutter. A minute, two perhaps, and the round piece of glass was in her hand. A single movement of her fingers and the lock clicked open.

Mattie slid easily from the kitchen sink to the floor, sent a pencil of light from her flash along the soiled linoleum, and spotting the swinging door passed through the butler's pantry to the dining room. After that she was familiar with the ground and no more light was needed when she went through the living room, found the heavy curtains and passed into the tiny library beyond. She knew exactly where the big couch was, across from the single window. The safe, too, close to that high-backed secretary and behind the framed portrait on the wall.

Not a sound did she make, not a bit of furniture did she strike as she moved quickly through the darkness. Inside the library, she took four long steps and raising her hand touched the frame of the picture.

Fingerprints! She thought of that and laughed to herself. Who'd bother about fingerprints. Once she had those type-written sheets, nothing mattered.

She laid the picture down on the floor against the wall, and placing her handbag beside it shot the rays of the flash upon the safe.

Deftly her fingers moved the dial—and then the click. Mattie sighed, thrust her hand into the safe and pulled out the sheets of paper. What a fool Marcco was after all! She had stood behind him while he opened it there in the light, and studied every movement of his fingers.

Mattie closed the safe, leaned down to replace the picture and paused, then she straightened and whirled around. There was a dull click, flooding the room with light. A soft voice chuckled.

"What a sweet little rat you are! First Zitto, and then me, and finally, I suppose, Satan Hall."

For a moment, only, Mattie faced Tonti Marcco; the cruel, narrow eyes and taunting lips. Then she made a quick dive for her bag upon the floor and the little automatic it contained.

MARCCO, FOR A big man, moved quickly. His foot came down heavily upon her wrist; his left hand shot up and gripped her by the throat. She couldn't help it; she shrieked out with pain. And he struck her, knocking her back as his foot lifted from her wrist. Then he struck her again.

She staggered against the wall as he tore the sheets of paper from her and thrust them into his jacket pocket. Then, as she tried to straighten her weakening knees, he almost lifted her body from the floor and hurled her onto the couch across the room from the window. Her head struck the wall and her body went limp for a moment. It was hard, turning her head, and she saw things through a mist. Marcco lit a floor lamp and snapped out the bright globes in the ceiling. He moved the lamp so that it shone down on her face and left the rest of the room in darkness. He was sitting, too, on the side of the couch. Through the glare of the light she saw his evil, grinning, cruel face. And then he was talking and she understood.

"You were early, my dear," he said softly. "And it is all a question of time. After Zitto put those fingers into your white throat I thought you might delay it a night. But you didn't. You thought like a man. What you did must be done quickly! Thought like a man, yes. But you are not a man. You are a very beautiful woman. And woman is a lure that kills men. A lure for Johnny Zitto because he hates you, or fears you, or distrusts you. And a lure for Satan Hall because he loves you, or wants you, or trusts you. Funny! You are here tonight to bring two men to this house. One from love and fear for you; the other from hate and fear of you. But it is all a question of time."

"What do you mean?" She only got part of it. "Time. A question of time."

"Time is important," Marcco said. "Important in life as in death. If Satan came too soon that would embarrass me; if he came too late— But of course they will come together." And then he leaned forward and started to talk, gloatingly, while his broad vest with the expanse of watch chain flashed in the light.

"My dear child," he said, "Zitto will be told how you crossed him and that you are a prisoner here. He will come immediately, for Zitto kills rats; and he will be told that he will find the type-written sheets you wanted for your own, so he will come alone. At the same time Satan will be told that Zitto is going to kill you here. I have arranged the time so that Satan will arrive to find you dead, and—well, if I know his nature, if half the stories about him are true, that will eliminate Johnny Zitto. A natural for me. No one will suspect my hand in it except you, and you will be dead. Love and hate and death, all very close together. But we have two hours to wait, you came so quickly. Then my friend will telephone them. It is all in the correct timing. Listen!"

When she turned her eyes from those cruel slits, he struck her brutally on the mouth. Blood formed on her lips. Her hand clutched at him, twisted in his watch chain. He jerked it free.

Marcco talked on and the girl's eyes widened in horror. It was a terrible way to die. By the knife, he said, and he seemed to take pleasure in torturing her by his description. And he was going to bind her there, before she died.

Time. Time! The words rang in her ears. One man lured there to kill another, and she dead between them. Time. Time! She didn't faint. She dug her nails into her palms, her upper teeth bit down on her lower lip. She had lived in the racket; she would die in it now. She wasn't afraid to die. But like that; like— And she wanted to live!

8

DEATH STRIKES

THE PHONE BUZZED in Satan's ear. He was fully awake in a split second. He always was. It was close to four o'clock. He sat on the edge of the bed, stretched himself and looked at the phone. He wanted to sleep, but this might be the commissioner, and after all— He picked up the receiver and said sharply into the mouthpiece:

"Yes—Detective Hall speaking."

"Right!" said a metallic voice, and to Satan's trained ear a partially disguised voice. "Listen. Johnny Zitto has Mattie in a house in the Seventies. Get the number." And the man gave the address, repeating it. "Now, if you want to see Mattie alive or get the murderer, hurry over there. Enter by the room that shows a light."

Satan said:

"Who are you?"

"Maybe not a friend of yours, but certainly an enemy of Zitto's," said the voice. "But to show I know things: Mattie got hold of some dope; information on big shots that would make them sweat. She snatched it from Marcco, and Zitto wants it. Well, don't go if you don't want to. Zitto left for a bit, but will be back any minute to—to kill her."

Satan had dropped the receiver back onto the hook and

was getting into his clothes. He swung his harness over his shoulder, tapped the gun lovingly with his right hand, then slipping another from under his pillow placed it in his jacket pocket. Trap? Maybe. But he didn't think so, and what's more he didn't care. He was going. He had seen the marks of Zitto's fingers on Mattie's throat.

Satan jumped into his flivver and shot across town. Around the corner from the number he sought, he left the car and hurried down the block. He was almost to the house when the purr of a powerful motor warned him of an approaching car. He slipped into an areaway and saw the big car go by. He thought there was just one man in it.

The car passed the house, stopped, and the man got out. He came hurriedly back down the street. As he passed beneath the street light, Satan saw his face; saw it just before the man turned and entered the basement to the house Satan sought. It was Johnny Zitto.

So Zitto was back. Mattie wasn't dead then. Or was she? Satan passed quickly down the street, entered the alley next to the house and almost at once spotted the light shining beneath the shade in the library window. He hopped the fence, crouched for a moment in the alley beneath the window. Then he spotted the shed that was just below it, and with quick, cat-like movements leaped and caught the copper gutter. He felt it give beneath his weight, then hold as he swung his body up on the slanting roof. He snaked his way to the window. The shade was drawn, but it was old and worn. Almost at once he found a hole in it and peered through. The first thing he saw was Mattie, stretched there on the couch beneath the lamp. Mattie, whose face was white, whose eyes were wide with terror, nameless horror that shrieked out silently, for the girl was gagged.

But there was more in her eyes than just unknown terror. She was watching something; eyes riveted in horror upon something. And Satan saw it. Beyond and above the lamp a figure was moving. The shoulders of a man, the dark sleeve of a coat, and above it the dimness of a face. But what Satan saw, and what sent his teeth tightly together and made his green eyes blaze, was what the man held in his hand. A knife; an ugly looking knife with a double-edged blade. And Satan's thoughts raced.

Zitto! He had doubtless entered by the basement then. Apparently he was not going to waste any time in making the girl talk. But how could she talk? She was gagged and—

Satan knew the truth even as he raised his gun to crash in the window. Zitto was going to kill her. Kill her! And the knife went up suddenly and started down.

Satan's gun cracked twice. He didn't fire wildly, blindly. He just fired quickly. And he didn't fire at the white hand that held the knife. There was no time for fancy shooting; knocking a knife from a moving hand, a hand that would in a second bring death to the girl. He fired at a steady target. At the white blotch of face. The distance was not great. Satan knew what a heavy forty-five would do at that distance if—if— But there had been little chance to aim.

There was just the two roars, almost as one; the tiny tinkle of glass. Satan had come erect, and, throwing up his elbow, crashed through the window and into the room.

Mattie still lay on the couch. Her face was still drawn, her throat still white; there was no red upon it. And the man he had hit—Zitto! The heavy slug had hurled him from the couch against the wall. He had turned, and even now Satan saw his huge figure toppling, saw in the dimness beyond the circle of light the man fall on his face, crashing between the library curtains.

Satan rushed to the girl, tearing the gag from her mouth, cutting the ropes that bound her.

"That's the kid," Satan said. "You have nothing to fear now. Zitto can't harm you now." He looked at the sprawled form in the darkness, lying there between the two rooms. "It's too bad it had to come like that. Somehow I always felt I'd get Zitto, but that I'd get him with a gun in his hand. So he— It wasn't like Zitto. He suspected you, Mattie."

"No, no." Mattie cried from the couch. "I wouldn't have double-crossed him. I couldn't, Satan. It had nothing to do with him. I wanted only my freedom. I—I—I never could rat out, not even on Zitto. I—" And suddenly rubbing a hand across her eyes: "What are you saying? Zitto dead? Zitto dead! How—when?"

"There, there," Satan didn't know what to do for a hysterical woman. He didn't know what to do for Mattie. "It's over," he said.

HE TURNED AND found the electric light switch and flooded the room with light. The body lay there by the curtains. The head and shoulders were hidden by the drapes that divided the library from the living room, and— The curtains moved. Distinctly Satan saw the curtains move at about the height of a man's head; a tall man's head.

"Stay where you are." Satan's voice was low and even. "You, behind that curtain! Now, swing back the curtain and stand still. Quick! or I'll spray it with lead."

The curtain moved, then jerked aside. A white face showed, then the face grinned. The man spoke.

"You can't get rid of me that easy, Satan," the man said. Satan cursed softly. The man in the doorway was Johnny Zitto. Then who— And Satan looked down. The head of the dead man was twisted slightly. One glassy eye looked up at him. It was not cruel and cold now; just cold. The dead man was Tonti Marcco.

"I always told you," said Zitto with a shrug of his shoulders, "I never went in for a knife." And with a sharp whistle: "What a nice little plot! But let the girl tell it."

And Mattie did tell it.

"Tonti Marcco was going to kill me," she said. "Kill me just before Johnny Zitto came. And then you'd come, Satan, and think—think Johnny did it, and— It was terrible. He was a fiend. He seemed to take pleasure in torturing me and telling me how I'd die. Two hours to wait. Two hours, while he sat there on the side of the couch. Time. Just a question of time." She shuddered. "He said my body must still be warm when you arrived, or—or—" and her hands went over her eyes. "I was working on my own, Johnny," she finally said to Zitto, "I— Maybe I wanted to, but I couldn't have ratted out."

"I guess you couldn't," Johnny said very slowly. "I'm sorry, Mattie, about—" He paused, and then: "But how did things go wrong? How did Satan get here on time, and—" He jerked a thumb toward Marcco and grinned.

"Time!" the girl gasped. "Marcco had to work it just right. And I—I got his watch from his pocket and set it back fifteen minutes. At least I hoped it was fifteen minutes; anyway ten minutes. My hand trembled so that I couldn't be sure. I did it before he bound me."

Zitto nodded his understanding.

"Those magic fingers!" He thought half aloud.

"Then to keep him from knowing! That was hard, very hard. Ten or fifteen minutes wasn't much for him to lose in two hours. But he wanted to look at the time shortly afterwards, and I fought and kicked and shouted, until he gagged me. Then I struggled and tried to get free. The big moment came when he did look, and he didn't know— didn't know, and I wondered was I wrong. Had I set it back enough? Had I, by mistake, turned it ahead? And would Satan come in time, or would he find you, Zitto, standing over my—my—"

"Forget it, Mattie," said Zitto. And turning to Satan: "Well, this is one bit of killing you can't hang on me." He looked down at Marcco, half raised his hand as if to grasp Satan's, looked at those green eyes, and shrugging his shoulders said lightly: "Much obliged, Satan."

"For what?" Satan looked at him steadily.

"Marcco was getting to be a problem and—Thanks for everything. You'll understand." And Johnny Zitto turned quickly, stepped over the body of Marcco and said: "It's your party. I want none of it." And he was gone.

The gun still dangling in his hand, Satan stood there. His left hand rubbed his chin. Then the front door closed and a moment later a motor raced, purred distantly and died away. Satan turned to Mattie.

"That information, Mattie?" He looked toward the safe. "In there?"

"No, not now," Mattie told him. "I—" and as if in sudden

decision: "Well—it's yours, Satan, to do what you please with. It's in Marcco's pocket. I saw him put it there."

Satan's eyes shone brightly as he knelt by the body. He hummed softly as he dug his fingers into Marcco's pocket. Why, it would bust the Zitto alibi in the De Grassie kill. He could go to Creighton with the very information that Zitto had, and—

Another pocket, the inside jacket one—and the hum died on Satan's lips. Both trousers pockets, then the hip ones, and he turned the body over roughly and looked under it. There were no type-written sheets. There was nothing that would— Satan came to his feet.

What had Zitto said?

"Thanks for everything. You'll understand."

And Satan did understand. Zitto had taken that information, taken it before he stood up behind those curtains; yes, taken it almost the very moment after Marcco crashed between those curtains at Zitto's feet.

"It's gone." Satan said half aloud. "I've lost again."

Then he looked down at Marcco and over at Mattie Hern. Well, maybe he hadn't lost after all. For Mattie was alive, and certainly Marcco was dead. And tomorrow was another day.

SATAN'S THREAT

Death Hovered Over That Locked
Chamber Like a Fluttering Bat During
the Last Hour of Conflict Between Johnny
Zitto and Detective Satan Hall

1

A CHINESE CUSTOM

JOHNNY ZITTO PACED up and down his office above
the Club Venice. Once he looked at the door to the hall,
which was slightly open; then, with a half grin, he entered
the little wash room and surveyed himself in a full length
mirror. The years—and not so very many of them, had been
kind to Zitto. He didn't dissipate. He took care of himself;
kept in training by playing golf. The swankiest club in the
East; the Ritz Meadows Club. Almost every Saturday
afternoon found him out on the links; occasionally, week
days, too. But on week days he was very late. First and
always, Johnny Zitto was a business man.

Now he took note of his broad shoulders, clean shaven
face, soft blue eyes; and with a more critical eye, the gray
suit. It was not a flashy suit. Just the right touch; just the
semblance of a stripe in it. He whistled softly as he adjusted
his tie, jerked down his vest and twisted his neck slightly
inside the soft blue collar that matched his shirt. Then
he lifted the flower from the glass above the porcelain
basin and placed it carefully in his lapel. The picture that
presented itself was not unpleasing; certainly not unpleasing to Johnny Zitto.

Leaving the wash room he returned to his office, looked

once at the huge, latest model burglar proof safe; then going to his flat desk pushed the edge of it until the rear right leg ran off the rug. Carefully he manipulated the leg until it settled squarely where he wished it to be. He went quickly to one knee, made a slight pressure with his thumb on a section of highly polished wood, slid that bit of wood easily back, and, sticking his hand in, brought out a little tin box.

Johnny's eyes glittered as he pulled out the typewritten sheets; the sheets he had taken from the dead body of Tonti Marcco. Marcco, whom Detective Satan Hall had so conveniently killed for him.

Johnny Zitto mulled over the names on those sheets; names of big men in the country who had at some time or other failed in their duty even to a criminal extent. This knowledge was worth a fortune to him. By the evidence which had been gathered over the years and listed carefully under each name, he could force these men to act under his orders. Business men, politicians large and small, men who made our laws, yes even national figures.

It was the same list of names that Joe de Grassie had taken years to gather, with the evidence against each one. Joe de Grassie who had formed the Combine, a national organization of crime, which through influence, bribery, blackmail and murder would control one great racket—one racket combining all rackets—labor, industry—and slip easily from bootlegging into the legitimate liquor trade once prohibition was ended.

"De Grassie!" Johnny Zitto sneered. It was De Grassie who had formed the Combine; gathered together the biggest criminal leaders in every big city. And he had

"You dirty little—" Zitto began. Fear and horror were
in Mattie's eyes, but she was not looking at Zitto

taken in Johnny Zitto. Johnny's lips curled. "Taken in was
right. Forced him in by kidnaping him, making him put
up money—and rather than lose that money, stay in the
Combine." Johnny smiled—held him in the Combine
until that night Johnny Zitto had shot De Grassie to death.
Oh, Johnny had liked the idea of the national combine,
but he wanted to head it; not be just a part of it. And now
he did head it. He had gone to Chicago, busted in on the
meeting of the big shots, recovered his money, and he left
that meeting as head of the greatest criminal organization
the nation had ever known.

Since then things had happened quickly. Johnny built
the Combine even bigger—even stronger. But there was
one danger. Detective Satan Hall—the most feared man
in the underworld today. Like the criminals themselves,
he, too, shot to kill, but he shot quicker and straighter, and

he was now bending every effort to get those sheets of evidence, break up this Combine—

On the surface Zitto scoffed at Satan Hall. But deep inside of him he was worried. Satan had shot to death some of his best men—and with the Commissioner of Police standing squarely behind him he was a real menace to Johnny Zitto. Satan liked Mattie Hern. How much Zitto didn't know. But he had killed men who threatened her; men who wanted her. Oh, it wasn't murder—at least not legal murder. But somehow these men had died—died by Satan's gun.

"Mattie Hern!" Johnny Zitto shook his head. Maybe she had first joined up with him through fear of others, perhaps stayed with him now through fear—for Johnny Zitto could, if he wished, slip the evidence to the police that would send her father to the electric chair. But Mattie— Mattie would stick. She would never break the code. She was born in the racket—lived in the racket—and now— well, Johnny hoped her head wouldn't be turned by her great good fortune. Yes, he had plans for Mattie.

LIQUOR! EVERY MAN in the Combine now was working toward that end—control of the legitimate liquor trade as soon as prohibition was repealed. Rotten politicians, rotten judges, rotten—oh, in a way, just the same breed of men who made bootlegging pay. The thing was easy—simple— Johnny had but to take that list of names, run a finger down it to send a national figure from his pedestal.

Although those typewritten sheets were worth a fortune to Johnny Zitto it was the little note clipped to the last sheet, scrawled in a hurried masculine hand, to which he now gave his attention; smiled grimly. This was personal—personal vengeance.

Then he replaced the papers in the tin box, slid back the board and moving the desk onto the rug again, looked over at the safe. An old Chinese custom! He grinned. The safe was impregnable to burglary, but not to a court order. There was money in the safe, of course. But that was a blind, as well as the safe. As to safe deposit vaults! He didn't trust them entirely. Where he used them, and many of them—under the names of friends, of course, a court order would reach them, too.

No, these typewritten sheets were too valuable to trust to anyone. His followers were loyal; Johnny ruled them with an iron hand. But the names on those sheets and the evidence against each name was worth perhaps a million dollars, properly handled. And after all, Johnny had had experience with men. His broad shoulders shrugged. A million dollars was a lot of money.

In a way those sheets were a white elephant. He didn't know just where to keep them—and he couldn't destroy them. If he wanted to make them public— He grinned. There was information there that would rock the entire nation; scandal that would sink to insignificance the already startling details of some of the crookedness of high and trusted officials.

But Johnny Zitto had no intention of making them public; at least, not as a whole. Only those who failed to take orders from him when the time came that he could use them need fear public shame or public retribution. He laughed as he lifted the phone. He wasn't the only big shot who had escaped prison.

"Send Mattie—" he started, and stopped. There were footsteps in the hall, a light knock on the half open door. "All right, Charlie—never mind." He hung up the receiver.

Before he went to the door he frowned. Mattie shouldn't have walked up like that; not until— But the frown left his face as he flung the door wide open and saw Mattie standing there. He had been thinking about Mattie lately; about Chet Barloff, Joe de Grassie, even Tonti Marcco; all three who had really died because of Mattie, unless— Johnny Zitto straightened slightly. Well, they had looked at Mattie and wanted her.

Mattie stood in the doorway; black eyes, black hair, delicate red lips, skin as— And as she walked into the room Johnny Zitto's mild blue eyes brightened. They followed every movement of that slim young form. It was the first time in years that Johnny Zitto had looked at a woman in that way. Before, it had always been: can she turn the trick; has she got the class for it—the brains for it? Will she have the guts when the time comes, or will she squawk all over her face when the finger's on her?

Now he was looking on Mattie as a woman—his woman. Mattie was in for a surprise; a pleasant surprise, when he told her! He shrugged his shoulders. Mattie had been queer that way. Or had she? Maybe, after all, she was just clever. He always knew she had brains. Maybe she had been waiting for just this moment. He closed the door, turned and faced her.

"I've been thinking a lot about you, Mattie." He ran a hand through her soft black hair and liked the feel of it on his finger tips. And when she drew back, "Forget the trouble we had. Things didn't go right that day that I damn near strangled you. As for De Grassie! I was a fool to turn you over to him. Things are going to be different now. I killed De Grassie because of you, Mattie."

"You killed him because of yourself," she said quickly, her black eyes on his bright blue ones. She had never been quite afraid of Zitto before; at least, in this way.

"Me and you both, kid." He dismissed that subject with a movement of broad shoulders. "You've been loyal, Mattie; you've stuck. There were times, perhaps, when I didn't understand. But those papers that I got from Tonti Marcco; you knew what was in them? You were going to bring them to me?" There was just the slightest hint of a question in his voice.

"I knew what was in them, but not the names of the people. And I was going to tell you about them, and ask you to—to let my father go; not threaten him through me any more."

Johnny Zitto laughed. It was a boyish laugh.

He opened the drawer of his desk, tossed a couple of thick packages of tightly rolled bills across it. Mattie's eyes bulged. They were crisp new bills.

"THEY'RE FOR YOUR old man, Mattie," he said. "He often talked about going into the ice business in Antwerp. He should be good on diamonds. Besides, we don't want him beefing around, putting on airs and blowing his head off along the Avenue. Here!" An envelope followed the money. "Passport, steamship ticket. It's first class, of course. I'd of gotten him the best suite on the ship, only he's shrewd and might guess and want to shake me down for a pile of jack. First class! The old buzzard should go steerage."

Mattie looked at Johnny Zitto, then she looked at the money and back at Zitto again.

"Are there any strings attached to this?"

"Hell! No." Zitto laughed. "You wanted the old man to have an 'out.'" He half waved a hand toward the safe. "And you earned it for him with those typewritten sheets. I've always been in the big money; in the millions, lately. Now I'm out of that."

"You're going to throw up the racket?" She picked up the money and stuffed it into her bag. Perhaps, after all, she had caught Zitto in an affable mood. She'd take advantage of it.

"Not exactly." Johnny Zitto grinned. "But I'll be in the billions now." His eyes blazed for a moment and he placed both his hands on Mattie's shoulders. Strong fingers bit into her flesh, but Johnny did not realize that. "It's true— true. One racket in the entire country. Prohibition's over, and hardly a drop of liquor will be sold in this country unless I pass it; maybe not even shipped into the country. Liquor, labor— But why bother you with it?"

He paused for a long moment, and then:

"You're out of all that. You're going to live, Mattie. Cars, diamonds, yachts—whatever the hell it is that a woman wants most. I was up looking at the penthouse on that new Park Avenue apartment. I forget how many thousand they spent decorating it, and I didn't give a damn. I'm having the place torn to pieces and fixed up again. Nothing will be too good for Johnny Zitto's woman."

Mattie jerked back. There was fear in her eyes; terror, perhaps. It wasn't immediate and physical. She didn't look at the closed door and fear that, despite her cries, her struggles, Johnny Zitto would crush her in his arms, mad with passion. No, she thought of her father; the crime that Zitto could roast him for. She thought of a week from now; a month from now, when Zitto, scarred in his weakest—or perhaps strongest spot; his pride, would—would what? And the "what" was too terrible—too horrible even to contemplate. That he would kill her seemed a simple and perhaps too pleasant solution to Zitto's hurt pride. But that he might throw her to Hertz— Sam Hertz, his right hand man since the death of Tonti Marcco, was something that filled her with horror; with loathing.

"So," she opened her bag, "there was a catch in it then."

"Catch?" Zitto seemed surprised. "There's no strings on it. Take that jack to your old man. We just won't want him around." And suddenly, "I've been a fool; grabbing everything, listening to the slogan along the Avenue: Johnny Zitto always has the best. And right under my eyes, under my hand, the finest bit of dress goods in the city"—he hesitated and then got it out, almost patronizingly—"yes, in the whole country— Imagine it! It took that half Russian Barloff and a couple of grease balls to let me know the truth."

"But—" Mattie was watching him.

"BUT— SATAN, EH?" Johnny Zitto's lips parted. "Satan Hall. I've got him in a jam. I've only got to spill the word and he'll be pounding pavements out on Staten Island or up in Kingsbridge."

"No, no." She shook her head. "It's a combination that even you can't lick; lick by influence, Johnny. The commissioner of police stands directly behind Satan."

Zitto did not catch the alarm in her voice, or if he did he took it for alarm for herself—not for Satan.

"Hell!" Zitto pinched her cheek. "You did me a big turn,

Mattie; a damn big turn, when Satan was thinking of you and I got that evidence. No, the commissioner won't be behind Satan any longer," and with a crooked twist to the left corner of his mouth, "or if he is he won't be commissioner any longer." He held out his hand. "Just like *that* he'll be eating out of my hand, taking my orders."

"What is it?" Mattie hardly whispered the words.

But Johnny Zitto pushed her toward the door.

"You ain't going to trouble your head about such things any more. You're going to spend your time looking pretty, thinking up ways to—well, to please me. De Grassie was right. A guy's got to have recreation. Women," he looked down at her by the door, "at least one woman has her place." And seeing the look on Mattie's face and not understanding it, "I know, Mattie. It's big. I guess I could have had any girl on the Avenue, or off it for that matter. And don't mind my way. I haven't got the time for playing around with cute tricks. Just believe me when I say I like you a lot."

The conceit of the man! But Mattie didn't think of that then. She knew that what Johnny Zitto wanted, he got— he took. She simply said:

"What of Satan—of Satan Hall?"

"Oh, I'll miss him." And the smile disappeared and a frown took its place. "In a way I'm kind of glad he's to drop out of things. I've had—well, half a feeling that it would be Satan who would finally knock me over. But that's out now. Still, we'll keep this quiet for a bit. I know it'll be hard for you, but don't get blowing about it yet."

And when she would have spoken he pushed her out the door.

"Just run up to that penthouse and see what's what.

Don't ask prices; get what you want. And, Mattie," as, in a dazed way, she passed down the hall and turned onto the little flight of stairs, "there ain't a store in the city where you can't get credit—or if you find one, tell them to give me a jingle. We'll have dinner together tonight, and I wouldn't be mad if you were just lousy with diamonds."

2

THE HOUSE OF DEATH

DETECTIVE SATAN HALL stood on the dock and watched the sailing of the steamship *City of Antwerp,* and noted with some surprise and considerable satisfaction the departure of Mattie's father, Jake Hern. There was a time not so long ago when Satan felt sure he could put the finger on Jake for murder. It was Zitto-money and Zitto-influence that sprung Jake, and it was also Zitto influence that caused witnesses to disappear and the memories of others to forsake them entirely. Since his release Jake had done little outside business in the underworld. He understood distinctly that Zitto could produce witnesses and evidence at any moment he wanted to. And he understood, as Mattie understood, that that instant would be when Mattie no longer took orders from Johnny Zitto.

There was something fishy about the whole thing. It couldn't be possible that Johnny Zitto didn't know about it. Or was he just through with Mattie? And that was what bothered Satan. Johnny Zitto was never through with anyone who worked for him. That is, not through with them while they lived. There was no secret about that. Everyone in the underworld knew it. As for the cops! Well, they had picked up enough stiffs in their day—or rather, Zitto's day, to make them thoroughly believe it.

Two quiet-clothes-men approached Satan where he stood partly hidden by several huge packing cases.

"Well, it's Jake Hern all right," the smaller of the two said to Satan, "And he sailed with the ship. His daughter, Mattie, saw him off. She's out on the pier now, waving." And leaning forward, "That right hand man of Johnny Zitto's was here, too. Sam Hertz, the hood from Chicago."

"What was he doing?"

The taller man shrugged his shoulders.

"Don't know, but he waited on the dock for the girl."

"You didn't hear why Jake was setting out—business trip?"

"Not a short one." The smaller dick shook his head. "He's been sending wires; getting them, too. Looks like regular business; honest business, though that's hard to connect up with Jake. Had one of the best rooms on the ship."

"No one else on the ship, up my alley?"

"Not up your alley, Satan. A few con men and the forger, Evans; and a couple of jewel thieves, I think. But none of the Zitto outfit. Want a tail on Hertz or the dame—or anything else?"

"No," said Satan, "not a thing."

He turned. Mattie and Sam Hertz were coming down the dock. Satan passed behind the cases and followed the man and the girl from the dock.

He whistled softly as they reached the street and a uniformed chauffeur opened the door of the expensive car. It was a big Rolls. Satan was puzzled. But he jumped a taxi as the Rolls pulled away, and followed.

Satan didn't know why he was trailing them. He wasn't thinking of Zitto then. He was thinking of Jake Hern, his sudden affluence—and now, Mattie with a Rolls. Satan sighed slightly. He liked Mattie a lot; how much, he was never sure of. He tried not to let himself think about that. But Mattie was a crook. Some day, maybe, it might be his duty to lay the hand on her shoulder.

Mattie had said she wanted to get out of the racket; that only her father held her to Zitto now. Distantly came the sound of the ship's whistle; ahead was the shining back of a fifteen thousand dollar car. Did that look like—

The Rolls swung over to Fourth Avenue, slid easily uptown, crossed the bridge and slipped around the Grand Central Station, then onto Park Avenue. Before a sky-scraper apartment it stopped; Mattie and Sam got out. She spoke to the chauffeur and they entered the apartment. The man at the door grinned and bowed as he swung open the door.

Satan dropped out of the taxi down the block, saw the Rolls pull from the curb, then sauntered down to the entrance to the building. He hesitated before the doorman, his hand in his pocket. It was one swell dump, he thought; should he part with a five or a ten? He took one more good look at the doorman and decided, with a little grimace, that it would have to be a ten.

"The lady who just went in—Miss Hern. There—"

Satan got no further. The dignified uniformed dummy unbended suddenly and became just another man.

"The penthouse on the roof; any one of the three end

cars," he said. "And they're getting damn sick of you guys. She wants to move in. Her friend's making a holler now about—"

And without finishing, the doorman hurried to the curb to open a car door for a big blonde with a little white dog.

Satan grinned to himself, and shoving the ten back in his pocket, walked between the marble pillars, down the long hall in the back and onto the soft rugs between the elevators and the row of small writing desks. But his smile was gone when he shot up in the car to the roof.

The elevator operator leaned out and pointed.

"The penthouse is up them stairs. There's to be a private car to it later, I think. Look out for the men with the ladder!"

SATAN STOOD AT the foot of those stairs until the men with the ladder reached the bottom. They were followed by a man with a pad and a pencil, and glasses.

Satan mounted the steps, passed down a wide hall strewn with strips of drapes and piles of plaster, and cans smelling of paint. There was a door at the end. It was wide open; held back by a huge hook.

He bumped into a man who was looking behind him, a half frightened, half hurt and indignant look on his over-red face. The man said:

"He's up here again, and he's raising hell. If he felt that way about it, why didn't he leave the place alone in the beginning? Besides, there's been so many here that we get in each other's way. Day and night, night and day. Now he throws us all out."

Satan tried to grin his appreciation, but didn't make a go of it. The "he" Satan felt sure was Sam Hertz. That he liked Mattie Satan knew; but then, many of them liked Mattie—had liked Mattie. That Mattie loathed Sam, he also knew. But that she feared him, too, was true.

Satan walked down the hall and peered into the living room, across another hall—at least, a turn in the main hall, where it widened out. This room was finished; and what a finish! Even Satan knew that expert hands, artistic eyes and a small fortune had decorated and furnished it. Nothing gaudy, nothing expensively offensive. It was a stage setting that seemed to belong. And the place was comfortable, from the soft low chair beside the stand under the lamp to the luxurious couch almost directly before the thick curtains of a small alcove.

A man in overalls passed him, and another was behind *him*. They grumbled audibly, but did not notice Satan. They passed out into the main hall and Satan heard their feet beating on the stone floor.

Then a voice. It was Mattie's. The words didn't reach Satan clearly, but the words of the man who answered her did. He said:

"If you're a wise girl, you'll save plenty. They'll be big boys, Mattie, and a girl like you should shake down a fortune in a year; maybe less."

The voice was close now; steps crossed from a soft rug to hardwood, and Satan looked back toward the main hall. Then with quick long steps he crossed the room, slid behind the couch and was in a tiny recess behind the curtains.

Between those drapes he could see into the room.

Sam Hertz and Mattie had entered the room.

"Well, I've cleaned the place out," Sam said. "We're alone, Mattie."

"Yes." She looked toward the hall. "And things will be delayed."

Mattie stood there, almost in the center of the room.

"Why," she asked, "did you put the men out?"

"Union hours." Sam Hertz grinned, his big mouth with its thick lips spreading across his face. "Besides, I wanted to talk to you."

"What did you want to say that you couldn't tell me with the men in another room?"

"Well, for one thing—that you're beautiful, Mattie." He raised his hands and she stepped back, nearer the couch. "And that I fancy beautiful women."

She looked toward the door again, but the squat muscular body of the man from Chicago blocked her vision.

"I think I'll be going now," said Mattie.

"No." Hertz shook his head. "I wanted to tell you something. I've been a fool. Like the rest of the Avenue, I believed—or at least half believed that you were different from the others. How does it go? Like Zitto said. A brain without a body! But I only half believed it because I've got eyes." And as he took a step forward, "And because I ain't such a bad guy with the ladies. Come on, Mattie; be regular. I can do things for you."

Mattie drew in her under lip.

"Do you know why I'm here; why I have this place, that car; why I've been playing the shops, the jewelry stores?"

"Sure!" said Hertz. "Sure, I know."

Mattie's eyes widened in surprise.

"And you talk to me like—like this?"

"Why not?" said Hertz.

"You don't know why I'm here, Sam." And raising her voice as the man moved so close to her that her legs were almost against the couch, "Tell me, then. Tell me."

Sam straightened. He was slightly surprised. Then he grinned.

"Johnny made you a proposition. He's got a list of big names; trusted officials who'll have to work in with him. Some in the city, some outside. He figured they'd have to be entertained along with the boys in on the Combine, from other cities. He figured he'd have to make a big impression. And he figured that this was the dump for it and that you were the dame. Maybe he bought you in, maybe just ordered you in. Johnny's peculiar that way. But"—his hands rested on her shoulders now—"I'm of the racket, I'm of the Combine. I'm entitled to some of that entertainment."

Mattie Hern's eyes widened.

"Did Johnny Zitto tell you that?" The words were no more than a whisper. They barely reached Satan, behind the curtains.

"No. He didn't need to. I've got brains, kid. I—" He stepped forward suddenly and crushed her in his arms.

The girl fought. Her hands came up, jerked at his wrists, clawed at his face.

SATAN'S LIPS SET grimly, his green eyes narrowed. A gun jerked into his right hand; his left reached for the curtains. For a moment he saw red. He didn't know if he'd close a finger on that trigger and snuff out Sam Hertz, or if he'd just step from behind those curtains and bring his gun down on the man's head.

Then he did neither, for Mattie had partly turned Sam

around in her struggle. Her head was thrown far back, her eyes were deep with fear; but the words she spoke, though her lips quivered, were loud and clear.

"Don't! You're a fool, Sam. I'm—I'm Zitto's woman."

Sam's arms dropped to his sides as if unseen giant hands had jerked them from the girl. His mean little eyes popped. His thick lips opened, closed with a snap, and opened again.

"That's—that's not true," he stammered as Satan waited, his right hand holding the gun, the fingers of his left clutching the inner folds of the drapes.

Then Sam said:

"Zitto don't go in for women. Zitto—"

His hands were rising from his sides again.

"Look around, Sam," the girl cried out. "The penthouse, the car, the jewelry, my father sailing for Antwerp. Can't you see? Can't you understand? You fool—you fool!"

"You sold yourself for your father! Zitto's woman, eh? Well," he clutched her suddenly again, "you're my woman now."

And Satan did nothing. For over the head of the struggling girl he saw broad shoulders; blond hair beneath a slouch hat; blue eyes, that weren't soft and gentle now. Blue eyes that were pin points of frozen water.

Johnny Zitto raised the cane he carried in his right hand and poked Sam Hertz in the back. His voice was low.

"Come—come, Sam," he said quietly. "What's all this clowning around?"

And Sam came. He spun like a top and stared into those cold and now cruel eyes. He tried to speak and couldn't. He made snapping sounds with his thick lips; and all the time Johnny Zitto smiled down at him with his mouth and regarded him fixedly with those hard blue eyes.

Johnny Zitto didn't speak again. He just stood there, waiting. Finally Sam's tongue came out and licked at his lips. He said:

"I didn't know, Johnny—I didn't know."

"And she shouldn't have told you." Johnny looked over at Mattie. "Not yet."

"Then it's true; it's true." Sam Hertz's voice raised. "I—God! Johnny, I didn't believe her."

Johnny Zitto's eyes shot fire, his lips closed tight. For a moment he was the common gangster; the Johnny Zitto of ten years back. His right hand slipped to his left armpit. Satan nodded from behind the curtains. Johnny Zitto was human after all and capable of great anger; uncontrolled passion even.

"You said—" Johnny started to snarl the words through the side of his mouth, and stopped suddenly. His set lips parted and his white, even teeth showed. Even the whiteness of anger seemed to go out of his cheeks as his eyes widened and smiled and became—yes, almost friendly.

"THERE, THERE, SAM," he said kindly as he laid a hand on the trembling man's shoulder. "Don't take it so hard. After all, Mattie's good to look at. It took me a long time to find it out."

"Yeah—I guess that's right." Sam's eyes were small now as he looked shrewdly at Johnny Zitto. Was he fooled by Johnny's apparent friendliness? And Satan wondered himself. Was it apparent friendliness? After all, Sam was a valuable man to Johnny Zitto; a very valuable man through the Mid-West. Maybe Zitto was willing to take it a bit for the sake of the Combine; the big money. Take it, at least until he was so firmly established throughout the country that nothing could shake him.

But Satan shook his head. That didn't seem Zitto's way.

"And now, Sam," Zitto was saying, "I've got big things in mind for you. I want you to go and see Regan out in Chi. I haven't liked his ways lately—his lip. Sometimes I was thinking—" He looked down at Sam and stroked his chin.

"You were thinking of me, out that way?" Sam's thick lips slipped back. "It ain't that you just want me out of the city?" He looked at Mattie. "You don't think I'll horn in on you now, knowing—"

"No, no." Zitto was very emphatic. "I know you won't ever horn in on me again, Sam. And I can't afford to leave you out in the West. I'll need you here; want to get you familiar with New York. I'll have to travel a bit; see things personally, and I'll need a man familiar with New York to leave behind." There was a pleasant look in Zitto's eyes before he turned from Sam; almost admiration as he said: "You're the boy I picked, Sam." He lifted the phone on the table, called the number of the Club Venice, and placing his hand over the mouthpiece, "There's some figures I've got hidden away. Charlie will show them to you. I'll want you to check them up with Regan's figures in Chi." And into the mouthpiece, "Zitto, Charlie. I've got a job for you to do with Sam Hertz. There's some figures I want him to have. You know them. Yeah, Sam will be coming right down. Take him up to number 116 with you." And placing the instrument slowly back in its cradle and turning to Sam, "That's done. Beat it along, Sam. You can trust Charlie absolutely."

Behind those curtains Satan nodded his understanding. He didn't know where 116 was, but he did know, or thought he knew, in a vague way, that number 116 was the house of death. Men who were taken there never came out alive. Their bodies were found later by the police, but never at 116. A deserted city street, in the out-lying parks, or perhaps floating in the East River! Satan's shoulders moved slightly. Wherever it was did not matter. Neither the police nor the citizens they served would miss Sam Hertz over much.

As he moved toward the door, with all the swagger back in his squat body, the assurance in his voice again, Sam said:

"You're a white guy, Johnny. Not a bit sore, eh?" He extended his hand and Johnny gripped it tightly.

"Not a bit sore. Good luck, Sam," he said.

"Good luck." Sam nodded. "And you're not thinking I'll ever bother Mattie again?"

"No," said Johnny Zitto, his blue eyes wide, smiling, friendly. "I'm not thinking you'll ever bother Mattie again, Sam."

3

JUST A MAN

SAM LEFT, AND his final friendly gesture was to close the outer door with a bang behind him. Satan wondered. Sam Hertz, the cleverest racketeer to come out of the Mid-West in years. Zitto had taken him in like a child. Of course Sam was going straight to his death. Charlie could always be counted on in a matter of murder.

Silent and straight, Satan waited. Wasn't it Johnny Zitto who said a guy never lost anything by listening? Satan had had a break; he'd listen now. But he didn't smile at that break. He was hearing things that he never expected to hear. Zitto never had had any use for women. He never thought in terms of sex. He always boasted of using just brains. And Mattie? Satan's green eyes narrowed; his thin lips were a single straight line as he looked over that luxuriously furnished room and thought again of the Rolls that had brought her here.

Johnny Zitto was saying to Mattie:

"So you told him, eh?"

"I had to, Johnny," she said. "It— Even then it helped only a minute."

"That's right." Johnny nodded grimly. "I saw that. But it doesn't matter. It had to come out." And putting both hands on her shoulders, "And don't misunderstand me, Mattie. I'm not ashamed of you. I was just waiting," he frowned slightly, "because of Satan."

"Johnny," dull black eyes brightened for a moment, "you're not afraid of Satan?"

"No. No. Hell! No." Johnny got the words out quickly. "I was thinking of your father. Men are funny. If Satan knew, he might have your father picked up when the ship docked at Antwerp."

"No." The girl shook her head. "You're wrong about Satan. Maybe he likes me, maybe he don't. Maybe he's just interested in me. But if he could have put the finger on my father, he'd have done it. I know Satan."

Johnny's eyes sparkled. He raised a hand and ran it through her hair, letting it slip down the back of her head until it rested on her neck.

"Maybe you know Satan, but you don't know yourself, Mattie. I've been a fool for years. After power; after money. What good is money if you don't buy what you want with it?" He pulled the girl close to him.

It was like Johnny not to understand the look in her large black eyes. Fear was there, Satan thought, as the girl half swung and faced the curtains.

Johnny Zitto suddenly crushed her in his arms. For a moment he held her passive body. Then she struggled, threw back her head and saw Johnny's blue eyes. She lost her head, threw up her hands and pushed at his chest with every bit of strength she had.

And Johnny Zitto looked straight into her eyes and read the truth there. Fear. Horror! He didn't believe it at first; he couldn't believe it. Then his hands dropped to his sides.

He took one step back, one forward, and raised his hand to strike her.

"You dirty little—" he started, and stopped. The anger left his face. Had he been mistaken? The fear and horror were in her eyes all right, but she was not looking at him now. She was looking over his shoulder. The fear was not of him then. It was—

Johnny Zitto's hand shot to his left armpit. He swung suddenly on his heels and found a gun sticking close to his stomach. His hand, that had been under his jacket, fell to his side—empty, as he looked into the green eyes of Satan Hall. Johnny Zitto didn't like what he saw in those eyes. He spoke quickly.

"It would be murder, Satan," he said, and cursed himself for the thickness of his voice.

Satan laughed. It was not a pleasant laugh, and he was not laughing at Johnny Zitto. He was not laughing at anyone unless it was himself. He had made a mistake; a grave mistake. Indeed, he had forgotten there was a gun in his hand. If there had not been, Johnny might not have pulled that hand from under his arm, empty—and then— Oh, Johnny was quick with a gun, but Satan was willing to have chanced it. Yes, he had made a mistake, and for that mistake Mattie must pay; the commissioner must pay— how dearly, he didn't realize at the time; and thousands of people throughout the State, throughout the nation, even, must pay.

AS THE LIGHT—THE light that had made Johnny think of "murder"—disappeared from Satan's eyes, Johnny spoke. His voice was not thick now. His words were clear. All his confidence, his assurance, was in his voice; a sneer, too.

"So, Flat-foot, you're not out pounding a beat yet. But you will be—you will be." And switching quickly and with a wave of his hand, "Nice diggings, eh? For a moment I thought that Mattie— But, there! Take that face of yours along and use it to frighten women; not guys like me."

"And the gun, too?" Satan grinned evilly. "I'm sort of watching over Mattie, Johnny, since her father went away."

"So, what?" Johnny shrugged indifferently, at least he hoped it was indifferently.

Satan juggled the gun in his hand.

"No use you and me kidding each other, Johnny. You always liked straight talk. I don't like you, Johnny. I do like Mattie. If I should have any reason to dislike you more— well," broad shoulders rose and fell, "the gun goes off."

"A threat to kill me, eh?"

"I guess that would cover it."

"Hadn't you better consult Mattie first?" Zitto sneered.

"No." Satan shook his head. "This is between you and me, Zitto. Now—on your way."

"Me?" said Zitto.

"Exactly. You!"

Johnny Zitto hesitated. He didn't take orders from anyone; he didn't have to. He looked again into Satan's green eyes; cruel, sinister green eyes.

No, there was no use in breaking Satan; no use in just exerting that powerful influence he had lately acquired to send Satan back to pounding a beat. Well—perhaps for a bit; just a day or two, to let him know the strength of Johnny Zitto. A day or two before he died. Johnny had thought of it before; many times. But never did he realize the necessity for it as much as at this moment. One thing was certain.

Satan had to die. And the place for it? Sure! Out on the lonely beat on Staten Island. Zitto grinned evilly. He'd do the thing right for once. He'd place a hundred grand; one hundred thousand dollars in cash right smack on the line for the rod who gunned Satan out. Until that time Johnny Zitto would not take a chance.

"I'll run along," Johnny Zitto tried to say lightly, though beneath his feigned calmness fires raged. "And, Mattie. Be nice to this tough dick." And then words he couldn't help hurling at Satan as he turned at the entrance to the hall. "Don't think you 'get' me for one minute on that gun threat. I know cops."

Satan shrugged his shoulders and said:

"It's gone off before, Johnny. And guys just like you didn't—didn't—"

"Didn't what?" Johnny sneered.

"Didn't like it," Satan finished simply.

And Johnny Zitto was gone, closing the door behind him.

Satan was a cautious man. He walked out into the hall, saw that Johnny Zitto had actually left the apartment, and returning to Mattie, said:

"Well, that's done."

"He'll kill you, Satan." She hurried over to him and took both his hands. "Why did you do it—do it for me? I'm not worth it."

Satan released one of his hands and scratched his head.

"I guess you're worth it, Mattie. As for his killing me! I wish—yes, I wish he'd take a crack at it."

"But he won't do it himself." Her hands were on his shoulders now. "Not that he's afraid, but he'll get others.

Besides, he's going to break you. Don't smile like that. I
know. I know! The commissioner's behind you and all that.
But it won't matter. He's going to, Satan. He don't bluff—
not Johnny. He don't have to."

"AND THIS THING—THIS thing you told Sam, Mattie,
about—about—" The words wouldn't come; they choked
in his throat. "It's not true. It's not true?"

It was some time before Mattie spoke.

"It's not true—not true yet," she said. And she did it. Her
arms were around his neck, her little body clinging to him.
Her hair brushed his cheek; then her lips. She was close to
him, very close. Involuntarily, unconsciously Satan's arms
were around her. Mattie was talking.

"I've always loved you, Satan, and you never cared;
couldn't care, I thought. Now—let us go. They're not going
to want you in the Department any longer. The commissioner—yes, even the commissioner isn't going to stand
behind you. It's too big; the Zitto influence. Get from
under, Satan. You and I. I— Remember about those type-
written sheets? I think I can get them, Satan. It's a fortune."
She ran on wildly when he pushed her from him and held
her so, his hands just above each of her elbows.

"Get them, Mattie?" he said hoarsely. "Get them!"

Her eyes were bright—brilliant.

"A million, maybe, Satan. At least a million. I told you
before and I tell you again. Properly handled they're worth
a million."

"I know, I know." Satan nodded. "Just blackmail."

"Trusted men. They betrayed that trust; they should pay.
And, Satan, it would be so much easier for them to pay
in—in cash."

"Get them, Mattie?" he said again.

"Yes, yes. For us. Only for us. For you and me. For our happiness, Satan." And before he could cut in on her, "Don't you see? I couldn't do it for the police; for the cops. I couldn't rat out on Zitto—not like that. And the cops. They're on the other side of the fence. They're the law. I've always hated the law and I always will. The law!" She laughed mockingly. "The law's not for my kind."

Satan never knew exactly how it happened. He never knew just how he had thought of Mattie before; he wasn't even sure how he thought of her now, as he held her in his arms. For a few—a very few minutes he knew that he was a man and she a woman, and that he loved her.

He couldn't speak. He didn't speak as he let her go and stood there looking at her—so white now; so beautiful. He just turned and walked toward the door. His hands were trembling; there were beads of sweat on his forehead.

Mattie followed him. As he opened the door she gripped him by the wrist, swung him half around.

"You'll— I'll get them, Satan. It may take a little time; and then you will—we will— Won't we?"

Bright green eyes stared at her. Thoughts were chaotic in his head, raced madly through in a jumbled mass. Just one thing was clear. He was not the machine he thought he was. A cog in a great wheel; a part of a great system that fought against crime. He was just a man. When he spoke to Mattie the words were his; at least, they seemed to come from his mouth. But they seemed like a thought only, as if he thought aloud. Yet the words were the truth. He knew they were the truth, and hated himself for it. But he spoke them just the same.

"Before God, Mattie, I don't know," was all he said.

4

ZITTO STRIKES

SATAN GOT THE message and thirty minutes later was in the commissioner's outer office, waiting. But his long legs couldn't stand the inactivity and his thin lips opened and closed and his oblique eyes twitched. In a way, he guessed what the commissioner wanted to see him about. Things had broken bad for the Department. Johnny Zitto had at length gotten control of the entire city; the entire nation, for that matter, falling quickly into line as Johnny exerted pressure to bear on certain former impregnable influences. The dream of the racketeer—a power so great as to be above the law—was about to be, yes, was being realized. Prohibition doomed; the repeal of the Eighteenth Amendment, that was to drive the racketeer from his lucrative profession, was now to drive him into legitimate business.

Johnny Zitto, and Johnny Zitto alone, was in a fair way to throw the entire country into chaos.

The door to the inner office opened and Roger, the commissioner's only son, stepped out. Satan smiled. He liked that young man; had always liked him and had been the one to tell the commissioner that the boy was young and his wild escapades would soon wear off. Yet, even the commissioner did not know just how wild some of those escapades had been. But Satan did. There was a woman back of them, and once Satan had shown him that the woman was no better than Satan had painted her, things had changed. Roger had settled down to hard work, graduated with honors from law school, married a childhood sweetheart; a daughter of a friend of the commissioner's, and started in on his career in the district attorney's office.

Satan smiled and extended his hand. Then the smile left his face. Roger's usual ruddy face was a deathly white. He half raised his hand to take the hand of Satan, then he shook his head, dropped his hand to his side, and pushing quickly by Satan, opened the outer door and stepped into the hall.

Satan looked at the inner door, marked PRIVATE. It was slightly ajar. He walked toward the small wooden fence, put his hand on the gate and snapped back the lock. The man behind the fenced looked up; his eyes bulged over his glasses.

"He didn't say for you to come in yet, Detective Hall," he said stiffly. "You'd better wait."

Satan shook his head.

"He's expecting me. I'm going in." The secretary came to his feet, stepping between Satan and the door. For five full seconds he looked at those green eyes. Then he shrugged his shoulders and stepped aside.

"Maybe you better, Satan." He forgot his accustomed front. And as Satan went to pass him he stretched out a hand and caught him by the arm. "There's trouble," he whispered hoarsely. "Big trouble! Do you know what I've been doing lately? Separating his private papers from the public ones. There's something wrong, something— God!"

Satan, it sounds impossible, about the boss. But I think he's going to quit."

"Quit—under fire?" Satan laughed. "Why, he couldn't; no more than I could. He's not built that way."

But the secretary did not smile.

"Wait until you see him," he said. "You'll know then."

Satan hesitated, looked at the secretary, started to say something about the commissioner's son, changed his mind, and slowly opening the door, entered the room, closing the door tightly behind him.

He had seen the commissioner only a few days before, and now he was shocked. The change in the man! Those quick, alert eyes were dull. There were pouches under them as if he hadn't slept, and the lines that led from his nose to his mouth were deeper. His hair! The gray of it seemed whiter; seemed— And Satan couldn't be sure of that. Perhaps it was the sallow complexion that made the hair appear whiter. The commissioner stared at him. His hand rested listlessly on the arm of his chair. He didn't get up and nervously pace the room while he talked. When he spoke now, the snap had gone out of his voice.

"I've been speaking to the district attorney," he said. "There's a lot of jealousy in his office; envy about your accomplishments with me, Satan. But I think he'll take you over."

"Take me over!" For once in his life Satan was really surprised. "What do you mean, take me over?"

"It wouldn't do for you to go back to regular duty; wouldn't do at all. You couldn't work that way; couldn't—" And seeing the strange look in Satan's eyes, he rubbed a hand across his forehead, shook his head once or twice, and then, "I didn't tell you. I'm resigning the end of the month; maybe sooner."

"Resigning? You! At a time like this?" Satan leaned on the desk. "When the city needs you most?"

The commissioner's smile was a sad one.

"They don't need me, Satan; not that bad. And they won't want me after a bit." He gripped the arms of his chair and came slowly to his feet. "You might as well know. That net of Johnny Zitto's; that net he got from Tonti Marcco, who got it from Joe de Grassie; that evidence against certain trusted officials. Yes, yes. I've been swept into the Zitto net, and like a hundred others I've got to pay for it."

"You! You?" Satan's mouth hung open; his thin green eyes were wide for once. And then, "I don't believe it. I don't—" He half looked toward the door. "It's your son—Roger."

THE COMMISSIONER'S HAND shot across the desk, slim fingers encircled Satan's wrist, bit into it with a strength that Satan never thought the little man possessed.

"We'll have none of that," he said sharply and with some of his former brusqueness. And then, his fingers loosening and his hands spreading far apart, "Forgive me, Satan. No man ever had a more loyal assistant; a finer friend."

Satan was always persistent.

"What has the boy done? I thought—"

"Yes, I know. His life has been as perfect and as satisfying as any father could wish for the past four years. There's the baby, too." For a moment the commissioner's voice faltered. "I thought it would make me feel pretty old, being a grandfather, but— You remember, Satan; I don't think I ever felt—" He paused, ran a hand across his forehead. "I've got to give him his chance; he's made good lately."

"And how," said Satan, "would that give him his chance? If you're out, and he makes good—then Zitto simply spreads the net a little."

"He wouldn't do that. He couldn't do that. He—he—hell! Satan, I'd have to get out anyway. It would embarrass the mayor; the whole administration."

"But it's nothing you have done?"

"No, no." He shook his head. "But that doesn't matter. Of course I've always said, and it was always true, that I had a free hand; that there were no politics in my office. But there's politics outside of it. They are my friends, they'd stick to me despite pressure. But you can't embarrass your friends."

"There's no other way?" And suddenly, "Can't you sit tight for a bit, until I look around? Johnny Zitto hasn't got a charmed life. All men have to die. There are those who'd be glad of the chance to knock him over."

The commissioner's smile was very tired, very hopeless.

"It's in black and white, Satan; damaging and damning. Zitto's death wouldn't help."

"But—time, Commissioner. Damning evidence in black and white has disappeared before. Can't you— Isn't there any other way?"

"There is," said the commissioner. "I can sit behind my desk and run the entire police department of the greatest city in the world, give my orders as I always gave them—with one provision. And that is, that those orders don't conflict with Johnny Zitto's orders."

"If you could stall for a bit— I know it would be hard for a man like you, but the end might justify the means."

The commissioner looked long and steadily at Satan.

"It wouldn't help you any," he said grimly. "The first order from Zitto is about you. Back to the Force. Back to a beat on Staten Island."

"So that's how it is," said Satan.

"And the second order—just this. Comes through Alderman Gray." The commissioner tossed a huge engraved card across the desk. "They're giving a dinner tonight. It's supposed to be to raise money for a new hospital, but it will turn into a testimonial to the 'East Side boy who made good.' Johnny Zitto is to start it off with a check."

"It's tough," Satan said slowly as he shook his head. "Very tough. I never looked at it this way before. I always thought guys in a jam like yours were yellow rats." He stopped quickly and bit his tongue. "Well, not exactly like yours—if you understand what I mean."

"I understand what you mean," the commissioner said slowly.

Satan reddened slightly.

"I see it different now—much different. Years of honest effort! One slip, or a slip they're not responsible for! It must be a temptation; a terrible temptation."

"It is," said the commissioner. "You try to think how you can hang on. You try to think that it will be someone else if it isn't you. Someone much worse. You think of your wife, your family, the girl who married into it and the baby that came. Five people; just five people, and you lie to yourself and forget the six million you serve and who trust you."

Satan rubbed at his pointed chin, rubbed at one pointed ear.

"Those are your thoughts." He nodded. "Now give me a chance to think on it. The dinner isn't so bad. You'd go anyway; it's a duty. You might spot just who is there, because they really back Zitto, and who is there because it's good politics."

"Are you going?" the commissioner demanded.

"Sure. Sure!" Satan nodded vigorously. "I'd like to see who's there. Just give me a few days, Commissioner; a chance to think."

"And the Staten Island beat?" There was no humor in the commissioner's voice, but Satan grinned.

"Put the order through. There's always a few days' notice. Sit tight for a bit, Commissioner. I couldn't work under anyone else. I just couldn't do it."

"What do you mean?"

"When you quit, I quit," Satan said emphatically. "I'll be with you, Commissioner, whether we sneak out like whipped curs or go down with flags flying."

"Hell!" said the commissioner, and for a moment anger blazed in his eyes. "You put it rather bluntly."

"Hell!" said Satan. "You'd want it that way."

And as Satan left the room the commissioner knew that he was right. He wanted it that way. Just that way.

As for Satan, he didn't exactly know what the thing was that Zitto held over the commissioner's head; this thing about his son. The commissioner hadn't told him and Satan hadn't asked. But he knew it must be bad—pretty damn bad. But he was going over and have a talk with Johnny Zitto.

5

A MESSAGE FROM THE MORGUE

"COME RIGHT IN, Satan!" Johnny Zitto called from the little wash room off his private office as he laid down his razor, pulled the plug of the electric heater that furnished the hot water, and then, humming softly, stood in the open doorway drying his face.

"I wanted to talk to you, Johnny." There was no expression on Satan's face. The features were hard, the chin perhaps more pointed, his eyes steady.

Johnny Zitto threw back a curtain, pulled out a shirt, slipped it on, tucked in the tails and with two quick movements jerked the hanging suspenders over his shoulders.

"I can remember," he said as he grinned into the glass, "when I considered this monkey suit something worn only by waiters and movie picture actors. Now—it's just as if I was born in it." He smoothed down the pleated front. "The color, though; I'll never get used to that."

"I want to talk to you, Johnny," Satan said again, and there was no change in his voice.

Johnny swung from the glass and looked at Satan; looked at him a long time. Despite the lack of emotion in Satan's voice, the unexpressive face. Johnny nodded. The narrow eyes and the whiteness of the skin along the high cheek bones told him the truth. Satan was like other men then. Inside, things were boiling. Well, Johnny didn't mind. A short while now, and just like *that*, pop—Satan would go over.

But he only said:

"Let's have it. I'm in an affable mood tonight. The dinner at the Towers is really for me. I'm as flustered as a young schoolgirl. Here, look at that." He tossed a sheet over to Satan. "Partial list of the guests." He grinned. "The papers will call it a 'representative gathering.' All there to pay me homage."

Satan read down that list of names and whistled softly. There would be columns on it in the morning papers. The reporters, with their tongues in their cheeks, would make a real story out of this. What else could they do? There was nothing against Johnny Zitto; not a blot on his name. They would know the truth of course; but after all, knowledge is not evidence and libel suits are sometimes very expensive. It would be a great story.

City officials; state officials; even government ones, and names that meant something in the financial world. Philanthropists, too. Some of them, of course; maybe many of them would be there in good faith, to pay Zitto homage. Ignorant good faith, of course; but they'd be there just the same. It wasn't every day that a boy came up from the city streets and planted down a check for a huge sum to build a new hospital.

And there, at the bottom of that list, but in larger type, was the name of the commissioner himself.

"Hot stuff, eh?" Zitto took the list and flipped it back on the desk. "Hardly believable."

"That's right," said Satan. "Hardly believable. But I wanted to talk to you about the commissioner."

"I see." Johnny grinned and his blue eyes gleamed. "I've heard that you're going back to pounding a beat. Staten Island, isn't it? Maybe I have some influence with the commissioner, but I don't believe in bringing politics into the police department." His grin broadened.

"We won't clown around, Johnny. I know. You're going to drive him out; drive him out for something his son did. Some time back, I guess."

"Drive him out! Out of office, you mean?" And the grin left Johnny's face. "Hell! No. That's the last thing in the world I want to do. I thought he understood that. He's the best police commissioner the city ever had, and he's going to be better."

"Going to take orders from you, eh?"

"Orders!" Johnny Zitto's eyes widened. "Suggestions maybe. I know the city pretty well. My advice isn't so bad. Men—big men listen to it, and—and like it."

"Got to like it," Satan agreed. "But the commissioner's built different. If you knew men you'd know that. He'll just resign, that's all."

"Is that all?" Johnny Zitto buttoned his collar and swung his head over his shoulder and sneered the words. "How about his son; his son's career; his son's start in life? Think it over, Satan. Even if the boy did beat the rap— Well, it isn't every guy who can rise above his difficulties, like Johnny Zitto."

"But," said Satan, "if the commissioner resigned there would be no reason to expose his son."

"No?" Johnny jerked at his tie, twisted his fingers a couple of times and straightened out the black bow at the ends. "Don't fool yourself on that; don't let the commissioner fool himself. Johnny Zitto makes men or breaks them. If the commissioner stands up on his hind legs and does the self sacrificing, loving father act—his boy takes the jolt. You know me, Satan. I have only friends and enemies; there's nothing in between."

"Nothing in between, eh?" Satan rubbed at his chin. "I'm not a friend."

"YOU'RE TELLING ME!" Johnny Zitto's eyes hardened for a moment, to soften again almost at once. Why get wrangling with Satan? He had made his offer of a hundred grand for Satan—dead. And it had been accepted; accepted eagerly by the best gunner in Chicago, the best in the country for that matter. Yes, accepted. Johnny was having hard work to keep the man in check until Satan was pounding the beat on the Island. It wasn't every day a lad could pick up that much jack for knocking over a cop; not in these times, anyway.

"And enemies die, eh?" It was as if Satan read his thoughts.

"Sometimes." Johnny was putting on his jacket now; pulling it down, but he could see Satan in the glass. He nodded inside. He was right about getting him out of the way. Satan was a killer, and Johnny was breaking him. For a moment he wondered if he did right by postponing the kill. He thought of Mattie, too; but Satan hadn't mentioned her name, not even once. That was bad; a very bad sign, Zitto thought. Satan wasn't a guy to open his mouth just to hear himself talk. He had made his threat up at the penthouse and let it go at that.

He swung and looked at Satan. Who the hell was that flat-foot anyway, that he could make him watch his step? For a moment his temper flared up, then died. He jerked a flat bit of cardboard from the desk and tossed it over to Satan.

"A pass to the blow-out at the Towers." He half sneered the words. "Twenty dollars a plate this, and honest cops don't have double sawbucks floating around. Take it, get a bellyful of real food and—and watch the little commissioner do his song and dance. Yep, to Johnny Zitto's music. Better men than he can ever hope to be are taking my orders and liking them."

He walked into the wash room and came out again, pinning a flower in his lapel.

"Not bad, Satan," he said. "Coming to the blow-out?"

"Maybe." Satan's face had never changed, and then suddenly, "What happened to Sam Hertz? His body hasn't shown up yet."

"No?" Johnny was giving the flower a final touch. "But it will—it will."

"And he was the wisest gunner who ever came out of the West; the quickest, too."

"They're all wise." Johnny walked to the door and opened it wide. His hat and stick were in his hands now, a dark top coat over his arm, the fingers of yellow gloves showing under his palms. "All wise, until they cross Johnny Zitto. Then they become dumb. That's a good thing to remember, Satan; a damn good thing to remember."

And Satan said very quickly:

"That's right, Johnny. I'm going to remember it."

Johnny didn't answer. He couldn't think of anything to

say. Zitto was nervous as he preceded the detective down that narrow flight of stairs to the room behind the bar. He always knew that Satan was a killer; everyone knew that. But he had never thought of Satan as shooting a man in the back; that is, never before. Yet he breathed a sigh of relief and wiped the perspiration from his forehead as he entered the bar.

Just before Johnny left Satan he did speak. It was a simple speech, but it shook Satan more than anything he had said before.

"Try to get over to the Towers if you can, Satan." Johnny threw the words lightly over his shoulders. "The commissioner's going to make a speech; a speech praising me. He don't know yet, but he is." And white teeth showed in an evil but triumphant grin. "He'll have about ten seconds to make his decision which side of the fence he's on."

And Johnny Zitto was gone.

Satan hesitated, was about to follow when a boy tapped his shoulder.

"A lady," he said, "wants to see you."

Satan followed the boy into the main dining room, past the few occupied tables to a booth in the rear, against the right hand wall. The girl in the corner of the booth was Mattie Hern.

"It's a wonder you came." She leaned across the table and talked low and fast as soon as the boy was gone. "I've tried the phone; you've been avoiding me." And when Satan did not answer, "Well, what are you going to do? It's dangerous; very dangerous, but I think I can get it. A million in those sheets maybe. A—" And looking him suddenly in the eyes, "You—you're not going to do it?"

"No," said Satan slowly, "I'm not going to do it."

"But— You didn't mean, then—the other day—you love me?"

"I DON'T KNOW, Mattie. That's the truth. I don't know. For a moment you made me forget everything. For a whole night even; maybe longer. Then I saw it; saw how these people you wanted to blackmail might be tempted, as I was tempted. How one misstep might ruin their whole lives. How the misstep of a friend, a relative, one very close to them, might ruin a good life. I saw it clearly, Mattie; very clearly, after talking to a man—a finer man than I can ever hope to be; than the city can ever hope to breed again. Mattie, get those papers; give them to me and we'll burn them—you'll burn them."

"Rat out on Johnny Zitto!" Her lips curled, her eyes flashed.

"What would be the difference; if you used them or burned them?"

"The difference!" She seemed surprised. "What I do for myself; for us, and what I do against Johnny; for the law, for the protection of those whose only claim to the respectability which they deny me is that they don't act in the open and haven't been caught. Don't smile, Satan, and don't preach, and don't try to understand something that a copper never can understand. Put it down to the code of the night. While Zitto lives, I can't. Don't you see, Satan? I just can't."

"So it's like that." Satan's hands spread and his shoulders moved. "If I can't understand you, Mattie, you can't understand me."

"I can understand that you won't grasp the opportunity

of a lifetime. The opportunity that can never come again, if you gum-shoed for the Force until you died of old age. And I'm not telling you this to change your mind. If my—my love for you can't do it, nothing can; nothing that I'd say can change it. The skids are under you, Satan. More than the skids. Zitto has marked you for death."

"Zitto has marked me for a long time, Mattie." Satan grinned. "If you can get those sheets, destroy them. There is some evidence that involves one of the finest, one of the squarest—"

Mattie laughed.

"I can guess," she said. "The commissioner of police. The natural enemy of my kind. I wouldn't raise my hand to—"

"I'll go under with him." Satan watched her through thin green slits.

"Sure. Sure!" Mattie nodded vigorously. "Because you're part of a system; a cog in a big machine. Because you'll always be a copper and never be a man. Because—"

A shadow crossed the table; a boy spoke.

"A phone call, Mr. Hall," he said.

Satan came to his feet, started after the boy, stopped and turned back to Mattie.

"You'll be here when I come back?" There was a question in his voice.

"No," said Mattie, "I won't." And before Satan could turn, "I won't be seeing you much from now on, I guess. You'll be out in the sticks and I'll—"

"Mattie!" Satan's hand reached for her wrist, then conscious of the presence of others, dropped to his side again. Mattie Hern slid quickly from the booth, turned without a word and walked rapidly from the dining room. When Satan reached the door she was gone.

Lieutenant Dane was on the phone.

"We picked up a stiff; maybe the one you asked us to look out for. No, no. It was in the back yard of a deserted house up in the Bronx. Someone put five shots in his stomach, then tried to carve something in his forehead with a knife. Looks like it might be one—one—six."

"Like it might be one—one—six? You can be sure it is one—one—six."

"Yeah? Well, suppose you go down to the morgue and have a look. Not a thing to identify him. But no one has had a look at him yet. Some of the boys will spot him if you're too busy to take a look-see."

"I'll go down." And with a snap to his lips, "It'll be a pleasure."

Satan hung up the receiver and left the Club Venice. Johnny was right. Sam Hertz was dumb. He'd look at the stiff, then send out the dragnet for Charlie, Zitto's bartender, who pulled a murder now and then on his off days.

6

ROGER'S CONFESSION

SATAN HALL DIDN'T go directly to the morgue. Things
were bothering him. He hadn't liked the look on the
commissioner's face; the dullness of his eyes, the slow-
ness of his step, which was usually so quick. He knew, too,
that back in that brilliant mind a great conflict was being
fought. Proud! Just! Straight, beyond even the suggestion
of a wrong. A man put into the position as the head of the
police by the will of a distressed and angered people.

He jumped a taxi and was driven straight to the home
of the commissioner's son. He'd see Roger and find out
exactly how bad things were. The commissioner saw only
the evil of bribery and corruption, but Satan knew there
were few things so bad that, given a break, money could
not fix.

Satan stood in the front hall embarrassed and uneasy
before the young wife of the commissioner's son. Her eyes
sparkled so; her welcome was so real; her pleasure in seeing
him so genuine!

"I tell you, Mr. Hall," she held both his hands as she
looked at him, "you've been hiding out on us lately. And
it's unfair. There, don't look so stupidly innocent. If it wasn't
for you we wouldn't be here. I wouldn't be so gloriously

happy. Really, Satan," and the brightness remained in her eyes though water filmed them, "we owe it all to you. Roger, myself, and"—she half looked toward the stairs and the nursery above—"and little Roger."

Roger took Satan into the library and closed the door. Satan looked at Roger and finally said:

"You haven't told her then."

"No." Roger shook his head. "Oh, she knows everything of the past, Satan; all you did. Even of the woman; everything but that single night. No one knew until—until Johnny Zitto sprung it on my father."

"It happened before your marriage, didn't it?"

"Yes, before." Roger turned and, dropping into a chair, buried his head in his hands, his elbows on his knees.

"I thought I knew most of it." Satan paused. He wasn't a man to pick and choose his words and he didn't now. "And most of it was pretty rotten, but it wasn't criminal. How bad is this?"

The young man raised his head.

"It was attempted murder." And when Satan did not speak, "It can't be fixed. It was Judge Thomas Holden I shot. Twice in the chest, while I was robbing his house. There, you know the worst now."

"Judge Holden!" Satan whistled. The sworn enemy of the commissioner. The convicting judge, the man who treated first offenders as if they were habitual criminals. Indeed, it was that very thing that had first brought him into disagreement with the commissioner; a disagreement that grew into a bitter feud.

Satan remembered that shooting, too. An attempt, and a successful attempt, to steal from the judge's safe affidavits that would convict a notorious gunman. The judge had come downstairs and surprised the man at the safe. He had fired once and missed. Then he fell to the floor so severely wounded that for weeks he was not expected to recover. But he did recover and today was meting out sentences. A stern, perhaps an honest justice, but one that was never tempered with mercy.

"My God!" said Satan. "How did you come to do that?"

"It's a hard story to believe." Roger looked up and talked fast. "But it's true. It was the girl, Satan—that woman. You know! She told me of a man; of letters she had written; of—I see it all now as a wild, unbelievable story. But I didn't then. I was infatuated with her; drink mad—call it what you will— She showed me the house, gave me the combination of the safe, and—I never knew it was the judge. It was another name she gave me. He came into the room, raised his gun and fired. I didn't shoot because of that; I didn't shoot because I was afraid of capture. I thought of what she had told me; of the young and innocent life she had pictured before she met *him,* and I shot him—shot him twice and fled. She's dead now, but you knew her. Perhaps you can believe me."

"Yes," said Satan, "I knew her and I knew you—then, and I can easily believe you. But the proof, Roger. It's not what Zitto knows, what she told him before she died. It's got to be evidence; legal proof."

"She didn't even know Zitto. She didn't tell him anything. It's far worse than that. I—I wrote out a confession."

"You what! How? When? Who did you write it for? Why?"

"I dropped from the window and thought I was safe. And there was a policeman. I don't know what I said to him; I don't know what I promised him then. But he recognized me. My father wasn't commissioner at that time, but he was a strong influence in the Department, and this policeman let me go that night. But he came to see me the next day.

"HIS NAME WAS Dunnigan—Edward Dunnigan. He wasn't over bright and I think he was honest enough. Maybe, in a way, he recognized what my father could do for him; but mostly, I think, he admired my father. The papers were full of it at the time and Judge Holden wasn't expected to live. The words of that cop stand out in my mind now. I can see him standing there while I pleaded with him. His hair was red and he was scratching his head and—"

"Yes, yes," Satan cut in. "Just what happened?"

"Dunnigan said he wouldn't talk if Judge Holden lived, but that he wouldn't go so far as to protect me if the judge died, and the charge was murder. He made me write out the confession. It was that, or—or— I wrote it, and that ended it. Dunnigan never bothered me again. I never gave him so much as a five cent piece. He wasn't a young man and I did get my father to make it easy for him at times. But he was shot to death last Christmas Eve and his wife, who was separated from him for years, got his effects. I don't know if Zitto bought that confession from her, if he found it, or what happened. But I do know that my father has seen it and that Zitto is pressing him; pressing him hard. I don't know what he's going to do."

"I know what happened," Satan said grimly. "De Grassie

or Marcco got that letter, and Zitto got it from Marcco." And suddenly jarring up the young man's head and looking him straight in the eyes, "It's tough, kid, but it's true. Crime always catches up with you."

"Can you do anything, Satan—anything?" Roger clutched him by both arms. "I don't care for myself. It's for them; for my father. God! He stuck to me when I needed him most and—and," his eyes popped, "I'd do anything—anything."

"Sure—kill Zitto," Satan said calmly. "I thought of that, but that would be only part of it. The evidence, the confession would have to be destroyed with him."

He turned and walked toward the door.

"Don't do anything, Roger," he said. "If I can get your father to sit tight for a few days something may—" But he stopped. What could happen? What could possibly happen? Zitto had planned for the commissioner to mark himself that night; mark himself with the stripes of the underworld, or his son with the stripes of the criminal.

It was a tough racket sometimes, Satan thought, as he left Roger in the library. If he could only pin the murder of Sam Hertz on Johnny Zitto! But he couldn't, of course. It would be just like any other Zitto killing. Elaborate alibis; alibis that could not be shaken.

Satan strode flatfootedly into the morgue. He nodded absently as the attendant talked to him. He was thinking about Charlie and the killing of Sam Hertz. He could understand that easy enough, but what he couldn't understand were the numerals 1—1—6 carved upon Sam's forehead. That was crude and foolish and not like the Zitto work. Did Charlie have a personal feeling against Hertz?

Satan's shoulders shrugged slightly as he stood beside the gruesome outline beneath the sheet. Sam Hertz, the cleverest and perhaps the fastest drawing gunman to come out of Chicago in years. Yet, when Zitto acted he was taken in like a child.

Almost indifferently Satan grasped the end of that sheet and jerked it back. His identification would be easy and unnecessary. But he would like to get a look at those figures. After all, Sam Hertz was a fool and—

Satan jerked back the sheet and looked down at the face of the dead man. The wind whistled back in his throat. Then, his first shock of surprise over, his lips parted and he grinned. Sam Hertz was not so dumb after all. Not by a long shot he wasn't. For the dead face Satan looked down at was not that of Sam Hertz. It was the face of Charlie, Zitto's bartender who went in for murder.

"The guy you expected?" The attendant threw the sheet over the body again.

Satan didn't answer him as he turned and left the morgue. The attendant wondered what made that evil face twist into a smile, or at least what he thought was a smile. He didn't see anything especially funny about that particular stiff, nor any other stiff for that matter.

Half unconsciously Satan's hand slipped into his inside jacket pocket and felt the thick bit of cardboard that he had almost absently slipped there up in Zitto's office. A ticket to the dinner; the dinner in honor of Johnny Zitto. He couldn't think of anything he could do about it. But perhaps he could give Zitto something else to think of and take away his appetite. He could tell him about his seeing Charlie down in the morgue.

7

THE COMMISSIONER SPEAKS

THE DINNER AT the Towers, according to the invitation, was not on the face of it to honor Johnny Zitto. It was to raise funds for the new hospital. But things were planned so that it would turn into a Zitto testimonial. Those in on the know were aware of that; planned that. The others— Well, there was to be Zitto's check—a substantial check, to start things.

In the anteroom of the great crowded ballroom that was necessary to accommodate the throng, Satan was hailed by several reporters. Jimmy Lewis, of the *Globe,* was the most persistent and the most enlightening.

"What the hell! Satan." Jimmy Lewis button-holed him. "Didn't you bring a wreath?" And then Satan's eyes, rather than his lips, asked the question, "For Johnny Zitto, of course. Don't tell me you don't know. The whole thing has turned into a field day for Zitto. Settleworth is the toastmaster, and he's been waving Zitto's check like the American flag. And now you! The guy that's been shooting Zitto's props from under him, turns up."

"I don't know anything about it," Satan said grimly as he started to push past.

"So—" Lewis blocked his path. "Will you state whether

you've changed your opinion about him; if you're still out to drive him from the city. If—"

"The damned—" Satan snapped off the sentence quickly. "No, I haven't changed my opinion about Zitto."

"No?" Lewis had a mean way of smiling. "But the commissioner has. Is it because you haven't changed your mind that there may be something to the rumor that you're going to track down lots with ragweed in them for the protection of hay fever sufferers, out on Staten Island?"

"A good cop," said Satan, "goes where he's sent."

"Come, come, Satan!" Lewis waved a hand toward the other boys. "We always give you a good break, and there are times when you're pretty free with a gun. Let's have the low down. Just because the commissioner has felt the pressure of the Zitto influence is no reason you should take it on the chin."

Satan remained silent. A long, lanky man from a morning sheet said:

"You know, the commissioner's going to speak. We understand he's going to laud Zitto to the skies. Now don't try to pull them evil eyes on us. The tip's a good one. What do you say?"

"I say this." The words just forced themselves through Satan's tightly set lips. "I know the commissioner and you know the commissioner. You know his record. Anything he does or says will be all right."

He pushed roughly by the little knot of eager faced reporters, saw another reporter signaling wildly from the banquet hall, and then he entered the big room.

He didn't have any trouble in spotting Zitto's table. It was close up under the speaker's table. And he didn't have any trouble in pulling up a chair and sitting down not far behind the ace of public enemies. Many chairs were pulled from the tables, others simply turned around. Some people, far in the back of the room, had moved to the front. There, at the long table about five seats from the toastmaster's right and almost above where Satan sat, was the commissioner of police; small, erect, his eyes set straight before him.

Settleworth was talking. His lips parted in a perpetual grin, his small round eyes sparkled benevolence, his voice was soft and pleasant to the ear. Settleworth, the ex-city official who had slipped from under before his name became public scandal and his body perhaps a public charge. There was no sign now in his huge frame and florid face that ill health had forced him to resign his "public trust."

THOUGH HIS WORDS were partly of the great institution, they were mostly of the man who had made it possible—Johnny Zitto, from the streets of New York, who "in the warm sunlight of his great business success had not forgotten those who lived in the cold blackness of sunless despair."

"I present to you now a man," Settleworth raised his voice, "whom you all know and respect. A man who has done more to rid this city of crime than any single individual; any dozen individuals. A man who can speak to you about the city's need for this great institution, and the city's greater need for the type of man who has made this institution possible—Johnny Zitto. This man has known Johnny Zitto, has watched him rise from the very gutters of the city, knows of the pitfalls which he faced, the temptations which he overcame, the burdens of false and malicious accusation that success all too often carries with it. And he will tell you nothing but good of—shall I say, our guest of honor tonight, though he came simply as an individual, buying his ticket just as if this check," and he waved an oblong bit of paper in the air, "this stupendous, generous check had never been signed by him. So," he turned, leaned far over the table, spread out his hand with his palm upward, "I introduce to you the Commissioner of Police of the City of New York."

The commissioner did not rise. He sat there staring straight ahead of him. If he had heard the words of Settleworth his face did not show it. The deafening applause that started, faded as he still remained seated. Satan watched him, his green eyes riveted on that fine face. Then he knew. Despite those staring eyes the commissioner had heard. For Satan saw him nod his head, raise his hands, place them on the table and come to his feet.

The applause that had subsided broke out again. Zitto was clapping, too, looking about his table where only the most respected citizens sat; leaders of social work, a banker who was noted for his philanthropy, a famous surgeon, and a religious leader or two. These men knew nothing of Zitto except what they had lately been told, which was plenty and not, of course, to Zitto's discredit.

Back further in the room were many who did not belong. But that was Zitto's pride and also his business instinct. It wouldn't hurt those associates of his to learn at first hand just how Zitto stood in the greatest city of the world with the police commissioner of that city.

The commissioner was talking. His first sentence was

heard clearly and if not exactly understood by all, brought a deathlike hush in that big room. He said:

"We cannot buy the respect of the people with money that is obtained with their blood." He paused a long time after that and then, "We can buy certain influences, certain public trusts and certain private acts through fear. That is exactly what Johnny Zitto has done tonight. But he cannot, while I am able to stand on my two feet, buy from me, force from me through threats—yes, threats that are all too real—the trust the people have given me. Some of you know the truth; some of you know because he has bought your bodies and your souls with money dipped in your neighbor's blood; some of you know because he has broken you on the wheel of your past misdeeds. But most of you don't know the man that Mr. Settleworth—the now pale Mr. Settleworth—wishes you to honor. Well, I give you Johnny Zitto." The commissioner's eyes flashed, his hand shot out, a finger pointed directly at Johnny Zitto. "I give you the name of the guttersnipe, who never climbed out of it but buried himself deeper into its filth. I give you Johnny Zitto; the real Johnny Zitto. Thief, gunman, racketeer, blackmailer, and murderer."

8

BEHIND THE DOOR

JOHNNY ZITTO WAS stunned. But there was nothing surprising in that. Satan, too, was stunned, as was every person in that room. Just a dead silence. Then Johnny came to his feet. His face turned from a dull white to a pasty yellow. He tried to speak but no words came. And then, as if to stamp with truth the commissioner's final word, his right hand shot to his left armpit.

Satan spoke softly from behind him.

"I wouldn't do that, Johnny," he said. And then, not quite so softly, "Or maybe it would be better."

Johnny felt the hard round surface against his back; Satan's shoulders almost touching his; the warm breath upon his neck. He knew that a single pressure of Satan's finger would mean his death, and that Satan stood so close to him that no one else could see that gun.

Then Johnny's friends came to his defense. They shouted and booed and scraped their chairs on the floor to drown out the commissioner's voice. But there was no need of that. The commissioner was finished; he sat down very slowly in his chair. There was no smile of triumph on his face. It was just a very sad and very tired face. He had done his duty to the millions he served as he saw that duty—his last duty.

There was no riot. Waiters gathered in little groups; detectives were in the room. The speakers' table was cleared. Two plainclothes men stood on either side of the commissioner, and though he waved them away they held their ground. Not much talk; some whispering as the guests left the room.

Satan followed Johnny Zitto from the banquet hall, watched him wave back those friends who came near him, saw his twisting lips, the burning eyes, the clenching and unclenching fingers as he sought the door. Heard him say to a man who was now out on heavy bail for jury fixing:

"Nix, Al—nix. The party's off. I've got other things to think of. I've got to strike now and strike hard."

Jimmy Lewis, of the *Globe*, was on Zitto's heels as were other reporters as he moved across that anteroom to a closed door at the end, marked A.

"What do you say, Johnny?" Lewis cried, and when Zitto only glared at him, "Going to let him get away with that or going to make him prove it? Hey, Johnny—we want a statement."

"A statement!" Johnny Zitto swung, his hand on the knob of the door marked A. "Well, I'll give you one. One that will drive the commissioner—" He wet his lips with his tongue. "What does the city think of a commissioner who'll protect a guy wanted for attempted murder of— What the hell do *you* want?" This to Satan, who pushed in front of Lewis.

"I want to talk to you, Johnny. Want to save you from being a fool as well as," Satan grinned, "what the commissioner called you." The door was slightly open now and Satan forced Zitto into the room. "You'd better listen, Johnny. You won't be sorry."

Johnny hesitated there in the open door. Behind him was a long table. The service was set. Satan understood. Johnny and his own boys had planned to celebrate quietly after the banquet.

"All right," Johnny said suddenly, and calling over Satan's shoulder, "Don't go away, boys. I'll write out a statement for you that will wipe the foreign news off the front page."

And they were in the room. Satan closed the door and locked it.

"Why that?" Johnny eyed him through half closed lids.

"You know the boys. We'll want this private."

"Go on. Bleat, copper—bleat!" Zitto hurled himself into a chair at the head of the table, swept a glass onto the floor, shoved a plate down the table, and taking a note book from his pocket placed it before him. "Go on," he said. "I'll write. Write stuff that'll make that yellow rat and you find the city too hot to hold you. Who'll believe that the commissioner didn't know his son shot Judge Holden? They'll believe that he's been protecting him over the years; protecting him while better guys took the rap."

"Listen, Johnny." Satan grasped the wrist that already held a fountain pen. "Don't write it; you can't prove it. That confession that Roger wrote I found tonight. I've got it now."

Satan didn't know why he told the lie. To gain time, he guessed. Johnny could easily prove it wasn't true—or could he? Perhaps the confession was hard to get at. But he wanted time—time to talk to the commissioner, even to Mattie again.

Johnny Zitto looked at him blankly, then his lips parted and his teeth showed.

"Where did you find it?" His eyes knitted.

Satan hesitated, and then:

"I didn't find it. It was given to me."

"Yeah? I don't believe that." Johnny jerked his hand free.

"Better believe it, Johnny." Satan tried desperately to put conviction into his voice. "Can't you see the truth? That's why the commissioner shot the works. You've got nothing on him now—on the boy."

And Johnny wondered. Things flashed through his head. Quick thoughts; fearful thoughts. Mattie Hern in the hall the other day when he was moving the table, Satan behind the curtains in the penthouse, and Mattie's explanation that she didn't know how he got there. Reasonable enough then—but now—now! He shook his head, ran his left hand through his blond hair. It wasn't true. It couldn't be true. Mattie— But the commissioner! No man would be such a fool as to throw up his job; condemn his son, just to—to— He came to his feet.

"It was Mattie then—Mattie Hern," he said.

"No, no." And Satan's hurry to deny it swept away Johnny's doubts. He didn't see; didn't understand; didn't even think of Satan's sudden fear that by his lie he had endangered Mattie.

ZITTO WALKED TO the window and stood looking out at the lights of the city. If Satan had lied to him it wouldn't take him long to find out. But why would he lie; why— And a new and sudden fear assailed Johnny Zitto. If Mattie had given Satan that confession she had also given him that list of names, with the evidence beside each name.

Instantly Johnny thought of the name of Creighton, a national figure. The man who had alibied Johnny the night De Grassie was killed; the night that Johnny had killed him. Creighton, the man Satan had interviewed and whose alibi saved Zitto from the chair. He half turned and looked at Satan. Did he have those papers with him, in his pocket now? They were bulky, of course, yet— And even if he didn't have them, Satan was the only witness to the death of De Grassie. If he did have them, and offered to destroy that evidence against Creighton, Creighton would retract that alibi. He'd—

But Satan hadn't mentioned Creighton. Why? Was it because he lied or was it because he hadn't seen the name; hadn't had time to see it? That might be it. That was it. Satan had hurried to the commissioner to tell him he had Roger's confession.

Johnny's eyes began to narrow and his lips to set very grimly. The shooting of Judge Holden by Roger couldn't stick without that confession of course, but it was still a good story. And if Satan were dead—dead!

And Satan wasn't watching him, he was leaning on the table. Satan—Satan, the killer. Everybody knew that he killed. Johnny had money, he had influence. A good lawyer could get him off on self-defense—self-defense! A dozen or more men had seen Satan push him into that room; "force" him into that room. Then the threat to kill him if he insisted upon telling the truth about the commissioner's son, the gun in Satan's hand, Johnny's quick dive and his own shot!

Reasonable? Well, what if it wasn't? But if Satan had lied! But he couldn't have. The commissioner wouldn't be such a fool. That he spoke out only because he thought it was right never entered Johnny's head. He had dealt with big men, and they didn't cut their own throats.

Johnny Zitto edged slightly toward the wall, turning his body slowly. Satan's side was to him; his right side. That meant that he would have to draw and swing. Draw and swing! Zitto wondered. Satan was fast, but so was he. Satan was—Satan was the cause of all his trouble; all— And thoughts went. Johnny dropped back a few years; nothing but animal instinct now, animal passion, animal lust to kill. Only his points of eyes held reason; they watched Satan's right hand upon the table.

Johnny spun on his heels and jerked out a gun. Even as he did so he realized his mistake. Satan had been waiting, watching—watching his shadow anyway. And Satan was not going to use his right hand. His left had flashed under his coat and out again.

All in a split second Johnny had these thoughts. But it was too late to draw back now. He was going to get in first shot; just one shot, if—

Big guns, both of them. Heavy guns. Just blazing death in the hands of two men who knew how to use them; wanted to use them.

Just two roars that came as one, two streaks of yellow blue flame that met, brightened and died, and two bodies that crashed to the floor. The battle of two deadly gunmen had been deadly.

Men pounded on the door, but the two silent figures on the floor paid no heed. Voices called hoarsely, feet ran over thick carpet. A body crashed against wood—another and another. The door groaned, shook, held, groaned again and the lock snapped.

Jimmy Lewis was the first man into that room, almost hurled into it by those behind him. Jimmy was not a big man, not a strong man; yet his body stopped, rigid—and stayed so with such strength that those behind him were held back.

Jimmy said, though he didn't know the voice was his:

"Two shots and two stiffs!" And although his words were flippant, his voice rose to a high falsetto and cracked eerily back in his throat.

9

GRAPEVINE OF THE UNDERWORLD

WITHIN FIVE MINUTES after those two bodies hit the floor; within four minutes after other bodies had crashed open that door; and within three minutes after Jimmy Lewis' voice had cracked back in his throat, that great system of the underworld, the grapevine, had flashed the word to the bar of the Club Venice.

No one seemed to speak it, no one seemed to even whisper it. Silent men still stood drinking against that bar. Yet everyone of those silent men had somehow heard that Johnny Zitto and Satan Hall had shot it out at last and that both men were dead.

Mattie Hern, passing through to that little visitors' room behind the bar, to make a telephone call, also heard the news. She didn't know then and she didn't know later who had told her or if anyone had told her at all, though she knew that someone must have. But the same story had reached her. "Johnny Zitto and Satan Hall are dead."

The thing shook Mattie. Shook her, inside, as she had never been shaken before. But outside! Mattie came from the night; the night that hides its emotions, its fears— yes, even its feelings of complete disaster. Maybe her face turned white, maybe her lips quivered slightly as they formed the unspoken syllables of the words, "Is it true?" Maybe, too, something rose in her throat, to drop back again into her stomach with a lasting sinking feeling when the man silently nodded his reply. Her father was free, of course. She thought of that. She was free, too. And she knew also that this dead silence was of the moment, of the hour, of a single night maybe. Then chaos! Guns would roar, smoldering hates would blaze into passions; physical passions. That was it. Hate, ambition and greed, the three horsemen of crime, would bring terror and death to the underworld.

And Satan! Her lips set tightly, her chin raised, she tried to keep her legs from caving in at the knees as she passed to the little room and dropped weakly into a chair. Satan might be alive now if she had—had taken those papers and given them to him. Mattie could not know that the very thing she thought would have saved Satan was the cause of the shooting; Zitto's belief that she had sold him out.

She rubbed a hand across her forehead, through the thick blackness of her hair. Those typewritten sheets; a fortune! A fortune up there in Zitto's room simply for the taking. She looked at the door to the stairs and shook her head. She didn't have the stomach for it. Not then. Tomorrow; the next day, maybe. And she came erect on that chair; a movement that sent her heart beating wildly. By tomorrow, later that night even, men—after the first shock of the news had passed, would be tearing that room apart. Or the police would—

Mattie jarred to her feet, glanced toward the stairs, gripped her bag, opened it with trembling fingers and glanced inside. As if forcing her feet she walked to that door, drew it open and slowly in the beginning, then more quickly mounted those stairs.

Mattie tried the door of Zitto's room. It was locked, but she knew that her quick deft fingers would be equal to it. There was only an ordinary lock; a simple lock. Zitto was a shrewd man. He knew the uselessness of bolts and chains and guaranteed locks against experienced hands that wanted to get inside. Heavy locks only invited trouble; were sign posts of valuable things within. Indeed, he wouldn't have had any lock at all if it wasn't for the high-priced cigars in his desk that would invite petty pilfering. Besides, men were always along that hall outside; trusted men. Always? Mattie looked down that hall. Everyone was below now; watching, waiting, wondering!

The hall was but dimly lit, and although Mattie carried a small flash in her bag she did not use it. Just a hand into her bag, a drop to her knees, and her fingers became steady; became those magic fingers that years before her father was so proud of, that not so many nights before had slipped into Tonti Marcco's pocket and set back his watch, saving her life.

The door opened. Like a shadow Mattie slid within, closed it behind her, found the latch above the keyhole and turned it slowly; silently. There were no windows in that room; the ventilation came from an especially controlled system. Without hesitation Mattie pressed the switch and flooded the room with light.

HORROR OR NO horror; empty nauseating feeling in the pit of her stomach or not, Mattie went to work. She was a smooth and fast worker, and she knew it. None more clever along the Avenue.

The desk was heavy and she had trouble moving it, and considerable more difficulty in setting it right—but she did. And there on her knees she found the secret of that bit of paneling and had stuffed the papers into her bag.

The thing was done. A million dollars that could soon be turned into hard cash was in her bag. Just the right party to work it. The right party! She nodded as she replaced the board and put her shoulder to the desk, lifting it back on the rug. Her black eyes sparkled. The right party? Why, there was no one cleverer than her father. She had a little money. She'd join him in Antwerp. Six months, a year perhaps; when things had quieted down they could return. Conditions would be better then. The victims on that list would be able to pay more, and the sense of security they had enjoyed over that year would make the shock more terrible to them; more valuable to Mattie and her father.

She walked to the door, and her knees began to play tricks with her again. And her stomach. Satan. Satan! He was dead and she loved him—yes, loved him more than she ever thought she could care for any living man. Living man! That was it. Living or dead, she loved him.

Those typewritten sheets! She had hardly looked at them. But of course they were what she wanted. They— Quickly she opened the bag and lifted them out. And the clipped sheet at the end detached itself from the larger sheet and dropped to the floor.

She picked it up and read it. It was Roger's confession. That was why Satan wanted the papers destroyed. The commissioner; his friend! Roger, who had made good after a wild youth. A wild youth! Mattie hadn't thought it was as bad as this.

She thought of Satan—of— Fear had been hung over her head by the misdeed of her father. It had—well, not made her a crook because she always was one, but it had kept her one. Now these others; the ones that must suffer with them! She didn't need the money; she wouldn't want money now. The good things of life; the pleasures it could buy would never be pleasures now—not with Satan dead. As for her father! He had twenty thousand dollars and was free. She smiled bitterly. Jake Hern would never need help from any man, not in the making of money anyway.

Truth is truth, whether Mattie recognized it or not. All these thoughts, she told herself, had something to do with her decision, if it was a decision and not just an involuntary act. But the truth was—that she was thinking of Satan when she walked into that little wash room and plugged in the electric heater. She was thinking that she loved Satan— maybe more, since he was dead, and that Satan wanted it that way.

Through dim, lifeless eyes she watched the red glow brighten; the thick sheaf of papers curl and smoke. After that she tore them off, one by one; then two at a time and even three as the heat increased. And the last to go, the last to crumple into black ashes and be dumped down the drain of the wash basin, was the confession of Roger, the commissioner's son.

Mattie sighed as she pulled out the plug and replaced the heater. She took a towel and carefully wiped away any semblance of wet ash. A fortune? Yes. She thought of that and wished she had done this thing before. But her head straightened slightly, and though the sinking feeling still clutched at her stomach, her legs did not give at the knees when she walked. Mattie had been true to the code of the night. She had been loyal to the living Zitto. Now she was loyal to the dead Satan. A dead Satan and a live love; a terrible, gnawing, remorseful love. She had made her decision to destroy those papers too late.

10

MIRACLES DO NOT HAPPEN

NO ONE STOPPED Mattie as she walked down the stairs and passed through the length of that bar. Men watched her of course; little sympathy in their faces, yet understanding. Some, even with an eye to the future. They had looked at her before of course, but those were covert glances. Now—Zitto and Satan were dead and Mattie was open prey.

"Anything new?" Mattie hardly breathed the words to Tony, at the door of the bar, and his answer, too, was a hoarse whisper.

"Not much. They've taken them to the Washington Hospital, and—"

Mattie's head swung. Big eyes were wide.

"They're alive—alive then!"

"I ain't sure. But the cops are hoping one of them will talk before— No one knows exactly what happened."

"Which one—which one? I've got to know which one."

"Hell!" Tony drew back. "Don't claw me like that, Mattie. I don't know."

"I've got to know. I've got to know." Mattie dropped her hands to her sides, and, moving quickly, passed into the main hall and out onto the street.

The George Washington Hospital was crowded and, temporarily at least, Detective Satan Hall and Johnny Zitto were laid in two small beds with hardly no space between them.

Mattie had literally to fight every inch of the way to that room. And then, if it hadn't been for Jimmy Lewis, of the *Globe*, she could not have gone that far. But at the door the bulk of four uniformed policemen made entrance impossible. They were not men you could talk to; men you could plead with. Jimmy Lewis knew that.

If it were not for the keen ears of the commissioner, who was inside that room and close to that door, Mattie would have been carried forcibly below and perhaps even held by the police.

The commissioner opened the door and put an end to the one-sided struggle, with low sharp words.

"Mattie—Mattie Hern," he said. "Satan wants you; come in."

"Satan! He wants me?" And the commissioner had to hold her arm as she started to sink, slowly. He wondered, too, at that change in her face; it seemed soft and kind, even good. It wasn't the face of Mattie Hern as he remembered it.

"He's called your name; wants you to get something for him."

"He's alive!" Mattie slipped through the open door, leaned against it for a moment when the commissioner closed it. "He's going to—to live?"

"I don't know. I don't know. That's the surgeon now. Dr. Hallington. None better in this part of the country."

Mattie swayed upon her feet, steadied, shook her head

and made her eyes take in that little room. The two white-clad figures; the big man who was leaning over one of the small beds, hiding the figure upon it. The other bed!

The other bed, where that gasping, terrible, hopeless—yes, rattling breathing came from. Mattie had seen death before. Now she drove her feet forward, forced her eyes to look at that gasping man. His eyes were closed, his mouth was open, his face was like fresh powdered chalk.

Her own breath sucked in, almost choking her. That man was Johnny Zitto.

The famous surgeon straightened and turned, and Mattie saw Satan. His face was as white as Zitto's, but his breathing was different. His mouth was a single red line and his face was hard set. One hand, upon the white sheet, was clenched tightly. Mattie moved to that bed, her hand grasped that closed one. Leaning down she spoke quickly.

"It's me, Satan—Mattie," she said. "It's Mattie!"

Satan's eyes opened; just twin slits of green. Then they widened; brilliant, feverish balls. He seemed to study the girl for a long time. His face worked; there was agony in it. Mental agony more than physical, Mattie thought.

"He won't know you." Dr. Hallington laid a hand upon her shoulder. "The fever—delirium."

But Dr. Hallington was wrong. Satan was a determined man. That will of his forced him—his own brain, his own thoughts—through the tangled mass of incongruities. His words were thick when he spoke, but the brain that controlled them was Satan's brain, unhampered by the delirium of a raging fever.

"Mattie," he said. "Mattie. Those papers, Mattie. The

commissioner—Roger. God! Mattie, I'd hate to go out not knowing that—"

Mattie leaned close to him, her hair brushed his cheek. Something wet splashed upon his face; Satan knew it, but Mattie didn't. She didn't know that she could cry. And she told him; whispered it all, her head close on the pillow. The final burning of Roger's confession she repeated over and over. And she knew that he understood. She knew it from his eyes, from his parted lips, from the fingers that crushed hers just once in his iron grip. Then they relaxed. The eyes closed; there was no pain in his face, no hard determination to his thin lips. If he thought at all, it was simply that a good day's work had been done. And Satan slept!

The commissioner was saying, and his voice shook:

"Satan—Detective Hall. Doctor, will he—will he live?"

The great surgeon smiled. "Absolutely!" He nodded his head. "It will be a miracle if he doesn't."

"And the other one—Zitto—Johnny Zitto. Will he live?"

This time Dr. Hallington didn't smile. He shook his head. He said simply:

"It will be more than a miracle if he does."